PETER DRAX
HIGH SEAS MURDER

ERIC ELRINGTON ADDIS, aka 'Peter Drax', was born in Edinburgh in 1899, the youngest child of a retired Indian civil servant and the daughter of an officer in the British Indian Army.

Drax attended Edinburgh University, and served in the Royal Navy, retiring in 1929. In the 1930s he began practising as a barrister, but, recalled to the Navy upon the outbreak of the Second World War, he served on HMS *Warspite* and was mentioned in dispatches. When Drax was killed in 1941 he left a wife and two children.

Between 1936 and 1939, Drax published six crime novels: *Murder by Chance* (1936), *He Shot to Kill* (1936), *Murder by Proxy* (1937), *Death by Two Hands* (1937), *Tune to a Corpse* (1938) and *High Seas Murder* (1939). A further novel, *Sing a Song of Murder*, unfinished by Drax on his death, was completed by his wife, Hazel Iris (Wilson) Addis, and published in 1944.

By Peter Drax

Murder by Chance
He Shot to Kill
Death by Two Hands
Tune to a Corpse
High Seas Murder
Sing a Song of Murder

PETER DRAX

HIGH SEAS MURDER

With an introduction
by Curtis Evans

DEAN STREET PRESS

Published by Dean Street Press 2017

Introduction copyright © 2017 Curtis Evans

All Rights Reserved

First published in 1939 by Hutchinson & Co. Ltd.

Cover by DSP

ISBN 978 1 911579 63 2

www.deanstreetpress.co.uk

INTRODUCTION

Eric Elrington Addis, aka "Peter Drax," one of the major between-the-wars exponents and practitioners of realism in the British crime novel, was born near the end of the Victorian era in Edinburgh, Scotland on 19 May 1899, the youngest child of David Foulis Addis, a retired Indian civil servant, and Emily Malcolm, daughter of an officer in the British Indian Army. Drax died during the Second World War on 31 August 1941, having been mortally wounded in a German air raid on the British Royal Navy base at Alexandria, Egypt, officially known as HMS *Nile*. During his brief life of 42 years, Drax between the short span from 1936 to 1939 published six crime novels: *Murder by Chance* (1936), *He Shot to Kill* (1936), *Murder by Proxy* (1937), *Death by Two Hands* (1937), *Tune to a Corpse* (1938) and *High Seas Murder* (1939). An additional crime novel, *Sing a Song of Murder*, having been left unfinished by Drax at his death in 1941 and completed by his novelist wife, was published in 1944. Together the Peter Drax novels constitute one of the most important bodies of realistic crime fiction published in the 1930s, part of the period commonly dubbed the "Golden Age of detective fiction." Rather than the artificial and outsize master sleuths and super crooks found in so many classic mysteries from this era, Drax's novels concern, as publicity material for the books put it, "police who are not endowed with supernatural powers and crooks who are also human." In doing so they offered crime fiction fans from those years some of the period's most compelling reading. The reissuing of these gripping tales of criminal mayhem and murder, unaccountably out-of-print for more than seven decades, by Dean Street Press marks a signal event in recent mystery publishing history.

Peter Drax's career background gave the future crime writer constant exposure to the often grim rigors of life, experience which he most effectively incorporated into his fiction. A graduate of Edinburgh Academy, the teenaged Drax served during the First World War as a Midshipman on HMS *Dreadnought* and

Marlborough. (Two of his three brothers died in the war, the elder, David Malcolm Addis, at Ypres, where his body was never found.) After the signing of the armistice and his graduation from the Royal Naval College, Drax remained in the Navy for nearly a decade, retiring in 1929 with the rank of Lieutenant-Commander, in which capacity he supervised training with the New Zealand Navy, residing with his English wife, Hazel Iris (Wilson) Addis, daughter of an electrical engineer, in Auckland. In the 1930s he returned with Hazel to England and began practicing as a barrister, specializing, predictably enough, in the division of Admiralty, as well as that of Divorce. Recalled to the Navy upon the outbreak of the Second World War, Drax served as Commander (second-in-command) on HMS *Warspite* and was mentioned in dispatches at the Second Battle of Narvik, a naval affray which took place during the 1940 Norwegian campaign. At his death in Egypt in 1941 Drax left behind Hazel --herself an accomplished writer, under the pen name Hazel Adair, of so-called middlebrow "women's fiction"--and two children, including Jeremy Cecil Addis, the late editor and founder of *Books Ireland.*

Commuting to his London office daily in the 1930s on the 9.16, Drax's hobby became, according to his own account, the "reading and dissecting of thrillers," ubiquitous in station book stalls. Concluding that the vast majority of them were lamentably unlikely affairs, Drax set out over six months to spin his own tale, "inspired by the desire to tell a story that was credible." (More prosaically the neophyte author also wanted to show his wife, who had recently published her first novel, *Wanted a Son,* that he too could publish a novel.) The result was *Murder by Chance,* the first of the author's seven crime novels. In the United States during the late 1920s and early 1930s, recalled Raymond Chandler in his essay "The Simple Art of Murder" (originally published in 1944), the celebrated American crime writer Dashiell Hammett had given "murder back to the kind of people who commit it for reasons, not just to provide a corpse; and with the means at hand, not with hand-wrought dueling pistols, curare and tropical fish." Drax's debut crime novel, which followed on the heels of Hammett's books, made something of a similar impression in the United Kingdom, with mystery writer and founding Detection Club member Milward Kennedy in the *Sunday Times* pronouncing the novel a "thriller of great merit" that was "extremely convincing" and the influential *Observer* crime fiction critic Torquemada avowing, "I have not for a good many months enjoyed a thriller as much as I have enjoyed *Murder by Chance*."

What so impressed these and other critics about *Murder by Chance* and Drax's successive novels was their simultaneous plausibility and readability, a combination seen as a tough feat to pull off in an era of colorful though not always entirely credible crime writers like S. S. Van Dine, Edgar Wallace and John Dickson Carr. Certainly in the 1930s the crime novelists Dorothy L. Sayers, Margery Allingham and Anthony Berkeley, among others (including Milward Kennedy himself), had elevated the presence of psychological realism in the crime novel; yet the criminal milieus that these authors presented to readers were mostly resolutely occupied by the respectable middle and upper classes. Drax offered British readers what was then an especially bracing change of atmosphere (one wherein mean streets replaced country mansions and quips were exchanged for coshes, if you will)—as indicated in this resoundingly positive Milward Kennedy review of Drax's fifth crime novel, *Tune to a Corpse* (1938):

> I have the highest opinion of Peter Drax's murder stories.... Mainly his picture is of low life in London, where crime and poverty meet and merge. He draws characters who shift uneasily from shabby to disreputable associations.... and he can win our sudden liking, almost our respect, for creatures in whom little virtue is to be found. To show how a drab crime was committed and then to show the slow detection of the truth, and to keep the reader absorbed all the time—this is a real achievement. The secret of Peter Drax's success is his ability to make the circumstances as plausible as the characters are real....

Two of Peter Drax's crime novels, the superb *Death by Two Hands* and *Tune to a Corpse*, were published in the United States, under the titles, respectively, *Crime within Crime* and *Crime to Music*, to very strong notices. The *Saturday Review of Literature*, for example, pronounced of *Crime within Crime* that "as a straightforward eventful yarn of little people in [the] grip of tragic destiny it's brilliantly done" and of *Crime to Music* that "London underworld life is described with color and realism. The steps in the weakling killer's descent to Avernus [see Virgil] are thrillingly traced." That the country which gave the world Dashiell Hammett could be so impressed with the crime fiction of Peter Drax surely is strong recommendation indeed. Today seedily realistic urban British crime fiction of the 1930s is perhaps most strongly associated with two authors who dabbled in crime fiction: Graham Greene (*Brighton Rock*, 1938, and others) and Gerald Kersh (*Night and the City*, 1938). If not belonging on quite that exalted level, the novels of Peter Drax nevertheless grace this gritty roster, one that forever changed the face of British crime fiction.

Curtis Evans

It was a stormy night in the fishing-town of Gilboro'. Rain carried by a south-westerly gale swept Union Street clear of pedestrians. It filled the "Lion and Unicorn", the "Ring of Bells" and the "Keel and Barge" with customers. The manager of the Plaza Picturedrome was quite satisfied with the weather and was sitting in the pay-box smoking a tenpenny cigar and making neat piles of pennies, sixpences and shillings.

A tram came grinding and swaying along the street and stopped at the corner. A girl, her chin buried in the tightly buttoned collar of her raincoat, stepped out and ran to the pavement. She didn't care tuppence for the weather, nor was she worried by a wet tail of hair which had escaped from the scrap of felt and straw she called a hat. She was looking for Larry. Two days ago he had promised to marry her after what could by no stretch of imagination be called a whirlwind courtship. For five years they had been walking out, sitting silent on seats on the front, in the cinema, eating suppers at Bent's Café down by the fish-wharf.

But now it was all fixed up. They'd chosen a house. Jessie's bottom drawer was full, and all that remained was to choose the furniture. As a matter of fact Jessie Miles had already made up her mind what they were going to have.

The windows of the Gilboro' Furnishing Company were filled with tables and chairs, chests of drawers and beds. On one of the tables was the plaster figure of a boy wearing blue shorts, a cap on the back of his head. He was whistling. Jessie had been afraid to ask how much he was, but she meant to have him.

She was so busy figuring out where he'd look best in the front room that she was startled when a hand gripped her arm. She said: "Oh!" spun round on her heel and looked up into the smiling face of Larry Hicks. His wide mouth was stretched in a grin.

"Sorry if I'm late."

"You're not. I was early. Come on, let's go in."

As Jessie took a step towards the swing doors of the Gil-boro' Furnishing Company the grin on Larry's face faded and he caught the sleeve of her coat.

"I've got something to say first."

"What is it?" Jessie was frightened. He was looking quite solemn, which wasn't like Larry.

"Oh, it's nothing much. Let's take a walk."

"But you said that you'd settle about the furniture." Tears were not far away.

"Yes, I know but . . ."

"What is it? Tell me." Jessie gripped the lapels of his coat.

"It's the money. I haven't got enough."

"But you said last night that you'd be able to make it up, and you don't need to pay for it all at one time."

"Yes, I know. I thought I could borrow a tenner from Carl Swanson, but he's broke."

They turned away from the shelter of the shop awning and faced the full force of the wind.

"Where are we going?"

"Down to the wharf."

"Why?"

"I want to show you the *John Goodwin*."

"Is that the boat Carl Swanson is taking out?"

"Yes."

"You're not going with him?"

"I haven't promised yet."

"Larry, you said you were going to give up the fishing."

"I can't get a job ashore so there's nothing else for it, and, besides, after one trip with Carl I'll have enough for us to start with. If we're lucky."

"Yes, if you're lucky. But if you're not and anything goes wrong?—you know what happened to the *Emily May*."

"Broke up with all hands. Yes, I know, but Carl's never been in trouble. He's made money every trip he's been on." They were nearing the end of the street. Before them stretched a long line of shuttered stores a hundred yards away across an expanse of glistening, wet paving-stones. The wind moaned and whistled through the alleys between the buildings. Low clouds were scudding overhead. "When are you sailing?"

"In the morning. On the first of the ebb."

A spatter of rain splashed in a wide puddle and Jessie put a hand to hold down the skirts of her coat which were whipping round her legs. She was very cold.

Larry, careless of the weather, strode on round a deserted lorry piled high with empty fish-boxes, and led the way down an alley. Jessie bent her head to meet a sudden blast.

A line of trawlers, wedged as tightly as sardines in a tin, lay bows on to the wharf. Larry stopped opposite one and said: "That's her. The best boat fishing out of Gilboro'. Electric light. Electric winches. New nets."

Jessie pressed closer to his side. She was trembling. "All the same I wish you wouldn't go. At least not with Carl Swanson."

But Larry wasn't listening. "More than twenty thousand she cost, and she's built on the lines of the old *City of Glasgow*. She was a ship! I've seen her busting home, taking it green over the forecastle. Full speed and first home. That was her ticket, and once Carl gets on board this old hooker he'll show 'em the way to catch fish."

"The *City of Glasgow* went down, didn't she?"

"Yes. Off Iceland. But that was a bit of bad luck. Fog. They didn't have wireless. It's different now."

Jessie said: "Let's go home."

"All right." Larry put an arm round her waist, but there was no responsive bending to his embrace. He glanced down at her and was going to speak, but suddenly changed his mind. Jessie had been like this before, but she'd always got over it. And every time his ship had docked she'd been there waiting for him, no matter what time of day or night it was.

On their way up to the town they had always stopped at the coffee-stall in the market-place for a cup of coffee, a pie and a talk with Sam Hopkins, who kept it. He'd always been the same ever since she'd been a kid at school. Old Hoppy with his funny little fringe of grey side-whiskers, shaven chin and quizzical grin.

He looked like an elderly, intensely respectable coachman, which was not very odd, because for thirty-five years he had been a coachman. An appreciative employer had left him a legacy which he had laid out on this coffee-stall, and he had become as well-known and respected in Gilboro' fish-market as Nelson is in Trafalgar Square.

The coffee-urn was Hoppy's greatest joy and pride, for it was made of copper and "took a lovely shine"; almost as good as the shine on the carriage lamps and silver-mounted harness which had been his charge for so many years.

"Let's have something hot. What d'you say?" Larry rattled coins in his pocket.

"I don't mind."

They were off the wharf now, threading their way between barrows, boxes and baskets, their feet scrunching on powdered ice.

"Look!" Jessie's grip tightened on Larry's arm. "Over there!"

Across the wide expanse of the fish-market, beyond the line of wooden stores, there was a street lamp. Its white light was flickering in the wind which whipped round the corner. Beneath it a man was standing leaning against the wall. The pin-point of a lighted cigarette glowed red.

There was something about him, something about the hunch of his square shoulders, the cock of his tweed cap, which told Jessie that it was Carl Swanson.

"Come on." She pulled at Larry's arm. "I don't want to have to speak to him."

"All right," Larry agreed, but as they turned he raised his right hand in greeting.

The glowing cigarette rose and then fell again in acknowledgment.

Hoppy grinned when he saw Jessie. He said: "What's he bringing you down here for? And at this time of night, too!"

"Two coffees. What are you going to eat, Jess?"

"I've got some fresh pies," Hoppy suggested. "And them sausage rolls are all right."

"I'll have a pie."

Hoppy took down a cup and held it under the tap of the coffee-urn. "I hear Carl's taking out the *John Goodwin* tomorrow."

"Yes, I'm going with him."

Jessie looked quickly at Larry and then down at the cup Hoppy set before her.

"He's had a job getting a crew."

"Damn' fools. They don't know where they're well off," Larry growled. "A share in any ship Carl takes out is worth twice one in any other."

"He drives his crew hard."

"I dare say, but you got to work these days if you don't want to finish up the wrong side of the line."

"It doesn't always work out that way." Hoppy put a pie on a plate and added a knife and fork. "Get that under your belt and you'll feel the better for it."

Jessie smiled at him.

Larry said: "What d'you mean?"

"He nearly lost his gear last trip."

"Do you mean he was poaching?" Jessie asked.

Hoppy nodded. "That's what they're saying."

"Well he wasn't copped, so what's the odds?"

Larry thrust out his jaw and leaned with both arms on the counter.

"Now, I don't want to start an argument," Hoppy said. "I was only telling you what I'd heard."

"When Carl brings in his ship with an empty hold it'll be time enough to knock him. It's jealousy! That's what it is."

"Maybe you're right." Hoppy took his pipe off a shelf and pushed down the dottle with a stubby forefinger. "Anyway, who's he got this time?"

"Dan Todd as chief and Tubby Stevens is going as cook."

"How about the deckies?"

"He's got 'em all."

Hoppy struck a match and sucked at his pipe. When he'd got it going he stuck his head out of the stall. "It's blowing and the south cone's still up."

"We'll sail all the same, at the turn of the tide."

"I thought you was going to give up the fishing."

"I'm going to make this trip."

"And then we're going to get married," Jessie said.

"That's right. I'm going to settle down after that."

Hoppy smiled through a cloud of smoke. "You've got to let me know when it's to be. I'll be there."

"I'll send you an invitation," Jessie said.

Larry had finished his pie. He drank noisily, and as he put down his empty cup he looked up the street. The tin clock beside the cash register said that it was half past ten. Jessie looked at it and said, "It's time I was getting home."

"D'you mind if I don't come? I've got to get my gear together."

"Of course not." Jessie put down her knife and fork. Larry put his arms around her and kissed her full on the lips.

"Promise me you'll look after yourself."

"Of course I will."

"You've got the socks I knitted you?"

"They're in my bag."

She clung to him. "Oh, I wish you weren't going."

"It'll only be for a month. Six weeks at most."

"I know, but still . . ."

"Now don't you worry. Just you fix your mind on the day we come back."

"Good night." And she was gone.

"What's the damage?"

"One and tuppence."

As Larry counted out the money Hoppy said: "She's a fine girl, Jessie. You're a lucky man."

"Yes, I know, but I wish she wasn't so strong against the fishing. It pays well."

"She's seen too much of it. Her dad went and her brother. It's cruel on the women—waiting and hoping." Larry picked up his change. "I'm going to get a spell of shut-eye. So long."

Old Hoppy leaning across the counter watched him walk away and saw him turn into the alley where Carl Swanson was standing. "He'll slip up one of these days," he muttered. "And when he does there'll be something to pay."

Carl took his cigarette out of his mouth, dropped it on the pavement and trod it out with the toe of his right foot. "All right for the morning?"

Larry nodded. "Yes. Is there anything I can do?"

"No. I just wanted to make sure you were coming."

"How's that?"

"I thought mebbe she'd have talked you out of it."

Larry laughed. "No fear of that."

"You never know with women."

"Jessie's all right."

Carl's eyes closed to slits and he nodded slowly. "We sail on the tide."

"Is it right you've got Tubby Stevens and Dan Todd to sign on?"

"Tubby's O.K., but I've got to have a word with Dan yet. You know what he's like."

"Those damned hens." Larry laughed.

Carl's lips tightened. "He's a good engineer and that's half the battle on a trip."

"And the cook's the other half."

Carl thrust his hands into the side pockets of his pea-jacket and sank his chin into his buttoned-up collar. "I'll be getting along. See you later."

Dan Todd had the lugubrious face of a sick horse—a horse which had consistently neglected to shave. At times he had the horse's capacity for saying nothing. Carl found him sitting in a broken-backed basket chair which creaked every time he moved. In his hands, held high to catch the beams of an oil lamp hanging from the ceiling, was a paper-backed book entitled *A Thousand a Year from Hens*.

Dan's long legs were stretched upwards to the ledge of a mantelpiece. Below them a fine red fire glowed. The window was tight closed and the smoke from a black briar was banking up on the ceiling in layers of blue-grey smoke.

"What cheer, Dan!"

A blast of air from the open door eddied the smoke and made Daniel Todd grunt, hunch forward in his chair and twist his head.

"Oh, it's you, Carl. Come in and shut that damn' door."

Carl Swanson threw down his cap, walked to the fire and stood straddling his legs. He was smiling. "I've just seen Larry Hicks."

"Which means you're making up a crew."

"Ay. In the *John Goodwin*. She's a grand ship."

Dan Todd turned down the corner of a page of *A Thousand a Year from Hens* and laid it on a chair. Then he took off his spectacles and put them in a metal case.

"I'm lucky to get her. She can do twelve knots and carry coal and ice for a two months' trip." Carl took a pouch from his pocket and began thumbing tobacco into his pipe. "There's a packet of money in a ship like that, and I know where I'm going to take her."

"They tell me she's got electric winches."

"And all new gear. The gaffer hasn't spared anything. You can have everything you ask for."

Dan stared at the glowing coals. He had forgotten all about his hens, the farm he meant to have one day, and the picture of himself with a bucket of mash on his arm, walking over the springy turf of the South Downs. He'd been there once on a visit to a sister.

Carl went on: "It's a chance that a lot of blokes would jump at. There's plenty wanting a ship."

Dan took a knife from his pocket and began to slice tobacco off what looked like a short length of tarry rope. "When do you sail?"

"In the morning." Carl turned to look at a clock on the mantelpiece. "Five hours from now."

"And you're still wanting a chief engineer." The hint of a smile pulled at the corners of Dan' s mouth. He knew well enough what Carl had come for.

"How about it?"

"The *John Goodwin*. I'll consider it."

"I can't give you long. If you don't want the job I'm going to see Tommy Black."

Dan Todd spat into the fire. "You won't do no good with him. He's been on the booze this last week back."

He heaved himself on to his feet and opened a cupboard door. "You'd better have something to keep out the cold." Whisky from a squat black bottle gurgled into a glass. "There's water in the back kitchen."

Carl laughed as he took the glass. "I'll be getting all the water I want tomorrow. Here's to a full hold."

"What time did you say you were sailing?"

"Four o'clock."

"The *John Goodwin*," Dan mumbled. "It's her maiden trip, isn't it?"

Carl nodded.

"I've never done the first voyage in any boat yet. It's mostly unlucky but still . . ."

Carl left the fire, sat on a wooden chair and picked up the book Dan had laid aside. "How are your chickens?"

"Not so bad. I've twenty pullets on the lay. Fourteen eggs a day since last Thursday. But tell us a bit more about the *John Goodwin*. Is she easy on the coal?"

To hear Carl Swanson describe the trawler, a casual listener might well have formed the opinion that she was little less inferior in comfort, steaming-power and stability to the *Queen Mary*.

At ten minutes to twelve Dan said: "I'll come with you. I don't like doing a maiden trip, but all the same I'll come. Ye did say she had electric winches . . ."

It was past midnight when Carl arrived at the lime-washed cottage in Hawkin's Court which had been his home ever since the day when, as a nine-months'-old baby, Mrs. Mather had taken him in and cared for him as though he were her own son.

There was light shining under the front door, and before he had time to lift the latch he heard footsteps shuffling along the flagged passage from the kitchen.

"I was wondering where you'd got to. Come along in out of the cold." Mrs. Mather shut the door behind him and put an arm on his shoulder. "You're soaking wet. Take off your coat this very minute."

Laughingly Carl obeyed. "You old tyrant!"

"I've been keeping your supper hot." She carried his jacket into the kitchen and hung it on the back of a chair before the fire.

"I'm going out in the morning."

A cloud passed over Mrs. Mather's face and she turned her head away. Too often had she heard these words.

"Wish me luck."

"Luck!" She laughed thinly. "It's more than luck you'll be needing in weather like this. Why don't you put it off a day or two?"

"Men must work."

"What ship have you got?"

"The *John Goodwin*."

"She's new, isn't she?"

"Yes. First trip."

"And tomorrow's Friday."

"Now come along, Granny. It's not like you to act this way. After all, someone's got to make a start."

"All the same, I wish you weren't going. I read your cup after you went out this morning."

"I don't believe in that."

"Maybe not, but it's often come true all the same."

The old woman knelt down, opened the oven door and took out a pie-dish. "The crust isn't what it should be. I was expecting you in earlier."

"I had to round up the chaps. Dan Todd and Larry Hicks."

"Are they going with you?"

"Yes."

"Jessie'll be wild. She was telling me Larry had promised her he'd give up the fishing."

"He's coming all the same. He's a good lad. One of these days he'll be getting a ship of his own."

Mrs. Mather put the pie-dish on the table and pushed up a chair. Then she poured water from a kettle on the hob into a fat brown tea-pot. "It's steak and kidney. I know that's your favourite."

When Carl had finished the meal he stood up and yawned. "We sail at four o'clock."

"Then away up to your bed. I'll call you in plenty of time."

Carl put his arms round her shoulders. "You and your tea-leaves. I'm going to make a bumper trip and when I come back I'll buy you a new shawl."

"I'd sooner have a piece of lino for the front passage. I had to throw out the bit that was there. It was all holes."

"You can have that as well." Carl swung himself on to the ladder that led up through a trapdoor to his room under the slates.

The south-westerly gale had lost nothing of its weight when Tubby Stevens, first cousin to a barrel in build, humped his bag on to the fish-wharf. Under his left arm he held a zither in a very new, shiny black case.

He was a cook, and a very good cook too, but he had taken a strong dislike to the sea during his first trip in a trawler. On that occasion the catch had been sold for £1,145, which, taking it by and large, is a very satisfactory price for the result of six weeks' fishing.

Carl Swanson had been the captain on that trip and, being as superstitious as the average fisherman, he had induced Tubby to sign on for another trip. The catch had been even better.

And so, in spite of himself, in spite of a burning desire to be somewhere where no one knew the use of a fish-net, Tubby Stevens shipped with Carl Swanson whenever Carl wanted a cook.

A passion for melody was strong within him, which accounted for the purchase of the zither which he was now carrying under his left arm. In his bag was a book entitled *The Twenty-Four-Hour Tutor*. Eight hours of earnest study of its contents had borne no more fruit than a halting rendering of "There's a Long, Long Trail". A melancholy tune and drearier than can be imagined when fingered painstakingly by Tubby.

A man in a canvas smock and sou'wester, who was standing on the forecastle of the *John Goodwin*, saw Tubby and hailed him in language which might have startled a Billingsgate fish-porter.

Tubby altered his course eight points and arrived at the bows of the trawler. The wind, now on his starboard quarter, assisted his progress to such good effect that he very nearly fell into the dock.

Impatient, if not willing, hands reached down for him, his bag and his zither. His hands clawed at a hairy coir rope. Some-one got a grip on the seat of his pants and Tubby was on board for better or for worse.

The mooring-ropes were cast off. A bell tinkled in the en-gine-room, the screw beat the inky water into a foaming spate, and the *John Goodwin* drew away from the wharf.

Carl Swanson, leaning on the bridge rails, told Tubby what he thought of him at some length. Larry smote him on the back with a ham of a hand and added his quota to the disapproval felt by the crew at being held up by a something something cook.

From below came the rhythmic whining beat of the engines, and, as the distance between wharf and ship increased, Tub-by resigned himself to six weeks of hell, during which time he would carry countless buckets of coal up a steep steel ladder from the stoke-hold to the galley, and many more fannies of tea down to the cuddy.

He walked aft and entered a low doorway cut in the en-gine-room casing. On his right was the galley, cold, and smell-ing of wet soot; on the left there was an opening in the deck and from it a ladder ran straight down to the cuddy. Tubby lifted his bag and dropped it. It fell with a plump; he followed it more slowly, clutching his precious zither tightly.

The cuddy was a triangular space in the stem of the ship, lined with bunks and two settees covered in shiny leather cloth. There was a stove at the apex of the triangle and Tubby set to work to get it going, for the southwester had chilled his body and numbed his fingers. Once lit, it would never be allowed to die until they were tied up once more at the fish-wharf.

When it was drawing well, Tubby looked out of a port-hole and saw, with the bitterness of a born landsman, the pierhead lights. They were paling in the first cold light of dawn. He saw the muffled-up figure of the assistant harbour-master and muttered: "Lucky swine!"

Then he stuffed a cutty pipe full of coal-black tobacco. The fumes resulting from the wedding of the flame of a match with the tobacco soon began to fill the cuddy. The skylights were screwed down and there would soon be a fug which would last for weeks, unless a sea was thoughtless enough to smash the glass. Smells of hot oil permeating along the shaft-tunnel from the engine-room, of paraffin leaking from a can in the corner, and of burning paint on the stove, joined and blended with the aroma of Tubby's burning shag.

A voice from the upper deck made it known that there was a real and pressing need for tea. Tubby groaned, and went up to the galley to stew some; hot, bitter and sweet was the way the trawlermen liked it, and they liked it often.

The *John Goodwin* cleared the pierheads and entered the Gilboro' River, which ran ten miles north before it made an eight-point turn to join the sea. The light in the eastern sky was spreading slowly over the sky—a cold, impersonal light.

Larry climbed up on to the gallery round the bridge where Carl was standing. "Doesn't look as if it's going to let up. The glass is away down."

"It'll take us a week to get on to the grounds. Plenty of time for it to ease up before then." Carl turned and called to the helmsman: "Keep her as she goes. Nor' by east." Then he walked to the port wing and looked across the flat grey marshes stretching away to a line of sand-dunes, the natural barrier to the open sea.

Larry joined him, and pointed to a building near the water's edge. "I hear Tom Ingleby's gone bust."

"I'm not surprised. It was a fool business to start. There's no money these days in barge-building, and anyone but Tom would have known that."

"He calls his place the 'Pride of Bedford', and Gawd, what a place it is!"

In the year 1879 the "Pride of Bedford", a proud, full-rigged ship, had raced the *Thermopylœ* home with a cargo of tea from Foochow. Then, when steam had spoilt that trade for sailing-ships, she had been laid up in the Gilboro' River. Forty years later, Tom Ingleby had bought her rotting hull, removed the best of her timbers, and with them had built a house raised high on piles above a mud-bank riddled with rat-holes and scored by the ever-sucking tide.

It was a crazy structure patched with pieces of tarred felt, linoleum and corrugated iron. Above the front door he had nailed the stem name-board of the ship, the Pride of Bedford. Somewhere among the marram grass lay the figurehead. On a slipway was the half-completed hull of a barge. Tom Ingleby's capital had given out before he had been able to finish her. But still he lived there in the graveyard of his hopes. In one of the creeks he had an eel-net, and in the winter he shot wildfowl on the marshes and sold them in Gilboro' market.

"It's his own fault he's gone that way." Carl said, with the contempt of one to whom success had come easily.

Ahead of the trawler lay the steel-grey ribbon of the river which led to the open sea. The bell of a buoy swaying to the swell clanged drearily.

Carl leaned over the rail and hailed a decky. "Tell that damn' cook I'm waiting for my tea."

The man acknowledged the order with an upward jerk of his head and clumped aft. Through the engine-room skylight came the clink of a steel shovel as the trimmers stoked the fires.

Ten minutes later Tubby arrived with a mahogany-coloured brew of tea in a fish-kettle. In one hand he carried a mug which he handed to Carl. "Dan says you've got a rotten lot of coal aboard. It took me half an hour to pick out enough as would do for the galley."

Carl dipped the mug into the kettle. "Cheerful as usual. Why were you late coming aboard?"

"Because the chambermaid in my hotel forgot to call me."

Tubby cared for no man, least of all for Carl Swanson.

2

IT WAS BLOWING a full gale when the *John Goodwin* arrived within sight of the Baarland coast after five days' steaming. The atmosphere in the cuddy had achieved a thickness which none but those with the strongest stomachs could stand. What it was like in the forecastle only the deckies knew, but they knew better than to complain to Carl. Bilge-water, foul-smelling, washed over the floor in spite of an hour's work at the pumps during every watch. Carl had forbidden Dan Todd to start up the steam-pump because that would have meant a loss in speed, and he was mad keen to get on to the grounds and shoot the trawl.

"A new ship shouldn't take in water that way," Carl had grumbled.

"Ye've got to give her time to take up," was Dan's reply. "She's green."

The coast of Baarland was a solid wall of fissured rock rising sheer out of the sea which ran up on to its face and fell back in foaming whirlpools of white-green water.

Carl rang down "Dead Slow" on the telegraph and called to the watch on deck to take a sounding.

The lead was armed with tallow, and a man clinging to the fore-shrouds swung it forward into the heaving waters. The wet line ran out. "And a half ten." The words, swept aft on the wind, reached Carl on the bridge.

"We're somewhere near it," he shouted to Larry.

With bent backs and straining arms two deckies hauled the lead on board.

"Bring it up here and let's have a look."

Carl took the lead and carried it into the wheel-house. There was sand and broken shells embedded in the tallow. Carl poked at it with a finger, muttered to himself, "We might as well give it a go," and then leaned out through a window. "Shoo-oot!"

At once from the deck the cry was taken up. Through the square of light of the fore-hatch bulky figures staggered on deck and shambled aft to the gallows.

"Port trawl!"

Larry blew down a voice-pipe to the engine-room, and when an answering whistle came, called: "Shoo-oot!" Then he turned to Carl. "You're taking a risk, skipper."

But Carl didn't hear him. He was thinking of full boxes, a full hold and a bumper pay-off. The best catch of the year and a pocketful of dollars.

Though the trawler was forging ahead at slow speed, a sea broke over her starboard bow and ran aft like a river, waist deep.

The voice of Dan Todd raised in anger was heard. He clambered up on the platform abaft the winch. He wouldn't trust anyone except himself to handle it. An electric winch! It was the first time he'd had a chance of handling one of them.

Larry shouted to him to heave up. Dan pulled over a switch, the motor whined and the heavy doors of the trawl rose slowly off the deck.

"Lower away. Smack it about with that damn' net. Pick it up. It won't bite you."

Into the frothing water went the long net. The doors were lowered. The towing-wire was paid out.

Larry turned his face upwards to the wheel-house. "She's all clear, Skipper."

Carl pulled over the telegraph. "Half ahead."

"Walk back on the winch. Stand clear."

The wire grating over the bulwarks tautened to a vibrating bar of steel.

Carl swung down the ladder on to the deck. "How much have you got out, Dan?"

"Thirty fathoms."

"Hold her at that." He put a hand on the wire. "She's fishing." He waited for a minute to make sure and then shouted to Larry to send the crew below. "We'll haul in four hours' time."

Dan Todd screwed down the cover of the switch-box of the winch and, choosing his opportunity, dropped on to the deck and made his way aft.

Down in the cuddy, Tubby was hunched up on the port settee with his zither on his knees. On the table was spread open at page five *The Twenty-Four-Hour Tutor*, and Tubby, oblivious to all else, was concentrating on the notes of "Swanee". He had mastered the first line and was picking it out for the ninth time when Dan came in, wiping his face with a lump of cotton waste.

"Where's that damn' tea?"

"On the stove. Help yourself."

"Carl'll lose his trawl if he doesn't look out."

Tubby stopped playing to say: "I wouldn't be surprised. Did it go down all right?"

"Yes, but I've never seen anyone fish in weather like this before. We ought to lie up in Haranger Harbour."

Larry came down, kicked off his sea-boots, took off his oilies and rolled into his bunk. The twanging of Tubby's zither made no difference to him and soon his snoring formed a background to "Swanee".

For four hours there was peace on board the *John Goodwin*, if one can except Tubby's assault on the zither, Larry's snoring, the beat of the engines and the wash of the seas on deck.

Then came Carl's shouted order: "All hands on deck!"

Dan Todd took up his station at the winch. The crew ranged themselves along the starboard bulwarks. Slowly the wire ground in until the doors rose to the gallows. Then came the net—empty.

"Shoo-oot!"

Once more the net was lowered on to the bed of the sea. The crew returned to their bunks in the forecastle. Tubby went round with his kettle of tea. Tea! The word would be written on his heart when he died.

Larry joined Carl in the wheel-house. "What about your having a drop of shut-eye?"

"Not before we get a good haul."

"There's no use your stopping up here."

"I'm all right."

"Have it your own way." Larry looked out into the black murk ahead and sucked hard to keep his pipe alight. "A day lost now wouldn't make no odds."

"I've come here to fish."

Larry said: "All right," and went below.

Three hours later a crack like the report of a twelve-pounder gun roused Larry from his bunk. He was wide awake in an instant. Before he'd swung his legs clear to the floor he heard the bo'sun shouting down the hatch:

"Trawl's gone!"

Larry felt for his sea-boots, slipped in his feet and jumped for the ladder. On deck men were shouting and swearing. He swung himself on to the casing and up the bridge ladder. Carl was standing by the starboard light-box, his back bent over the rail. When he saw Larry, he said:

"She's carried away." He paused and then, as an afterthought, said: "And there's two hands gone as well. The wire got 'em."

Larry looked down and saw Dan's white face upturned. "And thirty fathoms of wire."

Carl shouted to the helmsman. "Hard a-starboard." Slowly the ship's head came up into the wind and paid off to starboard.

"Going to pack up?" Larry asked.

"Like hell I am!" And then: "Get the starboard trawl ready."

Four miles away to port a light flashed twice.

Carl pulled over the telegraph. "Full ahead." Then he shouted down to Dan Todd. "Give her all she'll take."

Against the starlit sky, swept clear of clouds, rose the cliffs of Baarland. The sound of breakers on the rocks became clearly audible.

Larry stood quite still for a minute, then he went up to Carl. "Are you going to try inside?"

Carl nodded. "There's nothing else for it. We've got to catch fish."

"If the bogey man's about—" Larry began to say.

Carl cut him short. "I'll look out for him. Get that trawl out."

As the ship closed the land the sea became easier. Carl said: "This is better. Get a cast of the lead."

The first sounding showed rock, but on the second the tallow bore traces of clam-shells. Carl's mouth broke into a smile. "This is where we fill up."

He was right. The bag at the first haul was chock-full of fish which fell in a white, wriggling cascade when the purse-cord was loosened.

"Get her over again."

The bo'sun and a decky clawed seaweed clear of the mesh and refastened the purse-cord. The crew bent to heave the heavy, water-soddened line of net over the side. Then they turned to the fish-pounds and under the light of a yard-arm group, swinging from the fore-stay, began the work of gutting and packing.

The deck was clear of water now, the work made easier thereby, and soon the last shovelful of offal was pitched overboard and the hatch put back on the fish-hold.

Carl suddenly began to feel very tired; he had been on his feet for thirty-six hours. As he walked aft, there was the stagger of fatigue in his walk. He swung down the ladder to the cuddy. Tubby was there, bent over the table studying *The Twenty-Four-Hour Tutor*. Dan Todd was stripping off his jacket preparatory to turning in all standing. The bo'sun was already snoring in his bunk. The coals in the stove were piled high and glowed red. On the table were three dirty mugs, a basin of sugar and an open tin of biscuits, hard as granite chips.

Carl drew back the blankets in his bunk. Then he pulled off his sea-boots and climbed in. Thirty seconds later he was asleep.

On the bridge, Larry, with one eye lifting for a change in the weather, was wedged in a corner of the wheel-house. Above the wheel the roof-compass swayed lazily in time with the rolling of the ship.

Larry smoked his pipe through, then he went out of the door on to the gallery and flashed a torch down on to the trawl-wire. It was bar taut and led over the starboard quarter. The side-lights had been taken from their boxes and covered with sacking. It wasn't wise to advertise the fact that they were fishing within the limit. Abeam to starboard lay the Baarland cliffs.

Larry stamped his feet as he walked, and thrust his hands deep into the pockets of his lammy coat. It was perishing cold, and he thought of the cuddy and his bunk. Three hours more and they'd haul again. After that it was the bo'sun's watch, and with luck he'd be able to snatch four hours' sleep.

Three hours to go.

"What's that?" the helmsman called.

"Where?"

"Two points on the port bow. A white light."

Larry's eyes followed the direction but he saw nothing.

"I've lost it," the helmsman said, and left the wheel to lean out of a window and peer into the night.

"Are you sure you saw it?"

"Ay. Sure as I stand here. A white light."

"Maybe it's someone fishing. The *Maid of Perth*'s somewhere about. We were on to her on the wireless an hour or two back."

"Then what does she want to douse her light for?"

"Maybe she thought we was the bogey man."

"But we're not showing a light. It couldn't be that."

"You'd better steer a couple of points to starboard. Just in case."

The helmsman pulled over the spokes of the wheel.

Larry kept his eyes on the bearing on which the white light had been seen. For minutes he made no move. Then he swung round. "There is a ship out there. And she's not of our crowd. Go and call the old man."

Larry heard the thump of the man's feet as he dropped off the engine-room casing on to the deck, heard him run aft and heard his voice calling down the after-hatch: "Skipper! You're wanted!"

He could make out the black bulk of a ship now as the trawler rose on the swell and lost it as she slid down into the trough of a sea. She was showing no lights.

Then he heard voices. Carl asking, "What the hell have you done about it?" The clump of his sea-boots on the wooden deck and then he saw him jump for the ladder and swing himself upwards. He hadn't put on his oilies.

"Where is she?"

"Wait a minute." Larry raised his arm and pointed. "There! Just a bit to the right of the shrouds. D'ye see her?"

Carl said: "Yes, I've got her. Stop the ship!"

"What are you going to do?"

"Get the trawl in. Tell Dan to man the winch. Send the hands up on deck but don't make too much noise about it."

As Larry reached the deck a pencil of light shone out suddenly from the other ship, lit up a patch of sea, and started to swing round towards the *John Goodwin*.

"Put a cover over our number!" Carl yelled. "Dan! Where the hell have you got to, Dan?"

"I'm here." Dan Todd was at his post, one hand on the starting-handle of the winch. "What do you want? Heave in?"

"No, wait a minute."

Larry, with two of the deckies, was on the forecastle struggling with a tarpaulin. They were trying to get over the rail and lower it on the white-painted letters on the bow.

Carl watched the searchlight as it played round like an inquiring finger. It was coming nearer, nearer.

"O.K. here," Larry sang out.

"Then get down on deck. Hell and blast!"

The blinding ray of the searchlight fell right on the *John Goodwin*, swept on, stopped and returned slowly to its objective.

"Slip the trawl."

Dan Todd pulled over a switch. The winch motor started to turn, quicker, quicker, until its note rose to a high-pitched whine.

"Send all the spare hands to the stoke-hold. Get a full head of steam."

It was hell, this waiting. Carl's body was tense, his nerves strung up. His hands were gripping the rail. It was covered with ice but he didn't feel the cold. His eyes were on the rotating drum, on the glinting steel of the trawl-warp as it ran out.

"Give us that axe!" Dan shouted. He pulled over the switch and hacked at the hemp stopper fastening the warp to the drum. "Stand clear! She's going!" There was the sound of rope stranding and with a flick like the tail of a snake the warp had gone.

Carl leapt to the wheel-house and pulled over the telegraph to "Full Ahead".

Slowly the engines began to turn, worked up to half and then full speed. Vibrations ran through the ship and she lifted and plunged into the swell as Carl headed her seawards. But ever upon her was the merciless light of the searchlight.

The gunboat was a mile distant, but she was closing in quickly. Larry came up the ladder. He was breathing hard. "She's got us, Skipper."

"Not if we go inside."

"You mean the Skerries?"

Carl nodded.

"The channel's only two hundred feet. You'll never make it."

A ghost of a grin chased across Carl's set face. "That damn' searchlight'll show us the way. It's our only chance." Carl turned to the helmsman. "Steer west. That'll make him think." It did. There was a flash from the gunboat and then the report of a gun. Carl was grinning now. "They've tumbled."

Below in the stoke-hold Dan Todd and the trimmers were shovelling coal on to the fires. They were stripped to the waist and sweating and coughing; the dust rose in clouds as the coal cascaded out of the bunker door. One man carried a bucket of water from the engine-room, staggering to the roll of the ship, emptied it on the coal and returned for further supplies.

The second engineer was going round the bearings with a long-spouted oil-can; quickly, with practised movements, he opened a lid, poured in oil, shut the lid and went on to the next. He called out to Dan Todd: "She's running a bit hot, Chief."

Dan put down the ten-foot slice with which he had been cleaning a fire and came into the engine-room. "Whereabouts?"

The second engineer pointed to a bearing cover. "You try that."

Dan didn't speak for ten seconds, then he said, "She's not so bad." He noted the reading of the revolution counter then he looked at the pressure gauge. "We've got to keep going. Bearing or no bearing." He looked upwards suddenly. "Did you hear that? They've started with their gun. I doubt they've got us this time."

On the bridge Carl kept his eyes on the black shadow of a rock which rose a sheer forty feet out of the tumbling seas and which broke on its base. It wasn't more than a couple of hundred yards distant on the starboard bow. To port, seas were breaking on a long reef.

The searchlight left the ship, swept ahead and lit up the rock. A cloud of screaming gannets rose into the air and were swept to leeward on the wings of the gale.

"Half a point to starboard."

The seas were shorter and steeper now, and the *John Goodwin*, punching into them, pitched with a quicker motion. "We're losing her."

"She's stopped firing," Larry said.

"That's because she figures that I'll come out through the Spikerack Channel; he thinks he'll cop us there, but that's where he makes his blooming error."

The searchlight was suddenly switched off and minutes passed before Carl could accustom himself to the absence of light. "He'd like fine to see us pile up," Carl said to Larry. He walked round the gallery to the port side, stood there looking out for a minute or two, then he came back to the starboard side. "D'you think we've room to turn?" Larry looked at Carl for a moment, puzzled, then he said: "Yes, plenty."

"Hard a-port," Carl snapped out the order, went into the wheel-house and helped the helmsman to pull the wheel over. "When you get her round, steer east." He blew down the voice-pipe to the engine-room. "Tell the chief I want to speak to him. . . . Dan, you've got to get every blooming rev out of the old tub."

"She won't take any more. It's the coal. It's terrible dirty and the after-bearing's getting hot."

"Is there anything you can do for it?"

"Not unless we stop for an hour."

"We can't do that. We've got four hours' hard steaming ahead of us if we're to beat the bogey man."

"Well, we'll just have to hope for the best."

"O.K. If you want any more help, let me know." Carl put the plug into the voice-pipe and called to Larry. "Can you see her?"

"Ay. She's in about a line with the reef now, steering west."

"That's fine." Carl pulled out his pipe and filled it. He was beginning to feel better now. In the excitement of dodging the gunboat he had forgotten all about the lost trawls, that there was no other on board, and that for the first time since he'd been to sea as skipper he would have to take his ship into Gilboro' with only a score of full boxes in the fish-hold.

"Look there! He's got his light on again." Larry touched Carl on the arm.

Together they stood silent watching the questing beam. It was five miles away.

"Maybe he thinks we've gone ashore. He's looking round the Spikerack Channel. Let him. If we can make another couple of miles before he tumbles, we'll get clear."

Ten minutes later the searchlight was but a thin pencil of light. Carl ordered the helmsman to steer for the open sea on a course of south-west by west. Then he called down to the engine-room: "If you can keep her going like this for another hour, I think we'll make it."

As the ship drew away from the land the seas became longer, the force of the wind increased, and a never-ceasing succession of sea broke over the forecastle, flooded the foredeck until the fish-hatch stood up like an island in the midst of the frothing water.

Tubby unwisely tried to make his way forward with a fanny of boiling tea, met a breaking sea and was swept, struggling, past the galley door. He brought up against an extremely hard bollard, coughed up half a pint of water, swore and crawled to safety in the lee of the engine-room casing. There he lay for a moment, still swearing. Then, as the ship rolled to port, he made a dash for the galley door, got inside and shut the door. As he wedged it tight with the clips he thought of Gilboro', its pubs, its cinemas and his lodgings.

Water washed knee high, the fire was out, a pot which had once contained stew was lying on its side on the stove.

Well, it wasn't the first time he'd been washed out. He opened a cupboard and took out a canister of tea, a paper bag of sugar and a tin of condensed milk. Whatever happened the crew must have their tea.

He went to the top of the ladder leading down to the engine-room, saw the back of the second engineer bent over the circulating-pump, and hailed him: "Here, take this lot, will you?"

Then he followed the tea and the sugar and the milk down to the engine-room.

Dan Todd was sitting on an upturned bucket, reading chapter two of *A Thousand a Year from Hens*.

"I want a loan of a fire for ten minutes, Chief."

Dan put his finger in the page he was reading. He had reached the part where the author was dealing with the housing problem as applied to hens. "You want to boil tea on my stoke-hold fires?" Dan's tone implied that this was an insult, deliberate and unprovoked.

Tubby grinned. "That's the idea. I've been washed out up top."

"No one's going to boil tea on my fires. D'you see that gauge?" He pointed with an extremely dirty fore-finger. "I've got to keep the needle on that red line."

Tubby opened the canister of tea and spilled a good portion of its contents into the fanny. Then he took an opener out of his pocket and jabbed it into the top of the tin of milk.

"You could do with a wet, Dan, couldn't you?"

Dan made angry noises.

Tubby worked the opener round the lid of the tin, poured the milk into the fanny and added the sugar.

"Now all I want is a gallon of boiling water. Come on, Dan, be a sport. The old man'll be wild if he don't get his tea."

"And he'll be a damn' sight wilder if I let the steam go back."

"Just a gallon. You'll never miss it. You can give it me out of the boiler-feed. Tea's as important as steam in a trawler. You ought to know that by now."

"I'll tell you what I'll do. I'll give you your water if you don't play that damn' zither for twenty-four hours while I'm in the cuddy."

"Dan, you don't mean that. You can't! After all, what's wrong with a bit of music?"

"There's nothing wrong with music."

"You haven't heard me play 'Swanee'."

"I have. Five times—and every time was worse than the one before."

"That was because I hadn't quite got the hang of it," Tubby pleaded.

"You can have your water if you keep your zither in its box for twenty-four hours—and that's my last word."

Tubby looked at the fanny, at Dan, and then back to the fanny. He was weakening. "Make it twelve hours, Dan, and I'll start on a new tune."

"Twenty-four hours."

"All right. And I hope your hens get the croup."

Carl Swanson did not receive the results of this bargain, for he was marooned with Larry and the helmsman on the bridge. They watched anxiously for the lights of the gunboat, saw them draw clear of the land, saw the questing searchlight grow fainter and fainter until they could only see its loom in the northern sky.

"We're losing her," Carl said. "Another hour and we'll be well clear." He got on to Dan through the voice-pipe. "You can ease her up a bit. How's that bearing?"

The answer came distantly as from someone many miles away. "Not a great deal worse, but I'll have to watch it. The coal's the real trouble."

With safety came the realization of the present: both trawls gone, two men over the side and the fish-hold nearly empty! Black gloom descended on Carl Swanson, and he saw vividly the scene of the arrival of the *John Goodwin* at Gilboro'. There would be a crowd on the quay; Mrs. Mather, Jessie Miles, Hoppy and the gaffer, anxious to learn the result of the trip. And what was he going to tell them? That he'd lost six hundred pounds' worth of gear and had nothing to show for it.

He cursed the weather and the gunboat; his luck had let him down this time. He wouldn't take Tubby Stevens next trip; him and that damn' zither of his.

Carl's depression made itself felt all over the ship: in the forecastle, where the deckies lay in their bunks and smoked and read scraps of week-old papers. Two of them had gone; that had happened before in other boats and they had accepted the loss with a philosophy bred in the hardest trade in the world. But this time they'd lost their gear as well. There was little talk.

Down in the cuddy Tubby was sitting at the table, with his left side roasting at the stove. He was fingering the pages of *The Twenty-Four-Hour Tutor*, but he did not want to play his zither.

Dan came down the ladder. He was very tired and he moved slowly as he edged round the table to his bunk. Tubby dipped a mug into the fanny of tea and set it down before him. He pushed over a plate of corned beef. Dan drank his tea slowly and noisily because it was hot. Before he had finished it he was half asleep.

3

THE STEAMSHIP *Ivanhoe*, with a cargo of pitprops, and bound from Baltic ports to the Thames, ran into the same south-westerly gale that had caused the *John Goodwin* to lose her first trawl—a gale bringing snow and sleet which clung frozen to the rigging, the ratlines, and even to the wireless aerial swinging overhead.

Captain MacTaggart was a brave man, who for forty years had wrung a living from the sea. He had saved his money, had invested it, and had been lucky. At the age of sixty-five his life's dream became a reality. He was master of his own ship. That freights were low was his first bit of real bad luck, and he was having a struggle to keep the ship going.

He had cut costs all he knew, but even so he had had to sail on this voyage with the *Ivanhoe* uninsured. He had taken a cargo which had put her down to her marks and the decks were piled high with stacks of timber. The ship rose sluggishly to the seas. There was no life in her.

The mate who was on watch muttered to himself: "She won't stand this long," and shuffled across the bridge to where the captain was standing. MacTaggart, his short brown beard flecked with frozen spray, stamped his numbed feet on the deck. The mate called out to him: "Hadn't we better heave to?"

Captain MacTaggart peered over the canvas dodger, his eyes half closed to the driving sleet. "Like hell, I will. We're due in in two days' time and we're late as it is."

"She's making heavy weather of it." The mate was persistent.

Without turning his head, the captain said: "She'll come through all right."

The mate was about to reply but he changed his mind and went back to his position behind the wheel. He said to the helmsman: "Bring her up a point."

The helmsman grunted an acknowledgment of the order and put his weight on the port side of the wheel. The mate helped him.

Slowly the ship's head swung round to meet the seas bows on. She began to ride more easily and the next sea split on her stem and foamed aft harmlessly on either side.

The captain came suddenly alive. He shouted: "What the hell are you up to?" He worked his way along the rail, peered down at the compass card and gripped the wheel. "You're a point off your course. Bring her back."

The head of the *Ivanhoe* began to fall off and she rolled heavily to starboard.

"Look out!" The mate saw the sea coming and leapt to the wheel.

The captain said: "What the hell!"

The helmsman, fear in his eyes, was powerless to make a movement.

Crash! Five tons of green water broke over the port bow on to the stack of timber on the fore-hatch, burst its lashings and carried it bodily to starboard. The ship listed and hung there. Then came another sea, thirty feet high. The fore-mast fell with a crash and planks from the fore-hatch cover were swept along the deck by the force of water.

The ship was dead like a sodden log. The wireless aerial hung, a mess of jangling wires, over the bridge.

"Heave to!" The captain barked the order and lent his strength to pull over the wheel.

"She won't answer," the mate shouted above the roar of the gale.

"Get her hard over." The captain reached for the telegraph and rang "Slow ahead". "That'll ease her," he shouted, but it was too late. Another sea broke over the forecastle and poured down through the hatchway into the fore-hold.

"Get that wireless aerial rigged! Take all the hands you need and put the rest of 'em on to the hand-pump."

"Hand-pump!" The helmsman breathed the words to himself. "Blooming lot of good that'll do."

"And you! Wake up!" the captain yelled at the helmsman. "Get that wheel amidships . . . Now meet her. . . . Keep her like that."

The captain worked his way, hanging on to the rail, until he reached the starboard wing and stood there staring down at the wreckage. A shower of sleet whipped over the dodger and spattered in his face. The collar of his oilskin had come adrift but he made no attempt to fasten it. His hands gripped the rail, his forearms straight in front of him.

The water in the fore-hold was rising as each successive sea poured into it. He saw parcels of props washed out on the deck and their lashings break adrift. A man, staggering forward knee-deep in the swirling water, saw a prop swing towards him, was too late to avoid it and fell. The mate hauled him clear on the top of a hatch.

The man lay inert as a child's rag doll.

The captain stood watching. What had happened to the man didn't interest him. He was waiting until they could get that damned aerial rigged again. Then he searched the low-driving clouds for a sign of the slackening of the gale, but found none.

The ship was going down by the head and was slogging into the seas.

"Might as well send an S O S and get the crew out of it." He wouldn't go himself. What was the use? If the ship went down he'd be where he started when he first went to sea as deck-boy in a Cardiff collier. Sixty-five, and down to the bare bones. Too late to start again. Too late!

He turned quickly as a man slid down the inclined deck towards him. The ship had a heavy list to starboard, fifteen degrees, very nearly, and she was hanging there.

It was the mate. His face was like that of a drowned man and when he spoke his voice barely carried the two feet which separated him from the captain.

"Well! Can't you do it?"

The mate shook his head and croaked: "It's no good, Skipper. Sparks says he can't work his set unless we get the aerial right up off the deck. I had a try but it weren't no good; shorting all the time."

"Get all the hands up here." The captain fought his way to the chart-house. As he reached the door he called out to the helmsman to know if he could see any lights.

The helmsman wiped frozen spray from his eyes with the back of a numbed hand and shook his head.

The captain felt for the switch inside the door of the chart-room and pushed it down. The light blinded him, and seconds passed before he could fully open his eyes. A chart was spread out on the table. It was stained with the dregs of cocoa dripping from the lip of an overturned mug.

He wrenched at the door of a cupboard set high on the after-bulkhead and groped for the rocket-holder. Then he took down two rockets from their clips, fitted one into the holder and carried it out on to the open bridge. The mate followed him to the rail.

"It's no use, Skipper. There's nothing in sight."

"Well, we'll be ready if someone does come along." The captain fumbled at the lashings and leaned against the holder to keep it upright. "Tell the chief I want him."

The chief engineer, a brawny Tynesider, came up on the bridge. He said: "She's in a bad way, Captain. But I've got the pumps going."

"How's the steam?"

"Not so bad. We're making twenty revolutions and if the fore-bulkhead holds we'll be all right."

The captain gripped the chief by the arm. "You're a good one, Geordie. The fore-hold's full up, and if the hatch on number two goes, that'll be the finish. Is there any water in the engine-room?"

"Ay. It's just about a foot below the plates. I've got the ballast-pump on and that's keeping it down."

"Do you want any help in the stoke-hold?"

"Later on, I may. The mate's sent down two of the A.B.s and the cook's lending a hand."

At ten minutes after midnight the lights of a steamship showed up on the port quarter of the *Ivanhoe*. The mate saw her first and strength returned to him. He called to the crew huddled abaft the chart-house. "Get the boat out." They were sweating down on the falls, lifting the boat off her chocks while the captain fitted a lanyard into the rocket-tube.

The men at the boat stopped their work as the rocket whistled skyward and looked up as it burst in a shower of falling stars.

"She'll see that all right," one of them said.

The captain sent a hand to the engine-room with an order for everyone to come up on deck. He, himself, went to the engine-room skylight and, kneeling on the casing, shouted to the chief to leave the engines working slow ahead.

Then he came back to the bridge and asked the helmsman: "How's she steering?"

"Terrible slow in answering," was the reply. "She's carrying a couple of turns of port helm."

The captain looked down at the compass card. "The wind's shifting," he muttered to himself. "Gone round to west."

The helmsman said: "What?"

"Go along to the boat. I'll look out here."

The mate came on the bridge and asked: "Which side shall I get her out?"

"Starboard. I'll give you a lee. Call up that ship with the lamp and ask her to come close in on the quarter." The captain put a cold pipe in his mouth and sucked at it. "And get up a drum of oil. Lash it on the rail aft."

The motion of the ship was less now and she hardly rose at all to meet the seas, which were breaking over her port bow. The stack of timber on the fore-deck had jammed in the starboard alleyway.

The chief engineer, the second and third and the fireman were standing, waiting for the boat to be lowered. One or two had bundles in their hands. They were all looking at the steamship which was closing slowly on the *Ivanhoe*. They could see her forefoot as it lifted clear of the seas and the lather of spray as she pitched into them.

The mate sent the second officer to get the injured man into the boat. He was still unconscious and his face was white like the underside of a flat fish. Four men lifted him into the stern sheets of the boat and put a rolled-up oilskin under his head.

Then they helped to swing the boat out and lowered her until she was a foot above the bulwarks.

"Take the bung out of the drum," the mate ordered. "Now, all hands into the boat and settle down on the thwarts facing aft."

He stood watching as the oil streamed away to leeward, spreading into a wide fan, smoothing out the breaking tops of the waves.

The other ship had eased her speed and was lying off, three hundred feet away. A cluster of lights in a reflector hung over her side and showed a jacob's ladder rigged overhanging.

The mate watched the crew clamber into the boat; then he ran to the bridge. "We're all ready, Skipper."

The captain did not move, he did not even turn his head.

"We're all ready." The mate touched him on the shoulder.

"All right. Carry on. I'm stopping here."

"She can't last much longer. Come on."

"I'm stopping here."

The mate stood hesitant for a moment. He stared at the captain's resolute back. Then he said: "So long, Skipper."

Three hundred feet is not a great distance if traversed on the Serpentine, but with a gale blowing in the North Sea it is quite a different matter. Half an hour it took the heavily loaded boat from the *Ivanhoe* to reach her rescuer.

One by one the crew jumped from the boat on to the ladder of the steamship *Witney*, climbed up slowly, gripping at the frozen life-lines and were hauled on board.

Captain MacTaggart watched the empty boat drift astern. "Thank God they all got away," he muttered to himself.

The wind which had gone round to the westward now began to blow with increasing force. She couldn't last long in this weather.

MacTaggart lashed the wheel amidships, went into the chart-room and picked the log off the floor. It was wet with sea-water. He looked at the last entry made by the mate: "Longitude 61° 10′ N. Latitude 3° 04′ E. Fore-hold flooded. Fore-mast carried away." And the time: "10.15 p.m."

He unbuttoned his oilskin and fumbled with frozen fingers for a pencil. He wrote awkwardly: "12.45 a.m. Crew abandoned ship. Transferred by ship's boat to S.S. *Witney*."

He put the log in a drawer and went out on the bridge. A sudden snowstorm drove him back, and he shut the door and lay for minutes sprawled across the chart table, his feet braced against the starboard wall. The list had increased by a few degrees. He noted the reading of a spirit-level: seventeen degrees. He thought for a moment of trying to cast loose the deck cargo but dismissed the idea as soon as it was formed.

Smoke was streaming, flatly, from the funnel. The steam couldn't last long, and once the ship lost steerage-way it would mean that she would lie beam-on to the seas.

He fought his way up the slope of the bridge-deck to the ladder and climbed slowly, laboriously on to the casing and crawled to the engine-room hatch. As soon as he was inside, out of the bone-biting blast, the warmth began to make the blood run in his bare hands, causing a pain so sudden, so intense that he only saved himself from falling by crooking his arms round the ladder uprights.

Slowly the pain receded and his bent, numbed fingers straightened as he reached the engine-room platform.

Level with his head the piston-rods rose and fell. Steam was hissing from a leaky joint. The circulating-pump was turning over, jerkily, complainingly as though it was ever about to stop. There was a smell of hot oil and steam, and wet coal.

He stood for a minute or two in front of the counter. Sixteen revolutions. It wouldn't do to let her fall below that, especially the way it was blowing up.

He went into the stoke-hold and opened a furnace door. There wasn't more than four inches of fire on the bars. The door to the cross-bunker was open and on a heap of coal lay a shovel. He picked it up and worked for a time, throwing coal on the fires.

The heat from the fire made his face glow, and beads of sweat began to form on his forehead. It was heavy work with the ship listing the way she was, and his feet slipped on the steel deck. Once he fell sidewards and lay for nearly five minutes, breathing hard. Then he got up slowly and opened another furnace door. The fire was clinkered and glowed a sullen red where white flames should have been leaping up.

It was about all he could manage to lift a slice and break up the fused layer of coal, throw on more coal and slam the door shut with a reverberating clang of steel on steel.

That would have to serve until he got some sleep.

The needle of the gauge-glass was flickering round about sixty pounds' pressure and the circulating-pump was achieving a more regular beat.

On deck it was still snowing and there was a drift level with the rail on the starboard side. It was banked up on the light-box and he swore as he cleared it away from the glass of the lamp.

"Damn' lot of use it is anyway," he muttered. "I wonder where that flaming *Witney*'s got to?" The visibility wasn't more than a couple of hundred feet. Well, there was nothing he could do except maybe fire another rocket, so that the *Witney* could pick him up.

It soared into the blanket of snow and was lost.

He looked at the compass but did not take the lashing off the wheel. He was feeling faint, and staggered and nearly fell as his feet slipped on the freezing snow. What was the good of stopping up here? Clinging desperately to the ladder man-ropes he worked his way down to the boat-deck and along the lee side to his cabin.

He fumbled for the switch. As he pressed it down he remembered that the dynamo was stopped and struck a match to light the wick of an oil lamp above the bunk.

Then he took off his oilskins and sea-boots, dried his face and neck and hands with a towel, turned back the blankets of the bunk and crawled under them.

There was a flat bottle of whisky on a rack. He took it down and drank from it. Soon warmth came and with warmth sleep.

The grey light of a North Sea winter dawn was filtering in through the port-hole of his cabin when MacTaggart awoke, ravenously hungry.

For a time he lay feeling the motion of the ship. She still had a bad list to starboard but was hardly making any movement other than a slow lazy roll. The engines had stopped.

He raised himself on one elbow and peered out of the scuttle. The clouds were low but he could see the misty horizon five miles away. The ship was lying beam on to the wind and sea which had gone down since he'd turned in. He dragged his watch from an inside pocket. Half past six, it said.

Grey heaving seas, grey, low-hanging clouds, a fresh breeze from the westward. On the fore-deck was the confusion wrought by the gale of the day before. Most of the deck cargo was adrift and jammed in an inextricable mass between the hatch-coamings and the starboard bulwarks.

There was no sign of the steamship *Witney*, nor of any other vessel.

MacTaggart went into the steward's cabin, found a box of chocolate bars and ate one as he made his way to the engine-room. The steam had gone right back but there was still an inch or two of fire under the port boiler. If he could keep that going for a time there'd be enough pressure to work the ballast-pump, and he could start getting the water out of number one hold.

The *Witney* must be looking for him, and when she turned up he could get the crew back on board, pump out the hold and take the ship to her destination. When the fires were drawing well he shut off the steam to the main engines and opened it up to the ballast-pump.

Then he ate two more bars of chocolate and lit his pipe.

He'd have looked a damn' fool if he hadn't stayed on board! If some ship had come along, had found the *Ivanhoe* derelict and had salved her he might have had to pay half the value of the ship in salvage.

All that forenoon he worked at the fires and by twelve o'clock he was looking with satisfaction at a steady stream of water pouring over the side. The level of the water in the flooded hold was down by a couple of feet and the ship was already rising more easily to the seas.

Once he got the hold pumped out he could stow some of the deck cargo in it in place of that which had been washed out, but there would be plenty of time for that later on. Another ten hours' work would be needed with the pump before he could see the floors. If he could keep the steam up he'd be all right.

With the habit bred by forty years at sea he went up on the bridge into the chart-room and took the log out of the drawer. His hand was steadier than it had been the night before. "Noon: Steam on ballast-pump. Pumping out number one hold. Wind— west. Force 5-6. Sea—moderate."

Then he put the log away, pulled himself up the sloping deck to the port wing of the bridge and had a good look all round. There wasn't a ship in sight.

"Well, I'll be more use down below keeping steam than hanging round up here." He spoke the words half aloud to himself and went down on to the casing and into the engine-room.

All the morning he tended the fires. Then he heated up a tin of soup and found a tin of biscuits to go with it. It was harder work than he'd thought, shovelling coal, and at five o'clock in the afternoon he dropped his shovel. He couldn't go on at this pace. The water in the hold was down by four feet and that would have to do until he was rested. He went up to his cabin, lay down on his bunk and was asleep five minutes later.

4

LARRY WAS THE first man to sight the Ivanhoe lying beam on to the sou'westerly swell. When Carl came up, bleary-eyed from too much sleep and too much smoke, Larry said: "I damn' near missed her. Looks as if she'd been abandoned."

Carl picked up a pair of glasses hanging from a nail in the wheel-house and rubbed the lenses with a corner of his scarf. "There's no one on deck and her mast has gone. She looks in a bad way." He gave the glasses to Larry and then pulled over the telegraph to stop.

Larry said: "She's lost one of her boats," and looked at Carl. There was a question in his eye.

"We might as well have a look at her. Maybe there's something we can do." Carl's first thought was of salvage, but he didn't put it into words. That was too much to hope for on an unlucky trip like this. Both trawls gone, two hands lost overboard and an empty hold. It would be asking for another smack in the eye to think of salvage.

"Bring her a bit closer," he said to the helmsman. "And give her a touch ahead."

The *John Goodwin* crept up until she lay on the starboard bow of the *Ivanhoe*. "Get the boat out, Larry. You and me'll take a look at her."

Dan Todd was standing on deck by the engine-room door. He walked forward until he was under the bridge. "What d'you make of her?" he called up to Carl.

"She's floating. I'm going to see if there's anything we can do."

"You'll not be able to tow till we've got that bearing seen to, and that'll be a twelve-hour job."

"Time enough to think of that after we've been aboard of her." Carl was first in the boat as it was lowered into the water.

He unhooked the falls and called to Dan, "You'd better come, too, and tell us about her engines."

He picked up the stroke oar. Larry, in the bows, held the boat off the ship's side with a boathook. Two deckies clambered down into the boat and they set off. Carl and Larry and the two deckies pulling, Dan Todd at the tiller, a melancholy helmsman.

When the boat was in the trough of a sea both the *John Goodwin* and the *Ivanhoe* were out of sight. It took them twenty minutes' hard pulling before they ran alongside the starboard side of the *Ivanhoe*.

Carl jumped for the top of the bulwark and hauled himself on board. Larry followed him and the two of them plucked Dan from his position in the stem sheets and dragged him on board.

"Mighty me! What a blooming mess-up," were Dan's first words as he gazed first on the mast and rigging lying across a litter of scattered timbers, and then on all that remained of the hatch on the forward-hold.

"No wonder the crew's left her," he said as he slowly picked his way through and over the wreckage to number one hold.

Carl was there before him. Larry said, pointing to the level of the water: "This must have come in over the top. It doesn't look as if she's holed."

Dan nodded. "Ay. That's right enough. Else the water would be near up to the coaming." He rubbed his chin and looked aft. "If we could get a pump on it now we might save her before the weather comes in bad again." He turned to Carl. "What d'you think it's going to do?"

"We're past the worst of it. The glass is going up and the clouds are a lot higher." Carl walked aft. "Come on. let's have a look-see in the engine-room."

As soon as Dan Todd got his head inside the engine-room casing he said: "Gosh. That's funny."

Carl, who was close behind him, asked: "What d'you mean?"

"Do you not feel it? The place is warm. The fires can't have been long out." He climbed quickly down the ladder, and when his feet were on the engine-room platform he stood for a moment listening. Then he almost ran to the ballast-pump and squatted down on his heels. "Come and have a look here." He was pointing to a feather of steam seeping from the valve-box. He put a hand on the cylinder and then on the crank. "She's warm."

"How long d'you think it's been since it's been working?" Carl asked.

"I can't say." Dan straightened himself and looked round the engine-room. "That'll be the way into the stoke-hold." He pointed to an open door.

Beyond was a narrow passage between two boilers and, as he made his way forward, Carl felt the plates on each side of him. "They're cold," he said.

"That's damn' queer." Dan Todd muttered the words, and as he reached the open space in front of the furnace doors he walked crabwise over the sloping deck to the third boiler and opened the doors. "This is where the steam for that pump has been coming from. The fire's still alight." He picked up the shovel that MacTaggart had used and began throwing coal through the furnace door.

Carl watched him for a minute or two and then took Larry by the arm. They went back into the engine-room.

"I'm going to take her in. Are you on?"

"Of course I am."

"I'll see what Dan says." Carl went back to the stokehold.

Dan, who was bending down regulating a draught-plate, looked up when he heard Carl's footsteps. He said: "It'll be a couple of hours before we can do anything with that pump. The steam's gone right back."

"What about lighting up the others?"

Dan wiped his face with a scrap of cotton waste. "We could do that."

"And steam her in?"

"I don't see as there's anything to stop us if we had the hands."

"The more we have on board, the less there'll be to share out."

"Ay. I see what you're getting at." Dan was thinking of the farm he was going to buy one day; the hens he'd have and the gear; all the latest incubators and foster-mothers. But they cost money and he hadn't saved more than a tenth of the sum required.

"Could you manage on your own?"

"No. I'd like to have a couple of good hands but I might be able to make do with one. It depends on how far we have to steam."

"A hundred and twenty miles is what I reckon it is. How about Tubby? We'll want someone to cook."

"He'd do if he'll work."

"I'll see to that."

"Might as well have our bags over," Dan suggested. He was thinking mostly of his tin of tobacco and *A Thousand a Year from Hens*.

The boat returned from the *John Goodwin* bearing among other things Tubby Stevens cocked up in the stern on a pile of bags. He looked rather like a monkey, and there was the yearning look of a monkey for a nut in his eyes as he looked backwards to the *John Goodwin*. At least she was more or less whole, her masts were in a vertical position and her decks unencumbered with a pile of timber.

He held the zither-case on his knees with one hand and with the other steered a tortuous, unwilling course towards the *Ivanhoe*.

Carl greeted him with a laugh, hauled him on board by the waistband of his trousers and sent the boat back to the trawler. The bo'sun was to steam her to Gilboro' on his own at slow speed on account of the hot bearing.

"And now we'll have to find you a cabin," said Carl. He was feeling hearty and well pleased with himself. The bad luck of the *John Goodwin*'s maiden trip had been forgotten.

He was on top of the world again. His luck hadn't failed him after all.

He went up on the boat-deck and opened the first cabin door he came to and put his head inside. "Come and have a look in here, Tubby. Ginger-beer sailors! He's left his toothbrush behind." He stooped and picked up a photograph off the deck. "And a picture of his missis. Don't she look posh? And sheets in his bunk and all."

Carl Swanson had never had a cabin of his own before and he was as pleased as a child with a doll's house. He opened the drawers under the bunk. "And he's left his duds as well; no time to pack up seemingly." He looked at himself in the glass over the folding washstand, cocked his cap on the side of his head and grinned. "Fallen on your two feet this time and no mistake," he said to himself, and then turned and went out on deck, still grinning. Larry was coming up the ladder carrying his bag.

"Any place for me?"

"This is mine. Try next door."

Larry pulled at the handle. "It's locked." He put down his bag and was going to use his full strength when a voice inside the cabin wanted to know what the something hell was going on.

The grin was wiped clean from Carl's face and he stood for a moment quite still.

Larry muttered: "Well, I'm damned," and stared blankly at the door.

There was a shuffling of feet inside the cabin, the door opened and Captain MacTaggart came out on deck, the anger of a man awakened from his sleep in his eyes.

He looked at Larry, at the bag at his feet and then at Carl. Tubby was keeping out of sight and trouble round the corner of the deck-house.

Carl stepped forward. "Who are you?" he snapped. "I'm the captain of this ship. Name of MacTaggart. Where'd you come from?"

"I was just passing in my trawler and I came on board to see if I could do anything for you. You look kinda messed up. Cargo shifted. Wireless gone. Fore-hold awash." There was the hint of a grin on Carl's face as he spoke.

It riled the captain of the *Ivanhoe*. "Where's your ship?"

"I've sent her back to Gilboro'. Any objections?"

"Well, I'll have you know that I'm still captain aboard this vessel, but if you like to give me a hand to take her into port, I'll pay you for your trouble."

"That's fine. Then there's nothing to get het up about." Carl began to slice tobacco into the palm of his hand with a short-bladed clasp-knife. "There's four of us. Chief engineer, mate," he pointed to Larry, "a cook and myself. We'll get the water out of the hold and then we'll start steaming. Where are you bound for?"

"The Thames—Greenland Dock."

"We'll have to get that deck cargo cleared up a bit."

MacTaggart stuck out his chin. "I've told you that I'm skipper here and I'm going to give the orders. We'll have that clear before we go any farther. Come in to my cabin and I'll put it down in writing."

As the captain went into his cabin, Carl looked at Larry and winked. Then he struck a match and when his pipe was going lounged into the cabin and sat on the edge of the bunk.

The captain sat down on a hard chair and let down a flap which served for a desk. Then he had to find a pot of ink, a pen that would write and paper.

"We the undersigned agree," he wrote, and then scratched his head. He looked at a knothole in the desk for inspiration.

Carl craned his neck to see what had been written, then he leaned back across the bunk on one elbow. "Just say that we agree to help you salve the ship. You don't want to put no more than that."

The captain raised a suspicious brown bear of a face. His forehead was wrinkled as he gnawed the end of his penholder. "I'm skipper of the ship. That's got to go down."

"All right, put it in."

But the written word did not come easily to Captain MacTaggart. He struck out the lines he had written and started again. In fact he made two or three false starts before he completed the "agreement".

Carl read it through and signed it. He didn't much care what he put his name to, for an idea was forming in his brain, an idea which, if it bore fruit, would render any agreement of no account.

As he handed the paper back to the captain his eyes were narrowed and he was not smiling.

"Well, I'm going to have a look down below and see how the chief's getting on."

The captain blotted his signature, read the words for the tenth time, folded the paper and put it in his wallet. "Four of them," he said to himself. "Damn' pirates." He opened a drawer and took out a revolver, and weighed it in his hand. "Better keep this handy. You never know."

Someone was coming along the deck outside humming "Swanee".

The captain thrust the revolver back in the drawer under a shirt and turned to the door to see Tubby, who stopped humming to say, "What cheer, Skipper! Where d'you keep the eats?"

"What's that?"

"The eats. Munje. Grub. Food."

"And who the hell are you?"

"Cook, second engineer, fireman, steward and anything else that's wanted." As an afterthought Tubby added: "And I'm not so dumb on the zither neither."

This information gave the captain no pleasure. "I'll send for you when I want you. Now get out of here."

Tubby withdrew a foot from the sill of the doorway. "All right. Have it your own way, but the other blokes'll be yelling for tea and munje in half a brace of shakes and what am I going to tell 'em?"

The captain got up off his chair and as Tubby backed away he pulled the door shut and turned the key in the lock.

Tubby said something to himself about it being a blooming fine look-out and went to the galley. The fire he'd kindled was beginning to burn up, but except for a pot of doubtful grey, greasy stew there was remarkably little of anything to eat.

He opened up the draught-plate in the flue and then went down to the engine-room where Carl, Larry and Dan Todd were gazing with wrapt interest at the ballast-pump. It was turning over at a good rate and was making a great deal of noise about it.

Tubby put a hand on Carl's shoulder and said, "It don't look too good up topsides."

Carl spun round on his heel. "Is it starting to blow up?"

"No, it's that bundle of misery that calls hisself the skipper. He won't give me no chow."

"I'll be along in a minute."

"You want to go easy with him. He's got a gun."

"How d'you know?"

"I saw it in his hand."

"Don't you worry. I'll fix him." Carl turned to Dan Todd. "What d'you reckon she's doing now?"

Dan passed a hand across the stubble on his chin and said, "About two hundred and fifty gallons an hour."

"And how long is it going to take to clear the hold?"

"Tomorrow morning. Maybe a bit sooner than that."

"What about starting up the main engines?"

"We can't do both at once. It would be different if we wasn't so short-handed." Dan leaned over the guard-rail and fed oil on to the crank-bearing.

"I want to close the land as soon as we can. The glass is starting to drop back again."

"Well it's for you to say, but with all that water in the hold there'll be a big strain on the bulkhead if you steam the ship."

Carl said to Larry: "Let's go up top and see what we can do with the deck cargo. We've got to get some of this list off her." He took Tubby by the arm and propelled him towards the ladder. "And you can give us a hand."

By the time he had got up on deck Tubby had barely sufficient breath to ask what the hell was the good of them sweating themselves if they weren't going to get paid for it.

"Of course you'll get paid."

"But not as much as you said. This ship ain't no blinking derelict seeing as how her skipper's aboard."

"That won't make a lot of difference." There was a hard look in Carl's eyes as he spoke. He bent down and picked up the end of a heavy baulk of timber.

"What about making a new stack amidships and clearing this lot out of the alleyway," Larry suggested.

"That'll do for a start. We'll lash it back on to the superstructure and then we'll clear away the rigging."

Carl Swanson worked like two men, Tubby like a bad half; his hands were soft and his muscles unused to the lifting of heavy weights, but Carl kept him at it until they had cleared the starboard alleyway and had made a stack of pitprops on number two hatch.

Then he went to look for the captain. He found him on the bridge. "Will you let us have the key of the store, skipper?"

Without turning his head the captain said: "It's hanging up in the chart-room. Behind the door."

Carl gave the captain one long look and there was a sneer in his eyes; he gave an upward jerk with his chin as he went towards the chart-room door.

He saw the chart of the North Sea spread out on the table and thought to himself: "Well, if I couldn't bring this old tub in without that I'd blinking well shoot myself." He picked up a pair of dividers. "And all the gilguys, too. Ginger-beer sailors! I'd like to see 'em try to catch fish."

There was a row of keys with brass tallies hanging on hooks. He found the one he wanted and went back on to the bridge. "Whereabouts is the store, skipper?"

"Under the crew's quarters in the forecastle."

Carl hailed Tubby, threw him the key and told him where to go. "And see we get something good for supper."

Then he leaned against the rail and faced MacTaggart. "I'm going to start up the engines tonight."

"No, you're not. We've got to get that hold pumped out first."

"Have you seen what the glass is doing?"

"I have. And that's all the more reason why I'm going to get the ship seaworthy before we start the engines."

"It's risky stopping where we are. Twelve hours at five knots would get us into a bit of shelter."

"That hold's got to be dry before you put a pound of steam on the engines."

"There's four of us on board the ship," said Carl. His voice was hard and held a threat.

"I know. But I didn't ask you to come on board. Don't forget that."

Carl's right fist was clenched and he took a half-pace forward.

MacTaggart did not move.

Neither spoke for half a minute and then Carl said: "All right. Have it your own way."

"That is what I mean to do."

Carl walked to the top of the ladder leading down to the deck. "If you don't look out you'll lose your ship."

"If I do it'll be my own funeral."

Carl found Larry passing a rope over the timber-stack and he gave him a hand to haul it taut. It was getting on for eight o'clock and dark as pitch. The clouds which had been high were banking low on the southern horizon.

As he turned up with the last rope's end, Larry said: "Doesn't look as if we're going to have such an easy passage after all. What's the glass doing?"

"Twenty nine eight, dropping." Carl walked to the forward-hatch. "Dan's got a lot of water out. We'll have to rig up some sort of cover before we turn in."

"Battens and tarpaulins?" Larry suggested.

"Ay. That'll have to serve."

"We've got some of the list off her. She's riding easier, and as long as we don't drive her into it we won't get much water aboard."

"I'm not going to steam her till we clear the hold." Carl measured the width of the hold by eye. "Lucky that brace held up. All we want is half a dozen four by twos each side, nail 'em down and put the covers on."

Larry was thinking of Captain MacTaggart. "It's going to cut down anything we get for salvage, the captain being on board. There won't be more than a few hundreds in it for each of us."

"I'll think up something," Carl replied and walked aft looking for suitable timbers.

When Tubby told Dan Todd about the captain being on board Dan looked sour, and as he made up the fires he had no heart in his work. He'd been counting on something big; a sum that would free him from the drudgery of a trawler engine-room, the crowded discomfort of a cuddy—and now! He slammed a furnace door shut, looked at the needle in the gauge-glass and then picked up his shovel. All the way in it would be drive, drive,

drive. He knew Carl. And why the blazes shouldn't he have had a couple of deckies to help fire the boilers? Yes, he knew all about having to share the salvage award, but Carl could have made some arrangement to have paid them a fixed sum.

There was going to be trouble, too, between Carl and the skipper. Carl wouldn't cotton on to playing second fiddle. He never had. He'd once laid out his skipper when he'd been mate; and he'd got away with it. He always had. He was lucky.

The thought made Dan feel a little better. He gave the next fire a good rake-out and plenty of coal. When he'd finished in the stoke-hold he went into the engine-room and noticed, as he walked between the boilers, that the list had eased several degrees.

The ballast-pump was working at its full speed and the circulator was doing its job. There was steam to spare.

Down through the gratings overhead came the hesitant, maddening twang of "Swanee" being butchered to make a half-hour of bliss for Tubby Stevens. Dan opened up a valve and the hiss of steam drowned the alleged tune. He shut it down and tried another. She'd do. He'd warm through the main engines later on and have them ready when the order came to start them up. Tubby could take the middle watch on the fires. That'd put the clapper on that damn' zither of his.

The galley was looking quite inviting. The fire in the range was a six by six inch square of red coals and there was a pleasant bubbling sound from a pot. Its lid was tilted askew and from time to time it gave a little jump and fell back as though exhausted by the effort. A wisp of steam feathering out through the slit bore with it a very pleasant smell, a smell which would have given anyone an appetite. It spoke eloquently of onions, of mixed spices—Tubby had found a tin at the back of a drawer—of savoury meats. All of which was strange because the meat had not been long out of tin, the onions were not in their first youth and the carrots flabby. The secret of the tastiness of the stew was Tubby's; nor would he have told anyone where he had found the makings for the dough-boys which floated in it.

A very large, fat-bellied black tea-pot was standing on a box in front of the hot coals, its contents gradually achieving the bitter blackness of a trawlerman's brew.

Tubby, having finished work as a cook, had reverted to the role of an instrumentalist. *The Twenty-Four-Hour Tutor* was propped against a fish-kettle so that the oil lamp which hung above illuminated its pages. Dan Todd had resolutely refused to start up the dynamo and thus waste his precious steam in the generation of electricity.

Tubby was well pleased with himself; he had got the first line into his head and was nearly note perfect—nearly. He was taking it at full speed and his head was nodding approval when Carl came along the deck and wanted to know when the hell his supper would be ready.

Tubby fell foul of a couple of notes, retraced his steps and went through it all over again. He was the only man in the ship who wasn't scared of Carl Swanson.

Carl stood in the doorway. "Well, what about it?"

Tubby finished the tune and put the zither to bed in its case. "Dinner is served," he said, lifted the lid of the stewpan and sniffed. "I've got a lovely stew for you. And dough-boys. Where are we going to have it?"

Carl grinned. "In the saloon. I bet you've never eaten in a saloon before."

Tubby said something contemptuous about saloons.

Carl, on his way to the boat-deck, shouted, "Chow!" down the engine-room grating to Dan Todd who raised a blackened face and said; "I'll be up in a minute."

The saloon of the *Ivanhoe* was a rectangular room, twenty feet by ten, flanked on its long sides by the officers' cabins. Light and air were admitted through a skylight.

A long table took up most of the floor-space. A long settee ran along one side of it, chairs screwed to the deck gave seating-accommodation on the other side. At the end opposite to the door was a mahogany sideboard with cupboards and racks to hold glasses and bottles.

Carl lifted the lamp-glass of a swinging oil lamp and lit the wick. Then he stood looking about him. Very posh! Ginger-beer sailors! He stooped to the cupboard door of the sideboard, opened it, looked with appreciation on the array of bottles within and picked out one. "Finest Scotch Whisky. Twenty years in wood." There was a bit of stamp-paper stuck on it which bore the word: "Captain". Well, he'd never miss a tot.

It was a very generous tot that he was drinking when Larry came in and asked: "What have you got there?"

Carl gave him the bottle, saying: "Help yourself, it's on the house." His mouth twisted in a grin.

"Where's the skipper?" Larry asked.

"He was on the bridge the last time I saw him," Carl replied. He put down his glass and turned up the wick in the lamp. "He's a miserable old blighter."

The door was kicked open and Tubby, with a dirty sheet tied round his waist, came in carrying the stew in one hand, the tea-pot in the other. He saw the bottle which Larry had put down on the sideboard. "That's what I can do with," he said and put the pan and tea-pot on the table. He splashed whisky into a glass and held it up. "Here's to a successful trip."

Carl said: "Wait a minute. The chief's coming."

Dan Todd blinked in the light as he stepped over the high step of the doorway. His face was grey and smeary from the effects of hot water and soap on coal-dust and engine-oil.

"Come on, Dan. Fill up a glass and drink to—"

Carl stopped short and looked over his shoulder. Footsteps came shuffling down the passage.

As Captain MacTaggart came into the saloon Larry, with his glass half raised to his lips, became quite still. So did Carl Swanson. Dan Todd went on filling his glass and then he turned to look into the face of the captain of the *Ivanhoe*.

"Well, gentlemen. You've made free with my ship so I suppose I shouldn't be surprised to find you helping yourself to my drink." He lifted the bottle to the light. "That's going to cost you exactly two shillings and sixpence." He lifted the lid of the stew-pan, sniffed its contents and poured some of them on to a plate.

Then he locked up the cupboard, put the whisky bottle under his arm and, picking up the plate of stew, left the saloon.

Carl forced a laugh. "There's plenty more where that came from. Drink up!"

The toast was drunk in silence.

"Come on, Tubby. Dish out the stew. I'm hungry."

5

TWO THINGS RANKLED in Carl's mind as he ate his supper. The first was the presence and the attitude towards him of Captain MacTaggart, the second, the realization that the reward he would get for helping to save the ship would be only a fraction of the amount that would have been his due had she been a derelict.

Both touched his pride. He had boasted that his luck hadn't let him down and now it had. The sum they would collect wouldn't do much more than pay for the gear that had been lost on the *John Goodwin*. But that wasn't all that was worrying him.

He was thinking of what his fellow skippers would say when he got back to Gilboro'. They would jump at the chance of making him look a fool. Maybe he wouldn't get another ship. Gaffers were funny to deal with. As long as you brought in a full load they were all over you, lush you up to whatever you wanted, but if you had an unlucky trip it was different. He'd seen a lot of good men go under all because of a bit of bad luck. There were men working on the wharves, loading ice, stacking boxes, all because they'd slipped up once, only once.

And his pipe didn't taste good. He knocked it out and blew through the stem. God! He was tired. He would go and turn in. Tomorrow the hold would be clear of water and they could get steam on the main engines and steer a course for Gilboro'.

He went back into the saloon. Tubby was plunking away at his zither. Dan Todd was studying *A Thousand a Year from Hens*, a stubby forefinger moving along each line as he read.

Larry was lying on his back on a settee, smoking a cigarette.

Tubby stopped playing to say: "You'll never get to windward of that damn' skipper."

Carl sat for a time staring at the fire in the stove. Then he stretched his arms above his head and yawned. "Time to turn in." He stood up and took off his jacket, unloosened his scarf and pulled off his sea-boots.

Tubby went on plucking at the strings of his zither.

"I said it was time to turn in." Carl's voice was harsh.

Tubby looked at him, noticed the danger-signs and put his zither into its case.

Carl went to his cabin. He was utterly exhausted, but he couldn't sleep. He tried first on his right side, then his left. But the harder he tried, the quicker his thoughts raced through his head.

Captain MacTaggart! He couldn't get the man out of his mind; the way he'd come into the saloon, taken his bottle of whisky and walked out. He'd made him look a fool. No one had done that before and got away with it.

But Captain MacTaggart was captain of the ship and he, Carl, had signed that damn' agreement.

Dan Todd went on reading for half an hour. Then he went down to the stoke-hold and made up the fires. When he came back he said to Tubby: "Set the clock for twelve. You've got to keep the middle watch."

Tubby, who was half asleep, grunted: "All right."

Carl dozed, awoke and dozed off again. When the alarm went off at midnight he was wide awake. He heard Tubby in the next cabin get out of his bunk and go on deck.

He lay still for five minutes and then he got up. He didn't bother to put on his coat and he shivered as the full blast of the wind struck him as he came round the corner of the deck-house.

The treads of the ladder were slippery with ice and the iron rail burned his fingers as he gripped it. There was light enough to make out the wheel and the binnacle beyond. A loose corner of the canvas dodger was flapping angrily.

He sought the shelter of the chart-room. When he had slammed the sliding door behind him he struck a match and lit the oil lamp, waited until the lamp-glass had warmed and then turned up the wick. The chart was still on the table. There was a bit of rubber somewhere. His hands groped in the corners, found it and then set to work to erase the marking of the position of the ship made by the mate of the *Ivanhoe*. He brushed away the crumbs of the rubber and went over it again until not one trace of the pencil-marks remained.

Then he opened a drawer and took out the log and thumbed over the pages until he came to the one bearing the entries relating to the abandonment of the ship. Again the rubber did its work and when he had finished there was left no single word which spoke of the abandonment of the *Ivanhoe*, nor of her position when that had been carried out.

He put the log back into the drawer and raised his hand to open the door when he looked square into the face of Captain MacTaggart framed in the forward port-hole. He said: "What the hell are you after?" forgetting that a half-inch of thick glass separated them.

The face disappeared, the door was jerked open and the captain came into the chart-room. He said: "What's the game?"

For a split second Carl had no answer. Then a sudden rage seized his brain. He lifted an arm. The captain struck it down. He didn't speak.

The two men stood glaring at each other. Then Carl said: "What's biting you?"

The captain bent over the chart. The grin began to fade from Carl's face. Then he thought to himself: "What's the good, in here. There isn't room."

The captain straightened up and turned, leaning against the chart table. He looked Carl straight in the eye. "You're not going to do yourself any good, monkeying round like this. I told you before that I was still captain of this ship and if I were you I'd remember that." He walked to the door and out on to the bridge.

Carl stood looking at him as he went to the compass, and then he turned to the bridge ladder.

As his head disappeared from sight, Carl thought: "You damn' swine, I'll fix you."

The captain went to his cabin and locked the door behind him.

When he had undressed he took the revolver out of the drawer and put it on a shelf by the head of the bunk.

Carl remained on the bridge. The wind was getting up and the ship began to roll heavily. "If it gets any worse I'm going to start up the engines and get her head on to the sea," he muttered. "I don't care what that damn' fool says."

Spray was whipping over the weather-bulwark and above the whine of the wind Carl could hear the creaking of the timber-stacks. If they broke adrift again it wouldn't be so good. He should have ditched the deck cargo.

He went into the chart-house and read the barometer. It was steady at twenty eight nine five. That wasn't so bad. He walked out on to the bridge and worked his way up the sloping deck to the port wing. There was no real weight in the wind. "Just a bit of a squall," he thought, and looked down on the fore-deck. The cover on the fore-hatch was still in place and there wasn't much water coming on board.

Then as quickly as it had got up the wind eased and through gaps in the clouds Carl could see the stars.

And while he stood there with his back braced against a stanchion the idea that had come to him an hour or two ago returned. He thought: "I'll have to be careful. He's suspicious and he's got a gun."

He went into the chart-room and looked at the clock. Mac-Taggart had been gone an hour. He'd give him a little longer; another half-hour and then . . .

His right hand grasped the cold steel of a marline-spike.

From below came the sound of the clinking of a shovel on the stoke-hold floor-plates. The shovel was being wielded unskilfully and unwillingly by Cook-Steward Second Engineer, Tubby Stevens.

Smoke from the funnel, streaming to leeward, thickened. A wisp of steam hissed faintly from a faulty valve on the whistle.

Carl went down on deck and walked forward to number one hold, knocked out a wedge securing a tarpaulin and peered down into the hold. He dropped in a block of wood and heard it strike the surface of the water. "We're getting it down," he muttered. "It must be three feet lower since we started the pump."

He replaced the cover, drove home the wedge and made his way aft, and stood in the shadow of the bridge, listening.

Tubby must have finished in the stoke-hold by now. Perhaps he had gone back to his cabin. Carl walked round the fore-end of the deck-house on his toes. As he came to the saloon door he heard someone coming up the after ladder. It was Tubby. Carl saw him open the door of his cabin and go inside.

Now was his chance! He returned to the port side and with his right hand gripping the spike in the pocket of his coat he approached the captain's cabin, turned the knob of the door with his left hand and pushed. The door would not open.

"Locked!" Carl breathed the word. "Hell and blast!" He tried again, but the door was immovable. He looked at it stupidly, thought for one mad moment of trying to kick it in and then turned away and went to his own cabin.

The key was in the lock of the door, and as he turned it with the door half open a metal tongue shot out and fell a quarter of an inch. There was a notch cut on its underside which engaged in a pin, thus securing the door.

If the tongue did not fall, then the notch would not engage in the pin. He lifted it and then let it fall. There was not much strength in the spring; a wad of paper or a scrap of wood would hold it up.

It seemed simple enough, but twenty minutes had passed before Carl had shaped a splinter of wood of a size which would allow the tongue to emerge from the lock but would prevent it from falling on the pin.

Tomorrow he would put this piece of wood in place in the lock of the captain's door.

An engine-room in the grey light of dawn is not a place which attracts many people. Dan Todd was different, and in spite of his dreams of a chicken farm on the South Downs his heart was with steel, steam and coal.

So that when Tubby knocked on the door of his cabin at 4 a.m. he was actually glad, strange as it may seem, that it was his turn to attend with shovel and oil-can in the stoke-hold and engine-room.

He asked how the pump was working in the tones of a fond father inquiring of the progress of a favourite child.

"Champion," said Tubby, and disappeared with the celerity of a puppet pulled by a string.

"Champion," was the verdict of an amateur in matters of engineering, and Dan stopped by the gratings on his way to the engine-room hatch to confirm the opinion.

"Champion be damned," he muttered, as he listened to the laboured thrust and throw of the pump. "She's choking. That's what's the matter."

Dan Todd was an expert diagnostician. He swung down the steel ladder, ran to the pump and shut down a valve. Then he went into the stoke-hold. The pressure wasn't so bad but two of the fires were dirty. "I wish to hell I'd got a trimmer on the job instead of that damn' cook." Which was ungrateful of Dan.

He went up on deck and called Carl and Larry. "The strum-box is choked," he said. "If you want the hold pumped out we've got to clear it."

Carl said: "O.K. I'll give you a hand." He went forward to the hold, took off the cover and went down the ladder. Dan, who hated cold water, stayed at the top.

Carl continued on down the ladder until he was standing in water up to his waist. "Where is this blooming box?"

"Amidships. Right up against the after-bulkhead, I expect," Dan replied.

Carl felt with his feet and came on an obstruction. "I think I've found it." He took a deep breath and plunged into the icy water. His hands scrabbled on a grating choked with chips of wood and a hessian sheet wedged between the bars.

He was nearly exhausted and was numb with cold by the time the grating was clear, and when he reached the top of the ladder he lay for a minute bent over the coaming.

"It's all right now, Dan. You can start the pump again."

Larry and Dan helped him down to the stoke-hold and stripped off his dripping clothes before an open furnace door.

Slowly warmth returned, but an hour passed before he recovered his strength sufficiently to return to his cabin. He tried to sleep, but a rattling in the saloon woke him every time he dozed off.

He called out to Larry and told him to see what it was.

Five minutes later Larry put his head into the cabin. "It was one of the skylights in the saloon. The catch is bust but I've lashed it with codline; that ought to hold it."

At eight o'clock the pump began to race. "We're down to the bottom. She must be dry," Dan muttered to himself and went up on deck to look at the fore-hold.

Then he woke Carl and said: "All the water's out of the hold. Shall I start up the main engines?"

"Yes, go ahead."

Captain MacTaggart was smoking a pipe on the bridge when Carl found him. "Well, how are they getting on below?"

"The hold's dry." Carl walked to the telegraph and pulled over the handle to "Full Ahead", and as he heard the first sound of the engines starting he said: "What course d'you want us to steer?"

"West by south."

Carl spun the wheel and the ship's head came slowly round in obedience to the action of screw and rudder.

Larry came up the ladder. "How's she steering?" he asked.

"Not so bad."

"Dan says we won't do much more than three knots. He'll maybe be able to work her up a bit later when he's got the engine-room dry, but the water's not far below the plates."

The feel of a live ship under their feet cheered Tubby and Dan Todd, and as the engines settled down to a steady beat Dan nodded his head approvingly. "She's not so bad," he said, and stood with his eyes fixed on the revolution counter and his hands on the wheel-valve. "As long as we can keep up the steam we'll be in the River in a couple of days."

Captain MacTaggart walked out on to a wing of the bridge and stood there for a long time looking out ahead of the ship. Now and again he shot a sideways glance at Carl at the wheel. His fingers gripped the butt of the revolver in his pocket. He'd have to keep clear of that damn' pirate, and keep the door of his cabin locked at night. It was absurd, of course, but . . . He went down to the engine-room and found Dan Todd sitting on a bucket rolling a cigarette.

Dan looked up and said: "Well, we're homeward bound, Skipper. How are you feeling now?" He ran his tongue along the gummed edge of a cigarette paper.

"I'm all right," the captain grunted, and went into the stoke-hold.

Dan called to him. "We've got her up to sixty pounds. And that's not bad with only two of us on the job."

Dan heard him open the furnace doors, and shouted: "Are you going to take a turn at stoking?"

The captain came back into the engine-room and stood looking about him. He didn't speak.

Half an hour later, when Dan met Carl on deck, he said: "I think that damn' skipper's balmy. He's been down in the engine-room looking like a bloke what's seen a ghost."

Carl thought for a moment and then said: "I wouldn't be surprised if he jumped into the drink."

Dan looked surprised, and asked: "Why?"

"I dunno. He was acting queer when he was up on the bridge. Sometimes he'll answer and there's other times he's as dumb as a fish."

In the galley, Tubby, after a half-hearted attempt to learn "Down in the Cane Brake", gave it up and put his zither away. He went out on deck and lit a cigarette. Larry was leaning against the engine-room casing splicing a wire. He looked up, jerked his head in silent greeting, and then went on with his work.

Tubby, who craved conversation as much as he craved life ashore, said: "Well, Larry, what do you think about it?"

Without raising his head Larry replied: "What d'you mean?"

"This ship's lousy. I've never known anything like it. It's worse than it was on the *John Goodwin* after we lost our gear."

"It'll be all right when we collect the salvage." Larry spoke without enthusiasm.

"That's what I keep on telling myself. The weather's getting better, we've got plenty of chow and cabins to sleep in, but somehow it doesn't add up the way it should. We're going to have trouble. I feel it in my bones."

"The fore-hold's dry and we've got a good head of steam. There's nothing to worry about."

"Then why are you looking like a sick cat?"

"I'm not."

Tubby sighed and walked aft.

Dan Todd alone appeared to be oblivious of the blight on the ship. When he wasn't stoking the fires or looking after the engines, he read *A Thousand a Year from Hens*.

Captain MacTaggart stayed in his cabin until three o'clock and then Carl, who was keeping watch on his door from a position behind the port sea-boat, saw him come out on deck and go up on the bridge.

He waited until MacTaggart was out of sight and then he went quickly to his cabin. In his hand was the splinter of wood which he had taken so much trouble to shape so that it would fit into the lock of the door.

When it was in place he turned the key and noted with satisfaction that the tongue shot out but did not fall.

At eight o'clock that night Dan Todd, in the stoke-hold, was making Tubby clean the fires. "There's a bad clinker in the port wing that's got to be broken up."

Tubby cursed all clinkers as he lifted the heavy slice and rammed it into the fire. Then he tried to haul it back. "It's jammed."

"Let's have a try," Dan said, and spat on his hands. But he couldn't move the slice. "It's the fire-bars. One of them's burned out." He went into the engine-room and blew through the voice-pipe to the bridge.

Larry answered him. "What's the matter, Dan?"

"I'll have to let out the fires in the port-wing boiler. There's a bar burned out, maybe two, so we won't be able to steam any quicker till I get new ones in."

Dan went up on deck and into the fiddley, a store-room built in the engine-room casing, in which was a pile of firebars; he picked out two and laid them on deck outside the door and went to his cabin.

The wind eased during the first watch, and Carl went to his cabin after he had had his supper. But he did not sleep. He lay on his bunk and smoked a pipe.

There were three hours to go until he was due to relieve Larry on the bridge at midnight. Three hours. He turned down the wick of the lamp until the flame flickered bluely and went out.

It wouldn't be difficult if he waited till MacTaggart was asleep. But he'd got to hit hard the first time and give MacTaggart no chance to call out or to struggle. It was lucky the cabin was far from where Tubby would be sleeping. And as for Larry, he wasn't easily wakened.

There wasn't any risk. Not if he was careful. He would wait till Dan had gone down to stoke the fires. That would give him a clear half-hour.

He went over in his mind what he would have to do after MacTaggart was dead. A couple of fire-bars would sink the body. There was plenty of rope and twine in the store.

He raised himself on one elbow with the thought half formed in his mind of going to the store. Then he fell back on to the pillow.

Time enough to do that after midnight when there would be no one to see his movements.

At half past eleven he sat up and swung his legs on to the deck. He couldn't remain inactive a moment longer, and Larry wouldn't mind being relieved early.

Out on deck a light breeze was blowing, and the ship, which still had a list to starboard, was lifting slowly to the swell. He walked to the ship's side. Three knots; that's all they were doing. They should be going faster than that, now that the fore-hold was dry.

He turned and climbed the ladder to the bridge.

Larry turned his head and said: "You're early."

"I couldn't sleep. How's she steering?" He walked over to the wheel and looked down at the compass bowl.

"Not so bad. She's carrying a bit of port helm. About half a turn."

"Is Dan turned in?"

"I expect so, but he'll be up soon. He's keeping the middle."

"Well let's hope he knocks out some more speed."

Larry explained about the burnt-out fire-bars. "Dan says he'll have to wait till the morning before he can get the new ones in."

Carl put a hand on the wheel. "I'll take over."

For half an hour he kept the ship steady on her course. Then he lashed the wheel and took up a position by the starboard ladder. He could see the door of Dan's cabin.

Five minutes later Tubby came up from the engine-room and went into Dan Todd's cabin. Shortly afterwards Carl saw Dan walk aft to the engine-room hatch.

Now was his chance! The marline-spike was in his right-hand pocket. Then he remembered that he must get some cord from the store and went into the chart-room and struck a match. The key of the store was there, or should be, hanging from a nail.

"Damn and blast!" The key had gone. Larry must have it.

At that moment he heard the sound of grating footsteps on the starboard ladder. He went out on to the bridge and turned towards the ladder.

MacTaggart! He stared blankly into the captain's face as though he were seeing a ghost.

"Ay. It's me." The captain stopped on the top tread. His hands were grasping the rails on either side. He laughed, and as he laughed he showed white teeth. There was no humour in that laugh. It was mocking, scornful.

Carl felt anger rising within him. A vein on his temple began to throb. His head was hot. His hands were tightly clenched.

"I've just come to check the course," MacTaggart said. "And to see that everything's O.K."

"Then you can go right back to your bunk. I'm taking the ship in."

"Oh, so you think you're going to run this ship your own way, Mr. Trawlerman." MacTaggart loosened his grip of the rails and took a half-pace forward. "Faking the log isn't going to do you any good."

Carl's right fist shot out into the bearded face of Captain MacTaggart. Fingers vainly sought the rail. MacTaggart stood for an instant swaying and then fell backwards, crashing down on to the steel casing ten feet below.

There was murder in Carl's heart as he struck the blow.

Seconds passed before the full realization of what had occurred came to Carl Swanson. He took a deep breath and rubbed his knuckles on his coat. They were bleeding.

He waited for someone to come out of the cabins. Surely they must have heard the noise; Larry or Tubby Stevens.

He heard the clink of Dan's shovel in the stoke-hold far below. He heard the swish and smack of the seas against the ship's side, the creak of the timber-stack as the ship lifted to the swell and the steady beat of the engines. But that was all.

Carl walked down the ladder. He could see MacTaggart's face, the white of his forehead against the black steel deck.

One leg was bent under the body, the arms spread out. There was no movement, no sign of life.

Carl's heart began to beat quicker. He had seen men die; he had seen legs torn off by whipping wires; he had seen men drowning in the icy northern sea; he had heard men shrieking in agony, and had gone down into the cuddy and eaten his supper, smoked and slept soundly.

But now he felt sick. Half a minute had passed before he reached the foot of the ladder. He knelt down, put out a hand and touched MacTaggart's wrist. There was a groan and the head of the injured man turned.

"I've got to get rid of him. I've got to!" Carl muttered, and looked towards the bulwark ten feet away.

But first he must get the fire-bars and lash them to the body. He dropped down on to the deck and walked aft. As his hands groped for the catch of the fiddley door he stumbled over the fire-bars Dan had left out.

He picked them up and carried them forward. Then he lifted MacTaggart off the casing on to the deck. What he wanted was a length of twine or rope. Anything would do. He felt in his pockets though he knew there was nothing in them that would serve his purpose.

Then he remembered the codline lashing that Larry had put on the saloon skylight. That was just what he wanted.

When he had secured one end of the line to MacTaggart's waist and the other to the two fire-bars, he lifted the injured man, carried him to the bulwark and was going to drop him over the side when he remembered the agreement he'd signed.

His hands fumbled in the pockets of MacTaggart's coat and he muttered a "Thank God!" as his fingers closed on a folded sheet of paper.

Then he pushed MacTaggart over the edge of the bulwark.

He was sweating as he climbed the ladder on to the bridge.

Next morning Tubby, who had been on duty in the stoke-hold from 4 to 6 a.m., awoke and turned over in his bunk away from the light of a port-hole. He thought of the breakfast he should be cooking at that very moment. At last he summoned the strength of mind to leave his warm bunk, to struggle into his trousers and slip his feet into a pair of sea-boots.

As he passed the saloon he looked in and said: "Breakfast won't be long."

Larry was sitting on a chair, his head in his hands. He was alone.

Tubby stood at the door for a moment. Then he went up to Larry, touched him on the shoulder and asked: "Are you sick?"

Larry jerked up his head. "Hasn't Carl told you?"

"No. What?"

"The skipper went over the side last night."

"Suicide?"

"Looks like it. He was bats anyway."

"I knew something was going to happen."

"Well, I hope you're satisfied." Larry felt in his pocket and took out a flattened packet of cigarettes. He offered one to Tubby who took it. His hand moved slowly.

"Suicide!"

"That's what it must have been."

Tubby was staring at the deck. He didn't see it. His lips were forming the word, "Suicide! Suicide!"

Minutes passed before Tubby turned his head. Slowly his eyes focused on Larry. He said: "I was just thinking. It's funny, I mean him going like that. I've never been shipmates with a suicide before. It's unlucky."

From the boat-deck came Carl's voice calling for breakfast.

"Don't seem to trouble him much," Tubby muttered, and went aft to the galley. Breakfast! It seemed funny frying eggs and rashers and making tea when a man had committed suicide. Unnatural-like. He raked out the ashes of the fire and opened the damper full. It would be some time before the fire burned up. Well, Carl'd just have to wait.

Dan Todd came up out of the engine-room wiping his face with a rag. He stopped outside the galley door. Tubby was fishing a piece of burnt bread out of the ash-pan. "Did Carl tell you?" Dan asked.

Tubby turned towards his questioner. He said, "Yes," and put the bread on a plate.

Dan rubbed the stubble on his chin. It made a rasping noise. "I wonder why he did it? I had an uncle once who threw himself under a train at Nottingham. But he'd got cancer. I wonder if it was anything like that?"

"Maybe it was. You never know." Tubby put a tin tray on the top of the stove and loaded it with a plate of ham and eggs, a tea-pot, a jug of condensed milk and a bowl of brown sugar. "How did he do it?"

"Carl didn't say; just that he went to the skipper's cabin and found he wasn't there."

"What time was that?"

"I dunno. What does it matter anyway?"

Carl was sitting on the table when Tubby came into the saloon. He took the tea-pot off the tray. "I thought you were never coming."

"I've been stoking the damn' fires up to six o'clock." Tubby did not respond to Carl's mood of forced gaiety. He wanted to talk about the captain, to ask how it had happened and when, but there was something in Carl's manner which forbade such questioning.

As he poured himself out a cup of tea, Carl announced that they would be off the Gilboro' River by four o'clock that afternoon.

Tubby said: "I thought we were going to the Thames."

Larry kicked him on the shin.

It was an uncomfortable and a silent meal and Tubby was glad to get out of the saloon, even though it meant that he had to wash a stack of dirty dishes.

Carl went up to the bridge with Larry. He took the lashings off the wheel and turned it to starboard until the *Ivanhoe* was once more on her course for Gilboro'. The wind was a moderate breeze from the southward, there was little sea, and all that remained to remind them of the gale of two days ago was a long lazy swell.

"I'd better put in the log that we've altered course," Larry said.

"No. You needn't bother," Carl said. "We don't want to tell 'em everything."

Larry said: "O.K.; but there'll be an inquiry and they'll want to know why we didn't write up the logs."

"We're trawlermen, not ruddy ginger-beer sailors." Carl laughed and spat over the rail. "They won't expect anything from us, and they won't get it."

"There'll be an inquest."

"There needn't be."

"What d'you mean?"

"If we don't tell 'em anything they won't know anything. That's sense, isn't it?"

"We couldn't do that."

"Why not?" Carl was smiling.

Larry said: "Well, I don't know. But it wouldn't be right. And besides, if they find out where'd we be?"

"If none of us talks there'll be no trouble. There's only you and Tubby and Dan Todd. It'll be easy."

"But I don't see the idea. We haven't anything to hide."

"Ay, but we've got a hell of a lot to gain. If this ship was derelict when we came on board it'd make a difference to our pockets."

Larry looked at Carl, then he walked to the starboard wing and back. "Yes, it would make a difference. I see that."

"We'll just say there was no one on the ship when we came on board. We'll forget we ever saw MacTaggart. There's no one can say any different."

"What about the crew? They left the captain behind."

"He could have fallen over the side between the time they went and when we turned up."

"I don't like it."

"But you'd like to have a share of a salvage award, wouldn't you?"

Larry said "Yes," but his mind was troubled.

"There's nothing to be worried about. Leave all the talking to me. I've fixed the logs. It's not going to do anyone any harm."

"Except the bloke that's got to pay salvage."

"That'll be a company. It won't hurt them."

"All right."

"That's fine. Take the wheel and I'll go down and have a talk with Tubby and Dan Todd."

Tubby had finished washing up and was emptying a pail of dirty water over the side when Carl came along the deck.

Carl said: "I want a word with you."

"What about?" Tubby put the pail in through the galley door and dried his hands on a very dirty cloth.

"I've been having a yarn with Larry and we've decided not to say anything about MacTaggart being on board."

Tubby's mouth opened wide.

Carl explained about the salvage of a derelict. When he had finished, Tubby said: "Well, if you think it'll be O.K., I'm on." But his tone was doubtful.

"Of course it'll be O.K. Keep your trap shut; that's all you've got to do. It'll make a difference of thousands of pounds to us."

"Thousands!"

"Yes. You wouldn't say no to a couple of thousand, would you?"

"I'd buy a pub in the county of Rutland if I had that money. There's no sea near the place." The idea of a pub in Rutland pleased Tubby. He saw himself behind a bar drawing beer and drinking it and gossiping and telling the yokels about his life at sea. He'd have time to learn the zither properly; time to read the books he'd always wanted to read but had never found the time for.

Carl saying, "Well, that's settled," brought him back with a jerk on to the heaving deck of the *Ivanhoe*.

"Settled? What's settled?"

"That you'll say nothing about having seen MacTaggart aboard this ship."

"Oh!" Tubby thrust his fingers through his hair. He knew there was a catch somewhere.

"You won't have to tell any lies."

"But if I'm asked, what am I going to say?"

"That when you got on the ship there wasn't anyone on board. That's easy enough, isn't it? And don't forget the money you'll collect."

The temptation was too strong for what better feelings Tubby possessed. He nodded his head and said: "I'll do it."

Unlike Tubby and Larry, Dan Todd was an easy subject. He accepted the disappearance of the captain of the *Ivanhoe* without question and agreed readily to Carl's suggestion that he should forget that he had ever seen the man. "He's gone and I don't see that it'll make any difference if we don't say anything about him." Dan got up and stood looking at the steady rise and fall of a connecting-rod. "But all the same, I'm kinda sorry for the old geezer; the sea's terrible cold at this time of year."

"Then that's settled. You'll say nothing?"

"Ay."

Carl went up on to the bridge, and said to Larry, who was at the wheel: "I've fixed it up with the others." Then he walked to the port wing. "Here's where he must have gone over."

Larry said, "What's that?" and looked towards Carl, who was holding the loose end of a wire in his hand.

"This rail's been carried away. MacTaggart must have been leaning against it and it broke under his weight."

Larry left the wheel and joined Carl. He picked up the end of the wire and said: "Yes. That's how it must have happened."

Larry began to unreeve the lashing, and when he got it clear he stretched it out and showed a frayed end. "It's funny we didn't hear anything. You'd have thought he'd have called out. And besides that, either you or me have been here on the bridge all the time. I can't understand it."

Carl was silent for a moment. Dammit, he hadn't thought of that. He forced himself to think of a way out of the quandary. "I went down to the galley to make a cup of tea. That's when it must have happened."

"What time was that?"

"I don't know exactly. It must have been round about two o'clock."

Larry said: "I'd better fit a new lanyard to this."

"No, leave it as it is."

"O.K." Larry said, and went back to the wheel.

At midday the *Ivanhoe* was in the track of coastwise shipping. Carl went to the centre of the bridge. There was a pair of glasses hanging from the rail. He picked them up and looked ahead. "Keep her a shade to starboard, Larry. I think that's the Gap Lightship ahead."

There was no swell and the sea had no effect on the ship as she ploughed ahead at a steady five knots.

Ten minutes later Carl said: "Ay, that's the Gap all right. We'll be in in time for tea."

Larry went to the voice-pipe and called down to Dan Todd in the engine-room. "Keep her going, Dan. Only another four hours."

The thought of Gilboro' and Jessie Miles lightened Larry's spirits. He hummed a tune, a melancholy tune, but that was the way joy took him.

Carl stared stolidly ahead. In four hours they would be tied up at the fish-wharf at Gilboro'. He was bringing in a valuable prize and should have been well pleased at the prospect, but he wasn't.

He was thinking of Captain MacTaggart.

6

THE NEWS of the salving of the *Ivanhoe* was brought to Gilboro' by the depleted crew of the *John Goodwin*.

Jessie Miles had gone down to the fish-wharf to meet her at the grisly hour of 3 a.m., and had been the first person in Gilboro' to hear the news. She heard about the lost trawls and the deaths of the two deck-hands, but the news that Larry was safe was enough for her; more than enough.

She ran light-footed through the cobbled streets to Hawkin's Court and Mrs. Mather's cottage. She hammered on the door and roused many of the neighbours before the peevish, shrill voice of Mrs. Mather herself was raised in anger, thirsting to know who was waking her up at that time of the night.

A grudging: "Oh, it's you!" came through the crack of the half-opened door, and as Jessie pushed her way in Mrs. Mather grumbled at the cold wind, slammed the door behind her and turned the key in the lock.

"Now perhaps you'll tell me what it's all about." She pulled a shawl more closely round her shoulders and led the way into the kitchen. There was a handful of red coals in the grate; she picked up a poker and raked out the ashes.

Jessie said: "It's Larry. He's coming back tomorrow, or maybe the next day. I'm not sure which, but he *is* coming."

"And Carl? What about him?"

"Yes, and Carl, too. They're bringing in a ship that was wrecked and they'll get a lot of money for it."

"Where was it wrecked?" Mrs. Mather put a kettle on the hot coals and straightened her back.

"I don't know. Somewhere at sea. And now everything's going to be all right. Larry'll have plenty of money and we'll be able to get married and have that house and the furniture and everything. I'm going round to the shop tomorrow morning as soon as ever it opens."

"Today," said Mrs. Mather, looking at the clock on the mantelshelf.

"Well, today. It doesn't matter. Isn't it wonderful?"

"And Carl's all right?"

"Yes, yes."

"Sit down and take off your coat and we'll have a cup of tea." Mrs. Mather hobbled to the cupboard and brought out a tea-pot. She put it on the grate to warm.

Jessie pulled up a chair and sat down with her feet on the fender. She spread her hands to the fire. "They had a terrible time. They were caught in a storm and lost both trawls and two men over the side."

Mrs. Mather had had her fill of storms and of men lost at sea. Three of them! "But they got through all right? Carl and Larry?"

"Yes."

"Then that's all right." The old woman sat for a long time in silence. When the kettle began to sing she spooned tea into the pot and brought a jug of milk from the larder. "I'll have to think about getting his room ready. When did you say he'd be back?"

"Well, I don't know exactly. Either tomorrow or the next day."

It was still dark when Jessie left Mrs. Mather's cottage, and when she had gone Mrs. Mather climbed the ladder to the room under the slates with a lamp in her hand. She put it down on the chest of drawers and stood for a moment looking round. She'd given it a good turn-out the day before, beating the mats in the front yard and scrubbing the floor. The curtains were soaking in the tub ready for washing, and there were clean sheets on the bed.

Carl had laughed at her for giving him sheets and had said that blankets alone were good enough for him, but that had not made any difference to Mrs. Mather.

She'd have to air them, for it wouldn't do for them to be damp. And she'd light a fire and warm up the room. Later. Suddenly she felt very tired and had to hold tight to the head of the bed to prevent herself from falling. Silly, but she did really feel a little faint.

She climbed slowly backwards down the steep ladder, the flickering lamp in her left hand.

Carl was coming home.

The Gilboro' *Argus* carried a full and highly coloured account of the salving of the *Ivanhoe*. Everyone was talking about it down on the wharf; trawlermen, packers, buyers, lorrymen, ice hands; they all had heard the news. Smudgy photographs of Carl and Larry were on the front page of the *Argus*. They had been reproduced hurriedly from snapshots, and Jessie had been interviewed by a pimply youth, all neck and legs. And her photo was there too: "Trawlerman's bride plans home."

Old Hoppy did a good trade in gossip and coffee and pies and sandwiches and coconut buns. Yes, he knew Carl Swanson, and Larry Hicks as well. He'd spoken to Larry and Jessie Miles the night before the *John Goodwin* had sailed. Yes, sure, they were going to get married. She'd told him so herself.

The evening editions, published at noon, carried on the story which was in danger of becoming one of the century's most thrilling stories of the sea. They were heroes: all four of them. The reporting staff of the Gilboro' *Argus* dug into the past of Tubby and Dan Todd, but as neither of them were married and were not even engaged, they were only given a few lines. Larry was the only one with a real romance to his credit.

Mrs. Mather would have nothing to say to the press, though they hammered at her door and peered through the front-room window until she dislodged them with a wet mop. She drove the enemy back beyond the whitewashed wall and returned to her work of cleaning and polishing and scouring.

The paper said he wouldn't be back that day, but you couldn't be sure, and when dusk fell and she had placed a lamp in the window of the front room, the cottage was uncomfortably clean and the air full of the smell of yellow soap.

Jessie came round after supper, bringing an evening paper, but there was little in it of interest; no news of the *Ivanhoe*. There was, however, a "personal" interview with Mrs. Mather, which Jessie read aloud.

Mrs. Mather said: "The impudence of them reporters! I never said a word to them!"

At two o'clock next day a message came from the coast-guard station at the Point to say that the *Ivanhoe* had passed the bar light-buoy.

When Jessie told Mrs. Mather the news, she added: "Your tea-cup reading was wrong this time."

"Well, it's the first time that's happened," the old lady replied, torn between the loss of prestige as a prophet and relief at Carl's safe return. "I'll go and get my bonnet on and then we can start."

Down on the fish-wharf a crowd was gathering. In the wake of the storm had come a day of calm with a cloudless sky. It was quite warm in the sun, and men were standing about in their shirt-sleeves, women with their shawls unpinned.

A number of small boys were hanging over the rails at the lower pierhead, the entrance to the fish-dock. While they watched and waited they argued and shouted without ceasing.

Above, seagulls wheeled and dipped, shrilly screaming, as they fought for scraps of offal floating out on the tide.

"That's her!" The squeaky voice of one of the youthful watchers announced.

The men and women at the sheds pressed forward, screwing up their eyes as they looked down river to where a smudge of smoke was rising. From the market-place, from the streets, from the shops, more and more came running as the news was passed back. "It's them!"

Inspector Pollitt, looking very like a cylinder encased in blue cloth and silver buttons, was there with a sergeant and three constables. It was a big day for Gilboro' and the inspector wanted to be the first to welcome Carl Swanson; if he could get his picture into the papers he'd be very well pleased and so would his missus.

Inspector Pollitt had served in the Gilboro' police force for thirty-two years and had seldom had the chance of distinguishing himself. A succession of drunk and disorderlies and common assaults were all that he had had to deal with, together with a few petty thefts and once in a while a burglary.

The inspector was keeping one eye on the cameraman from the *Argus*, the other had been commissioned to look out for the mayor in case he should come along and steal his thunder.

Two miles down the river Tom Ingleby was standing in the living-room of the Pride of Bedford.

He put down the dish-cloth he had in his hand when he heard the sound of the *Ivanhoe*'s whistle; one long blast she sounded as she rounded the bend. He knew all the ships which traded regularly to Gilboro', but this was a stranger to him. He pushed open the door leading to the verandah and, avoiding a rotten plank, walked out.

Yes, she was a stranger all right. He put a hand inside the door and lifted a telescope from a rack. *Ivanhoe*—he spelled out the name on her starboard bow, and as he swung the glass to the left he drew in his breath quickly. Her mast was gone! She'd been in trouble.

A man on the bridge waved a greeting, but he did not reply. He wondered vaguely what had happened to the ship as one might speculate on the fortunes of someone on the other side of the world.

On the bridge of the *Ivanhoe* Carl was standing with his arms on the rail. He had a cigarette in the corner of his mouth. He turned to Larry, who was at the wheel, and said: "He's still alive. Poor old blighter! It would send me balmy living in a place like that." He stood up and threw away his cigarette. "Well, I suppose we'd better be getting ready to go alongside. You look out forward—send Tubby aft and see that he's got his lines clear."

Larry jerked his head in reply and left the wheel.

There was a half-smile on Carl's face as his hands gripped the spokes of the wheel. He was thinking of his meeting with his gaffer. "Ay, I lost all the gear, but I've got something here that'll pay for that *and* leave a bit over."

And he had. He was bringing in the *Ivanhoe* and most of her cargo, and there was only Larry and Dan Todd and Tubby Stevens to share the prize with him.

The fish-dock was in sight now, right ahead; he could see the crowd of people against the sheds. They were waiting for him! His mouth widened to a satisfied grin.

As the *Ivanhoe* ran in between the entrance piers the small boys raised a thin cheer, and Carl raised his arm in reply. Then he rang down, "Dead Slow", to the engine-room and the *Ivanhoe* nosed in towards a vacant berth at the quay. Carl could see Mrs. Mather and Jessie Miles standing beside her, his gaffer, Inspector Pollitt and his men. It was a grand turn-out. A great deal better than he had expected. There was a man with a camera.

Larry threw a heaving-line clear and true; it was caught and hauled in. Tubby was doing his best, but his legs and his arms would keep getting in the way, and Carl had placed the *Ivanhoe* right alongside before he had managed to pass up the stern-line.

When the ropes were fast Carl called down through the voice-pipe to Dan Todd. "Finished with the engines," and swung down the bridge ladder on to the deck.

Inspector Pollitt gave him a hand up on to the wharf and was pleased to hear the click of the pressman's camera as he did so.

Carl made straight for Mrs. Mather and hugged her. Again the camera clicked, and someone in the crowd shouted, "Hurrah!"

"It's good to have you back. Carl." Mrs. Mather's fingers gripped tightly on his arms. "But you gave me a rare fright, and I'll thank you to stick to your own job next time you go fishing."

Jessie was busy with Larry. Tubby, with a rope in his hand, grinned up at the crowd. A man said: "What cheer, Tubby! Are you learning to be a sailor:"

A passage was cleared through the crowd to where the gaffer's car was waiting, and they drove to the gaffer's office, where there was a bottle of champagne in an ice-pail and plates of sandwiches. Everyone who could get hold of a glass drank Carl's health, and then they all went out into the street to have their photographs taken.

It was a great occasion.

When Jessie had taken Mrs. Mather home. Carl told his story to the press, and in doing so did himself more than justice. If he hadn't turned up when he did the *Ivanhoe* would have sunk. There was no one on board. Her fore-hold was full up with water, but they had managed to light up one boiler and get a pump going. They had worked all tight getting a cover on the hatch. He, Carl, had never seen such weather and never wanted to again.

On board the *Ivanhoe*. Dan Todd was drawing the fires. He didn't hold with all this cheering and speech-making. When, he'd finished in the stoke-hold he meant to go straight to his lodgings and have his tea and a pipe, and spend the rest of the evening in the backyard with his hens.

"Ay, it was a tough job, but we brought her in"—Carl concluded his story. When the reporters had gone, a man who had been sitting very quietly in a corner of the office came forward. The gaffer introduced him as "Mr. Innes, my solicitor. He'll look after your claim, Carl."

Mr. Innes, a small man, rusty and brittle, accorded Carl a cold, dispassionate gaze. Facts were what Mr. Innes craved, and when he got them he had a habit of twisting and turning them inside out and asking dry, matter-of-fact questions which took the fire from the most thrilling story of the sea.

He had listened to Carl, as he talked to the reporters, with an unbelieving smile on his dried-up face. "Yes," he seemed to say. "That's all very well for the papers, but what I want is the truth, the plain unvarnished truth with none of your fancy trimmings." He said: "I must get all this down in writing."

"Tomorrow'll be time enough for that," Carl replied. "There's no almighty hurry, is there? The ship won't run away."

Mr. Innes agreed grudgingly that this was true enough, but went on to speak of writs, arrest and bail, not one of which expressions Carl understood. His mind was fixed on the night out he was going to have and the retailing of his story to an admiring and receptive circle in the private bar of the "Keel and Barge".

He looked round for Larry, but Larry had gone off with Jessie Miles. Dan Todd wasn't anywhere about. There was only Tubby left to perform single-handed the functions of a Greek chorus to the saga of the seas.

Mr. Innes held out his hand and got it well crushed. Through the tears which filled his pale-blue eyes he said: "Well, tomorrow then, Mr. Swanson. At my office. Ten o'clock sharp."

"I'll be there," said Carl carelessly, and hastened Mr. Innes' departure with a hearty slap on his shoulder blades. "And you'll want the others as well, I suppose. Tubby and Dan Todd and Larry? I'll bring 'em along."

Carl took Tubby with him to the "Keel and Barge", and acknowledged the chorus of greeting with a wave of his hand. He ordered a double Scotch, and was feeling in his pocket for the money when the landlord said: "This is on the house, Mr. Swanson." He filled a glass for himself. "And here's your very good health."

This was going to be something like a night, Carl thought to himself. Someone offered him a cigarette, someone else struck a match. They crowded round him. "Struck it lucky this time, Carl."

"What does it feel like to be rich?"

"What sort of trip did you have?"

"Is it true she was a derelict?" The shrill pipe of an old man sitting at a table hunched over his tankard cut through the buzz of talk.

"That's right," Carl answered. "Not a living soul on board when we got to her. Water was within four feet of the coamings in her fore-hold, the deck cargo shifted, and her mast and gear lying right across everything."

A full glass was put in his hand, and as he lifted it he said: "Here's to the lads who helped to bring her in." He put a hand on Tubby's shoulder and pulled him forward. "Come on, Tubby. You're in this too. Name your poison."

"A pint of mild."

Carl laughed. "Beer! On a night like this! Not blooming likely. Give him a Scotch and spare the water. He's had all he wants of that to last him a twelve-month." The men at the dart-board gave up their game and crowded round the bar. Everyone wanted to hear Carl's story at first hand and were ready to pay for the privilege in whisky.

The gale which had smashed the hatch of the *Ivanhoe* and had carried away her mast increased in force. The work done by the crew became that of supermen; men who needed no sleep nor food nor drink.

Reluctantly Carl admitted that the latter part of the trip had been uneventful, but returned quickly to the events of the first night and splashed on the colours with a heavy, alcoholic hand. Tubby did his best to fill in the gaps, but whisky to him was an unaccustomed tipple, and he soon found it more comfortable to be seated, and contented himself with an occasional, "Yes, that's right. That's what happened."

At ten o'clock Carl found himself in the street, still the centre of an admiring, cheering crowd. It was then that Inspector Pollitt, in plain clothes, appeared with a sergeant, and broke up the gathering and put a friendly arm through Carl's. "Now, come along, Mr. Swanson. It's best for you to get to your bed."

Carl said that Pollitt was a good old stick, his best friend who wouldn't let him down, and allowed his wavering footsteps to be guided in the direction of Hawkin's Court.

"Good ole Pollitt. Good ole Pollitt. I'll do the same for you one of these days." Which eventuality, of course, was most improbable, but the promise was well meant.

Mrs. Mather nodded her old head and pursed her lips as she led Carl down the narrow passage to the kitchen. She made him drink a cup of tea before she let him go to bed in his room under the slates.

Tom Ingleby stood six foot two in his waders. He had a greying black beard and brown, kindly eyes.

On the night of the arrival of the *Ivanhoe* he rowed up the river from the Pride of Bedford with three sacks of eels in the boat, and, as he bumped them up the steps on to the quay, he reckoned up in his mind that they would fetch thirty bob as near as no matter, and would keep him in grub for a month. He would be able to pay Hoppy what he owed and there would be enough over for an ounce or two of tobacco.

It was heavy work for a man of sixty-five, and he was glad to be rid of his load at Saloman's store.

With rounded, bent shoulders and a swinging stride, he made his way to Hoppy's house and opened the front door.

Old Hoppy was sitting in the kitchen in a basket chair, with his stockinged feet on the burnished steel fender. When he heard Tom Ingleby's shuffling step in the passage, he called out: "Come along in out of the cold. How are you keeping?"

"Not so bad. I'll be letting you have the money next week."

"There's no hurry for that. You know that well enough." Hoppy leaned forward and raked dead ashes from the grate.

Tom sat very stiff and very upright in a hard kitchen chair.

For a time the two men sat in silence, and then Hoppy said: "There's been a great to-do in the town today. Carl's just done a bit of salvage."

"What ship?"

"The *Ivanhoe*. He found her derelict in the North Sea."

Ingleby ran his fingers through his beard. "I was wondering what had happened to him. He wasn't on the bridge of the *John Goodwin* when she passed my place."

"He's struck it lucky this time all right. And not for the first time neither."

"Yes; and he's worked hard for all he's got. I don't suppose bringing in the *Ivanhoe* was exactly boy's work." Tom Ingleby shaved thin slices off a rope of black twist into the palm of his hand, and as he stuffed the tobacco into his pipe he went on: "Do you see anything of Mrs. Mather these days?"

"Not a terrible lot. She doesn't go out much, but Jessie told me she was keeping pretty spry. That's Jessie Miles who's walking out with Larry Hicks."

"Did you hear what sort of time Carl had with the *Ivanhoe*?"

"It's all in the papers. You can read it for yourself." Hoppy turned in his chair and stretched out a hand to the table. "And they've got his photo as well."

Tom Ingleby took the paper and held it to the light.

"I wouldn't have recognized him by this. He's got a lot fatter since the last time I saw him." But for all the deprecatory tone there was pride in his voice and he sat quite still for a long time, staring at the photograph.

He only laid it aside when Mrs. Hopkins came in, carrying a bulging string bag.

Tom got up and muttered: "Pleased to meet you, ma'am." He wasn't at his best and brightest in the company of women, for he had seen too few in the past thirty years.

Mrs. Hopkins took the shawl from her head and revealed grey hair drawn tightly back into a bun. As she emptied the bag she said: "Supper won't be long, and I've got a treat for you. Sausages. Fresh pork ones, and I got a pot of paste as well."

It was a treat for Tom Ingleby to have his supper cooked for him, and the smell of the sausages, hissing and jumping in the pan, was pleasant. No meal that he had eaten in the loneliness of his house down the river had ever tasted half as good as the suppers cooked by Mrs. Hopkins.

When the table was cleared and Mrs. Hopkins had taken the tray of dirty dishes into the scullery, Hoppy brought out the draught-board, and during the next half-hour few words were spoken. Draughts, as played by Tom Ingleby and Hoppy, was a game to be taken seriously.

Tom had three crowns against Hoppy's two, when the cuckoo clock aggressively announced that it was ten o'clock.

"I've got you this time," Tom Ingleby said.

"I'm afraid you have." Hoppy put the pieces into their box. "When'll you be up again? Next Wednesday?"

Tom Ingleby stood up. "Maybe before then. It depends on how the eels run." He said good night, picked up the old felt hat he always wore and went out.

When he was gone, Hoppy muttered: "He's had a tough time. It seems a pity that he can't—"

"What's that?" asked Mrs. Hopkins, who came in from the kitchen at that moment.

"Nothing," replied Hoppy quickly. He folded the draughtboard and put it away in a cupboard.

Jessie Miles was happy, completely, utterly happy, as she walked with Larry's arm round her waist along Union Street to the picture house. On the way she stopped in front of the furniture shop and said: "Now we'll be able to get everything we want, even the boy. I never realized I wanted him so much till now."

Larry stared at the statuette for almost a minute before he spoke. "We mustn't be in too much of a hurry, Jess."

"But why ever not?"

"Well, there'll be lots of things to see to and fix up before we get our money."

"But you will get it, won't you? Hoppy said you would; he had a cousin once who was in a boat that saved another. He said there was never any trouble about a thing like that."

"All the same, I'm not going to spend the money until I see it. When it's safe in the bank'll be time enough."

The light went from Jessie's eyes. She said: "Oh well, don't let's argue about it now." She tried to fix her mind on the house they were going to have, the furniture and the boy, but somehow the image would not form. She fought back the vague, uneasy fear that had come into her mind with Larry's words.

Larry looked down at her and smiled. "It's only a question of waiting a little longer."

"Yes, of course." Jessie smiled back at him. "And now, if we're going to see the big picture, we'd better hurry."

When the picture was over and he had seen Jessie home, Larry walked down to the market-place.

The remnants of the crowd from the "Keel and Barge" had come to anchor at Hoppy's stall, rather from a disinclination of their legs to carry their owners any farther, than from any wish to eat or drink.

Hoppy was polishing up the tea-urn, but at the sound of Larry's step he looked round. "Glad to see you, boy. How are you?"

"Not so bad. I'm glad to be back."

"I'll bet you are. Pie? They're nice and hot."

"No, thanks. Just a cup of coffee." Larry took his cup and helped himself to a spoonful of sugar. "Have you seen Carl?"

Hoppy grinned. "Yes. He's been making a night of it. Pollitt saw him home."

"Pollitt?"

"Yes. That's fame for you. If he'd been a decky on the jag he'd have been on a plank bed by now."

One of Carl's late audience, who was maintaining an upright position with some difficulty, said: "And what that man's been through you wouldn't believe."

"Yes, I would. I was with him." Larry winked at Hoppy. "It's been a high tide at the 'Keel' seemingly."

"And Carl hasn't half been telling the tale neither."

"What do you think about it yourself? Will we get much out of it?" Larry asked.

Hoppy wiped down the counter and leaned on it. "That depends on what the ship's worth. What would you say would be her value?"

"Well, a trawler costs more than twenty thousand, and the *Ivanhoe's* three times the size of any of 'em."

"And there's her cargo as well."

Hoppy ran his fingers through his hair. "Seventy thousand won't be far out for the value of the ship and cargo, and if you was to get a quarter of that I wouldn't be surprised."

A quarter of seventy thousand was a sum quite beyond Larry's ability to calculate. "Fours into seven . . ." he began.

"It's seventeen thousand as near as no matter."

"Seventeen thousand pounds!"

Hoppy nodded. "And it might be more. You never can tell. It depends what sort of story you put up, and you can trust Carl not to leave anything out. He told them at the pub that the water in the fore-hold was four feet below the coamings when he got on board."

"Are you sure he said that?"

"That was what was told to me. You'd better ask him." Hoppy jerked his thumb in the direction of a man at the end of the counter. "He was there when Carl was telling 'em all about it."

Larry repeated his question and received confirmation of Hoppy's statement.

"Isn't that the way it was?" Hoppy asked.

"Yes, I think so," Larry replied, and finished his coffee. "Well, I'll be getting along. Good night."

Larry walked quickly up the alley which led to Hawkin's Court, and as soon as he came in sight of Mrs. Mather's cottage he looked for a light in the top window. There was none. He knocked on the door, waited and knocked again. From within Mrs. Mather querulously demanded to know who was disturbing her sleep.

When she opened the door and saw Larry she said: "Oh, it's you, is it? He's gone to bed."

"I've got to see him."

"You'll have a job to wake him."

"That's all right. I can find my way up."

Mrs. Mather was quite right. Carl was hard to rouse. He grunted and said: "Go to hell!" as Larry gripped his wrist and spoke his name.

"Carl, you've got to wake." Larry shook him by the shoulders.

Carl opened his eyes and focused Larry with difficulty. "What's the matter?"

"I've just heard you've been spinning the yarn."

"Well?"

"You said that the water in the fore-hold of the *Ivanhoe* was four feet under the coamings when we got to her first. That's not right and it's not what you told the gaffer and Mr. Innes."

"Innes? Who's he?"

"The solicitor."

Carl pulled himself up in his bed and sat with his back against the head-board. "What does it matter what I said about the fore-hold?"

"You've got to tell the same story all the time. If you don't, people'll think there's been some funny business and start asking a lot of questions. Dan Todd's all right. You can trust him to keep his head, but Tubby's different. He might give the show away."

"I'll see Tubby in the morning."

"Yes, but you've got to make up your mind what you want him to say. Whether the hold was full up or not."

"What d'you think?"

"I dunno." Larry sat down and pulled a tobacco pouch from his pocket. "I don't like it."

"You've got nothing to worry about. You leave it all to me."

"But I've got to know what to say if I'm asked the question."

Carl yawned noisily. "Then say the hold was awash." Carl slid down in his bed and drew up the blankets under his chin.

Larry got up and put his pipe in his mouth. A string of tobacco hung down over the bowl. It flared up as he applied a lighted match. "These lawyers are the devil, asking questions. You'll have to watch your step."

Carl yawned and turned on his right side. "Good night. Thanks for coming along."

In the kitchen Mrs. Mather caught Larry by the skirt of his coat. "Is there anything wrong?" Her eyes were anxiously questioning.

"No, of course not." Larry took the pipe from his mouth and laughed.

But as she shut the door behind him Mrs. Mather was troubled. She stood for a time with her hand on the latch. Carl had been a good friend to her. But . . . As she turned bedwards she shook her head slowly from side to side. The tea-leaves had said there was going to be trouble.

7

THE OFFICE OF Mr. Innes was situated over a baker's shop in Union Street, nearly opposite to the Gilboro' Furnishing Company's showrooms. It consisted of two rooms: one where his clerks typed and talked and smoked cigarettes, and the other where Mr. Innes deliberated on the problems brought to him by his clients.

On the morning of the day following the arrival of the *Ivanhoe*, Mr. Innes was sitting at his desk, and though a basket of papers lay by his right hand he paid no attention to them. He was waiting for Carl. The clock on St. Jude's church had struck ten o'clock a quarter of an hour ago.

For the third time Mr. Innes pulled a warming-pan of a silver watch from his waistcoat pocket. Those who failed to keep appointments punctually gained but a lowly position in Mr. Innes' estimation.

He made a disapproving, clucking noise and began walking up and down his room.

While he was rehearsing what he would say to Carl when he did at last condescend to arrive, there came from the outer office what can only be described as a confused noise. A clerk came in and said: "They're here," and was half through an inquiry as to whether Mr. Innes would see them now when Carl rolled in.

He told Mr. Innes that it was a lovely morning, in a tone which brooked no denial, and sat down in the only comfortable chair in the room. Larry, Dan Todd, looking more than ever like a sick horse, and Tubby Stevens, grouped themselves behind him. They looked as though they were posing for a photograph.

Mr. Innes said, "Quite so," twice, and sat down. Then he coughed and picked up a pen. Now that Carl had arrived, his intention of commenting on his unpunctuality faded. Carl, in a small room, was rather overpowering.

"You want a statement from me. Is that right?" Carl asked.

"Yes, yes. Just tell me your story in your own words. And please speak slowly as I shall have to take it down." Mr. Innes dipped his pen in the ink. "First of all I want the day and the time when you boarded the *Ivanhoe*."

Taking a statement was, to Mr. Innes, a serious matter, and Carl was tired of the whole business by the time the last sheet was blotted. Then it was Larry's turn, and after him Dan Todd and lastly Tubby.

Tubby was signing his name when the telephone bell rang. Mr. Innes lifted the receiver and said: "Yes? . . . Innes speaking. . . . Yes, I am acting for Mr. Swanson. . . . What's that?"

The booming voice of Inspector Pollitt at the other end of the wire said: "The body of MacTaggart has just been brought in."

"Who?" asked Mr. Innes.

"MacTaggart. He was captain of the *Ivanhoe*. I thought I'd better let you know. I expect there'll be an inquest either tomorrow or the next day and we'll want Swanson and his men to give evidence."

"Quite so. Quite so. I'll tell them. Good-bye." Mr. Innes put down the receiver. He looked at Carl. "The body of the captain of the *Ivanhoe* has been recovered."

Carl half rose. "That can't be true. I——" Then he stopped speaking and dropped back into his chair. "Who told you?"

There was a look of faint surprise on Mr. Innes' face as he said: "Inspector Pollitt. And why shouldn't it be true?"

"I don't know," Carl mumbled. "But he wasn't on board when we got to the *Ivanhoe*."

Mr. Innes arranged the papers on his desk into a neat pile. "Well, we shall hear all about it at the inquest. Your presence and that of your crew will be required. I will communicate with you as soon as the date is fixed. That will be all for the present."

Out in the street, Larry said: "Now what the hell's going to happen?"

Carl said: "Nothing. We're all right."

"But if it's found out he was on board," Tubby began.

"It won't be if none of us talk."

"You can trust me," Tubby replied.

Carl looked at him for a moment. "For the sake of your health, I hope that's true." Then he said to Larry: "Come on along to the 'Keel'; I want a drink."

The red-brick piers, ten feet high, which supported Gilboro' council-chamber had, for three hundred years, kept its floor clear of the tides which used to sweep across the saltings when the moon was full and a nor'westerly gale was blowing.

Since the sea-wall had been built in 1888 and the river dredged, the fish-market no longer suffered from a surfeit of sea-water. The fishermen, opportunists ever, then took to storing their nets and baskets and warps under the council-room.

The resulting smell, a compound of Stockholm tar, hemp rope and fish, permeated through the cracks in the flooring above and fought a successful battle with the odour from the waxed oak panelling of the council-chamber.

And to make sure that no one should forget that Gilboro' depended on the sea for her livelihood, there were models of ships on brackets round the room, models of barques and brigs, of fishing-smacks, of Chinese junks, and one of a Deal galley.

The long, low-roofed room had served the town well as a meeting-place for the councillors, as a county court on Wednesdays, and as a police-court on Mondays and Thursdays.

Today it was to house the coroner, a crowd of witnesses and spectators, and a jury gathered in from the quayside and wharf.

An old man with the neck action of a tortoise, who acted as cleaner, caretaker and usher, was engaged in arranging chairs for the jury and for those whose importance was such that they were accorded a place at the broad oak table.

When he had finished this work, the caretaker fussed about with paper and blotting-pads, pens and pots of ink, moving slowly with a deliberation due to age and a touch of rheumatism. Then, when the last detail had been completed, he shuffled to a window and looked out.

The open space between the council-chamber and the wharf was dotted with groups of men talking. Now and again a head turned in the direction of the outside stone stairway leading up to the council-chamber door, but no one felt inclined to make the first move. Smoking was not allowed in the chamber.

At a quarter past ten Mr. Fleming came importantly round the corner from the High Street. He was a great bull of a man who had won hundreds of county court cases by virtue of a booming voice, a blustering, bullying manner and a complete inability to recognize defeat. He was also possessed of a shrewd common sense and was a very fair judge of character.

At the moment he was carrying a fat black brief-bag and was followed by a stocky little man in a shiny blue serge suit.

Hoppy, leaning on the counter of his stall, said: "That's Fleming. He's acting for the owners of the *Ivanhoe* and he's got the chief officer of the *Ivanhoe* with him. I saw his picture in the paper this morning."

Someone asked what his name was and Hoppy drew a folded paper from a shelf. "Pennington. John Pennington. And I bet he wishes now he hadn't lit out of the *Ivanhoe* as quick as he did."

Two newspaper reporters followed Mr. Fleming and John Pennington up the stairs and their example was followed by a group lounging on the balustrade.

The caretaker, his head weaving to and fro, greeted Mr. Fleming with the news that it was a fine day and the expectation that there would be a big crowd. He spoke with the satisfaction of a cinema manager when he tells the doorman to put out the "House Full" boards. He rubbed the palms of his hands together.

Mr. Fleming nodded and threw his hat on to a chair, put his bag on the table and unfastened its straps.

The reporters, reinforced by two men from a London news-agency, filed into their places and brought out notebooks and well-sharpened pencils. The caretaker left Mr. Fleming and asked if there was anything they wanted. He was an expert at drawing out the odd sixpence or shilling, and was not disappointed on this occasion. The man from the *Argus* asked him what he'd done with the body.

He was busy thinking of an answer to this one when the door opened and Mr. Innes came in. He gave Mr. Fleming a nod as he walked across the room with neat, mincing steps. When he had placed his bag on the table and his bowler hat carefully under a chair he turned to Carl, who was close behind him. "You sit over there till you're wanted." He pointed to the rows of high-backed, pew-like benches.

Dan Todd, who followed Carl, had no expression on his face, Larry was nervous, he kept his eyes on the floor; Tubby caught the caretaker's eye and grinned. He was also very nervous.

The room was filling up now with a shuffling, murmuring crowd who showed a strange desire to avoid the front bench.

A policeman, looking very odd without his helmet, brought in a pile of clothes and put them on the end of the table. He had a typewritten sheet in one hand and he checked each article, making a tick with the point of a well-sucked lead pencil as he did so.

Inspector Pollitt's entrance momentarily stilled the talk on the benches, but as soon as he was seated it broke out again.

The caretaker mustered the jury. Then he went to the top of the stairs. Everything was ready. Inspector Pollitt had assured him that the witnesses were present. He looked out across the market-place and then back into the room at the clock. It was close on the half-hour.

A figure on a bicycle, pedalling hard, shot out of a side street, swerved and steered straight for the chamber.

"He's coming."

"He" was the coroner—a thin, worried general practitioner with a limp, yellow moustache. He got off his cycle and ran up the steps two at a time.

"Silence in court." This was the caretaker's big moment. The buzz of talk died.

The coroner nodded and smiled to Pollitt, to Mr. Fleming and to Mr. Innes, as he squeezed between a fat juryman and the table to his desk set on a foot-high dais.

When the jury had been sworn he said: "Well, gentlemen, it is your painful duty today to decide the cause of death of one, Roderick MacTaggart. You will listen to the evidence and ask what questions you think necessary. I will give you such assistance as lies in my power and you will then retire to consider your verdict.”

It was a speech which the coroner knew by heart; he rattled it off like a boy at school repeating a well-learnt lesson.

“We will first take evidence of identification. Mr. MacTaggart.”

A man came forward and sat on the coroner’s right hand. When he had been sworn he said that he had identified the body as that of his brother, Roderick MacTaggart.

The coroner expressed his sympathy and said that he supposed that no one wished to ask any questions. His supposition was correct and Mr. MacTaggart gave way to Captain Small, a trawler skipper, who advanced slowly, crabwise, across the floor. He was crumpling a tweed cap in mahogany-coloured fingers. His face was of the same colour, which made his eyes look even bluer than they were in fact.

He swore to tell the truth, the whole truth and nothing but the truth.

The coroner was not the man to waste his own or anyone else’s time and before the last word was out of Captain Small’s mouth, he said: “Now, Captain, what do you know about this affair?”

“Well, sir, we was coming in from the grounds when my mate saw him a-bobbing up and down. ‘Harry’, he says to me—”

“No, we don’t want to know what anyone said. Just tell us what you saw yourself.”

“Well, I thought it was a fish-trunk at first, but as soon as I got my glasses on to it I saw it weren’t no fish-trunk, but a corp.”

“And you got it on board your ship?”

“That’s right, sir.”

“Whereabouts were you when you found the body?”

“As near as I can figure it out, sixty miles south-east from the Gap light-vessel.”

The coroner said: “Thank you,” and looked at Mr. Fleming.

Mr. Fleming stood up. “There are just one or two questions I would like to ask this witness.”

The coroner said: “Certainly, Mr. Fleming.”

“Now, Captain. How did you fix the position of your ship?”

The witness turned towards the solicitor. "Fixed my position? I didn't say I did no such thing. There weren't no call for me to fix my position."

"That is exactly what I thought, Captain. But tell me, how did you know where you were?"

"By the time it took me to steam to the Gap lightship; six and a half hours was the time between picking up the corp and when I was abeam of the Gap."

"Did you make any allowance for the set of the tide?"

"I did. We was drifted down three miles to the southward, I reckon."

"Thank you," said Mr. Fleming, and sat down.

The next witness was the police-surgeon, who examined the body.

The first question put to him by the coroner was: "Can you tell us, Doctor, how the deceased met his death?"

"Yes, sir. By drowning. His lungs were full of water."

"Are you quite sure about that?"

"Absolutely. There was a fracture of the skull caused by contact of the head with a flat surface. It was such an injury as may be suffered by a man falling backwards on to a road or pavement. I have had experience of similar cases."

"Was it a serious fracture?"

"Oh no. The skull was of average thickness and I think there can be no doubt whatsoever that had the deceased not fallen into the water he would be alive now."

"And is that all you can tell us?"

The doctor said: "Yes, I think it is," and then corrected himself. "No, there was one other injury though it, too, was of a very slight nature and could not have contributed in any way to the death of Captain MacTaggart."

"Perhaps we'd better have it all the same, Doctor," the coroner suggested.

"If you please, sir. It was a bruise about the size of a half-crown on the right cheek of the deceased and situated about one inch below the point of the cheek-bone."

"In your opinion was it caused before or after death?"

"Before, undoubtedly."

Mr. Fleming asked the doctor why he should think that, and was given a technical explanation of which he did not understand one word. Neither did the jury but they contrived to look very wise.

The coroner looked out of the window at nothing. He was thinking of one of his patients on the far side of the town who had gone down with influenza. He hoped that it wasn't the start of an epidemic.

His thoughts returned to the inquest to hear Mr. Fleming asking the doctor how long he thought the body had been in the water.

"That's very difficult to say with any degree of certainty. I should put it between six hours and forty-eight."

Mr. Fleming was satisfied and sat down.

The police-constable who had brought in the pile of clothes was the next witness. He took the oath without expression in his voice nor apparent appreciation of its meaning.

"The deceased was wearing an oilskin coat. Name of maker: John Gordon, Whittingham. It was belted round his waist with a length of cord. One button was missing from the collar. There were no articles in the pockets. Under the oilskin the deceased was wearing a pair of pyjamas." The constable wetted his thumb, turned over a page of his notebook and took a deep breath. "On his legs were a pair of thick woollen stockings and sea-boots."

The coroner leaned across his table and picked up a piece of cord. "Will you please demonstrate to the jury how you found this round the waist of the deceased."

The constable took the cord and stood up. "It was like this, sir. Tied in front with the two loose ends about eighteen inches long."

Carl Swanson sat rigid, his forearms flat on his knees. He was staring woodenly straight ahead of him. A faint sound, it may have been a sigh of relief, escaped his lips when the cord was replaced on the table and the constable sat down.

Mr. Fleming had no questions to ask but he wrote down something in his notebook.

"Is Mr. Pennington present?" the coroner asked.

The chief officer came forward and took the constable's place in the witness-chair.

He had been chief officer of the *Ivanhoe* and had left her on the night of November 24th in company with the others of the crew. Captain MacTaggart remained on board. At that time the water in number one hold was up to the coamings and there was, in his opinion, no chance of saving the ship; the deck cargo had shifted, she had a heavy list to starboard and the mast and wireless aerial had been carried away.

Mr. Fleming underlined the words he had written heavily with a blue pencil and made a star in the margin. He must go into this matter of the amount of water in the hold later.

"What was the state of the stoke-hold fires at the time you abandoned the ship?" the coroner asked.

"Two of them were alight in the port boiler," Pennington replied. "But the water was coming over the plates and it was only a question of time before they were put out."

"Have you any idea what was the ship's position at this time?"

"No, sir, I'm afraid I can't remember that, but I made an entry in the deck log and I put the position on the chart."

"Where is the log?"

"I have it here, sir," Mr. Fleming replied. "But there are no entries in it as spoken of by the witness." He handed the log to the coroner.

"But this is very curious. Are you quite sure?" The coroner turned over the pages until he came to the one for November 24th, the day of the abandonment. He turned to Pennington. "Please come here a minute and explain it to me."

The chief officer bent over the log. A minute passed as he examined the entries. Then he said: "Someone's rubbed out what I wrote."

The coroner lifted the log to the level of his eyes so that the light from the window shone on the surface of the paper. "Yes, there has been an erasure." He passed the tips of his fingers over the paper. "It's quite rough on this line. Let me see the chart."

Mr. Fleming spread the chart on the table and held down its curling sides with two books.

The coroner picked up a magnifying glass and held it over the chart. "Can you show me the place where you fixed the ship?" he asked the chief officer.

The chart had seen much service; it was dirty, there were many pencil-lines on it and several places where a rubber had been used.

"Our course from the Skaw was east by south, and as near as I can remember we had run a hundred miles from there." Pennington put his forefinger down on the paper: "That, I think, would be our approximate position."

The coroner said: "Let me see," and looked through the glass. "There has been an erasure there but there's another here, and here. I'm afraid we shan't get much assistance from the chart." He leaned back in his chair and turned to the jury. "You have heard the evidence of Mr. Pennington. Perhaps you would like to examine the log and the chart."

The foreman, whose life's work was plumbing, handled the chart gingerly. The other members of the jury crowded round him and there was much whispering and pointing. Two of them were looking at it upside down and none of them had more than the haziest notion of the respective positions of the Skaw and England. However, after much talk the foreman said that he was satisfied and handed the chart back to the coroner.

He was given the log and there was a further discussion. When it was over Mr. Fleming asked the chief officer if he had made any other record of the place of abandonment.

"No, I put it straight into the log."

"How did you fix that position?"

"By dead reckoning. I allowed a speed of eight knots from the Skaw on the east by south course."

"And that, of course, was only an estimate?"

"Yes, sir. And now I come to think it over I think that the speed of eight knots may have been rather high."

"Can you remember what you wrote in the log?"

"Not the exact words, but I did say something about abandoning ship."

"And there is no trace of that entry in the log now?"

"No, sir."

"Are you sure that this was the log in use at the time?"

"It was the only log we kept on the bridge. The engineer's log was lost over the side when we were getting into the boat."

The coroner thanked the chief officer for giving evidence and sympathized with him over the terrible time he had been through. Then he called Carl Swanson.

Carl gave a short account of the fishing-voyage on which he had been engaged prior to his falling in with the *Ivanhoe*. He had, he said, lost both his trawls owing to bad weather-conditions and omitted to describe his poaching efforts and subsequent chase by the Fishery Prosecution gunboat.

With regard to the position of the *Ivanhoe* when he boarded her he could give the court no assistance except that he stated that before beginning the voyage to Gilboro' the ship remained stopped for twelve hours while the fore-hold was being pumped out; thereafter they proceeded at a speed which he estimated as three knots for twelve hours. After that speed was increased to about five knots and the Gap light-vessel was sighted twelve hours later.

Mr. Fleming made a calculation in his notebook and when his turn came to question Carl he asked: "I have worked out the distances you have given to the court and I make it that you steamed in all ninety-six miles to the Gap light-vessel. Do you think that figure is correct?"

Carl grinned. "I'm sure I don't know. I never used the chart."

"Then how did you know what course to steer?"

"I just guessed at it."

"What course did you, in fact, steer?"

"I dunno. I had a good idea about where we were and I took a cast of the lead now and again; that told me all I wanted to know."

"I suppose you saw the chart on board the *Ivanhoe*?"

A wary look crossed Carl's face and he said: "No. I tell you I never have no truck with charts. None of us fishermen has."

The coroner leaned forward on his desk. "Do you mean that?"

"Yes, sir. It's nigh on twenty years since I went on my first trip and all that time I've hardly ever seen a chart used on board a trawler. The way we tells where we are is by getting up a bit of the bottom on the lead."

The coroner said: "I'm sorry to have interrupted you, Mr. Fleming. Will you please continue?"

"Did you at any time go into the chart-house on the *Ivanhoe*?" Fleming then asked Carl.

"Yes, I did."

"Did you see there a chart of the North Sea spread out on the table?"

"No, I didn't."

"Did you see the ship's log?"

"No."

"Now please think very carefully about this because, as you know, Mr. Pennington, the chief officer, has told us that when he left the ship the chart and log were in the chart-house."

"They may have been, but I didn't notice them."

"By the way, how much water was there in the fore-hold?"

Carl stuck out his chin. "It was full right up to the coamings."

"Are you sure about that?"

"Of course I am. Why shouldn't I be?"

Mr. Fleming said: "Very well. That is all I wish to ask you."

The coroner looked at the clock. If he could wind up now there would be time for him to pay two or three visits to his patients before lunch. He turned in his chair and faced the jury. "Gentlemen, there are no more witnesses, unless you would like to see the other members of the *John Goodwin*'s crew who brought in the *Ivanhoe*."

The foreman, whose business was slack, said that while he had no wish to hear any more witnesses he, speaking for the jury, would like to pay a visit to the *Ivanhoe*.

The coroner sighed and said: "Very well. We will go there straightaway."

There was a grating of chair-legs on the bare wooden floor. Mr. Fleming bundled his papers into his brief-bag. As far as he was concerned his work was finished.

The caretaker opened the door and, led by the coroner, the jury filed out.

Old Hoppy watched them walk across the market-place to the wharf and said to a customer: "Well, that hasn't taken 'em long. There'll be a crowd along in a minute." He turned up the burner under the tea-urn and put six pies into the oven.

The coroner walked quickly to the wharf; the jurymen almost had to run to keep up with him. When he came abreast of the *Ivanhoe* he called out to the watchman and asked to be taken up on to the bridge.

"Now, here we are, gentlemen. That is the chart-house."

The foreman and two others went in, could see nothing but a pencil with a broken point on the desk, and came out again. They stared vaguely about them: at the wheel, at the binnacle and at the engine-room telegraph.

The coroner was saying: "Well, I don't think there's anything to interest us—" when a juryman, eager to justify his position, called out: "I say! Come and have a look at this."

"This" was a frayed end of a lanyard which had once secured the top wire of the guard-rail in the port wing. The other jurymen, led by the plumber foreman, crowded round him.

Someone said: "That's where he went over all right. The line must have broken when he was leaning on it."

There was a murmur of agreement. The foreman said it was a good thing he had suggested coming. The coroner looked at his watch and said: "Well, it seems to be a clear case of accident. We needn't waste any more time here."

But however clear it may have been to the coroner, the foreman refused to be hurried. He and his friends pottered about the ship for another ten minutes before they returned to the council-chamber.

The coroner's mind was made up and he was determined to make up the minds of the jury in the shortest possible time.

"Gentlemen, you have heard the evidence and you have had the opportunity of inspecting the *Ivanhoe*. There has been no suggestion of foul play, therefore I do not think it necessary that I should go over the story again. It is fresh in your minds. However, if there is any point on which you would like assistance, I will be happy to give it."

The foreman said that they would like to retire to consider their verdict and, with a fleeting, weary glance at the clock, the coroner said: "Very well." He would have liked to have added: "Don't be all day about it," but didn't.

Five of the jury seized the opportunity to have a smoke. The foreman, straddling before an empty fireplace, said: "Well, lads, what d'you think? Accidental death?"

"That's what it looks like," said a little man who was having trouble in getting his pipe to draw. "But there is no point in rushing it. I don't like that business about the log. Someone's monkeyed with it."

"That's right," said a fish-porter. "But all the same, I don't see that it signifies a lot."

"No more do I. MacTaggart might have done it hisself," suggested the man who kept the whelk-stall on the wharf. "We saw the rail that was broken and that's the end of it as far as I'm concerned."

"All right, lads. What do you say? The deceased fell overboard by accident. How does that sound?"

There was much argument between the foreman and the fish-porter as to the form of the verdict. The others listened apathetically.

The usher poked his head round the door. "The coroner wants to know how long you'll be."

"We're just coming," the foreman said. "Come on, lads, what do you say? Accidental death?"

Pipes near their end prompted unanimous agreement, and the foreman said: "All right. Let's get back." He had suddenly realized that it was past opening-time.

The coroner, who was smoking a cigarette on the top of the steps, was recalled by the caretaker and by the sound of tramping feet.

As he settled himself into his chair he asked: "Are you all agreed upon your verdict?"

The foreman cleared his throat and stood up. This was, if not the proudest moment of his life, a most important one. His name would be in the papers that night and to a man in business in the town that meant something.

"We are of the opinion that the deceased, Roderick MacTaggart, met his death by—by—er . . ." The foreman glanced down at the scribbled note he had made on the back of an envelope. "By falling over the side of the steamship *Ivanhoe*." It didn't sound as good as he thought it would.

"I take it you mean accidental death?"

"We do," said the foreman, slightly offended.

"And that the cause of death was by drowning?"

A juryman pulled at the foreman's coat. "That's right. Tell him we agree."

The foreman grudgingly admitted that the coroner was right and felt that much of his personal thunder had been stolen.

The coroner wrote down the verdict in its amended form, and as he blotted the words he said: "Well, that is the end of the case. The witnesses may go."

Inspector Pollitt, vaguely disappointed that there was nothing for him to do, that there had been no startling revelations that merited an inquiry by the police, picked up his cap and returned to the police-station to go through his daily reports and correspondence.

8

As Mr. Fleming pushed his way through the crowd at the door he felt a hand on his arm. It was Pennington, the chief officer of the *Ivanhoe*.

"Hallo. Do you want me?"

"Yes, I'd like to have a word with you, Mr. Fleming, if you're not in too much of a hurry."

Mr. Fleming was about to say: "Come and see me tomorrow morning," and then he changed his mind. "We'll go to my office. It'll be more comfortable there." There had been something in Pennington's tone which revived the suspicions aroused during the inquiry.

Mr. Fleming's office was not comfortable, but it was certainly a better place in which to talk than the draughty market-place or the stuffy council-chamber.

He pushed through the swing door into the outer office and strode on down a short, dark passage to a glazed door on which, in black letters, was printed: "P. Fleming. Private."

The first impression Pennington received was that of papers, tin boxes and a mouldy smell. Two dirty windows faced on the High Street, and because Fleming disliked fresh air and noise they were shut tight. Beneath them was a stack of black metal deed boxes each bearing a name in gold lettering.

A bookcase, which covered a wall on the right, was filled with books: law reports and textbooks, seldom used and covered with dust.

"Take a chair," said Fleming. He took off his coat and hat and sat down at a wide mahogany desk. Then he unrolled the chart and spread it out before him. "Now, what have you got on your mind?"

"Well, I don't know if there's much in it, but you remember the skipper of that trawler who picked up the body said he was six hours' steaming from the Gap lightship at the time?"

"Yes. I remember that."

Pennington laid a long black ruler across the chart. "That was his course up to the lightship. Now, if I mark off his run of sixty miles to this point we are still nearly forty miles from where the *Ivanhoe* was abandoned."

"Of course, you are relying on your memory as to the accuracy of that position."

"Yes," Pennington admitted. "But I don't think I'm far out."

"Of course we could get confirmation from the *Witney*, the ship that picked you up," Fleming suggested.

Pennington said: "No, not for some time, at any rate. She's sailed for a Chilean port." He thought for a moment and added: "You could send a wireless to her."

Fleming straightened his back and walked over to the window. "Yes, we could do that. But such a message wouldn't be accepted as evidence. It's very difficult." He came back to the chart and checked Pennington's calculations. "Yes, there's forty miles to be accounted for, but couldn't the explanation be that MacTaggart steamed the *Ivanhoe* that distance on his own."

"Quite impossible. The fore-hold was full right up and he'd never have dared to get under way until he'd got at least half the water out of her. If he had done so the bulkhead would have gone."

"That reminds me, Carl Swanson is reported as having said that the level of the water in the fore-hold was four feet below the coamings when he got on board."

Pennington looked surprised. "When did he say that?"

"It was in the papers this morning."

"But when you asked him in court he said that the water was up to the coamings."

"Yes, I know. I don't know which is the true story."

"Well, whichever way it was, the skipper could never have steamed the ship a mile, let alone forty."

"Are you sure about that?" Fleming turned quickly towards the chief officer.

"I'm not an engineer but I do know a bit about pumping, and I know the steam was right back at the time we left. It would have taken a couple of hours to have got the pressure up again."

"And Swanson did say in evidence that the *Ivanhoe* remained stopped for twelve hours after he boarded her, so that they could clear the fore-hold of water."

"I don't like that fellow," Pennington said. "He's got a damn' sight too good an idea of himself. And all that stuff about not using a chart! He was lying through his teeth. He must have seen the chart and have rubbed out my working."

"Yes, that's quite likely, but it doesn't take us anywhere. He salved the *Ivanhoe*; there's little doubt about that, and he'll have to be paid."

"The whole job stinks."

Mr. Fleming said: "What do you know about the tides in this part of the North Sea?" He pointed to the chief officer's suggested position of the abandonment of the *Ivanhoe*.

"They never run more than a quarter of a knot. And if you're thinking that the body could have drifted thirty-six miles in the time, I'd say it was impossible."

Fleming rolled up the chart and tied red tape round it in a neat bow. As he put it on a side table he said: "What was the state of the ship when you left her?"

The chief officer leaned across the desk. "I tell you, Mr. Fleming, I never thought she'd last another hour. The deck cargo had got adrift and she had a fifteen-degree list. There was three feet of water in the starboard alleyway. The scupper ports had jammed shut and the water couldn't get away."

"So you thought that the only thing to do was to abandon the ship?"

"I did. We all did. There was nothing we could do, and when the *Witney* came up the skipper told us to launch a boat."

"Yes, and what happened then?"

"We got the starboard boat over the side. When the crew were in it I told the skipper we were ready, but he wouldn't budge. I tried all I knew to make him change his mind, but he wouldn't."

"Where was he at this time?"

"On the bridge, standing out on the starboard wing. He was a wonderful man but terribly obstinate. He wouldn't admit he was beaten."

"The *Ivanhoe* was all he had," said Mr. Fleming. "And she wasn't insured."

"I didn't know that."

"And by the time she's been sold and the salvage claim has been settled there'll be precious little left for the widow."

"You're going to sell her, then?"

"I'll have to. By the way, how was it that the *Witney* didn't stand by the *Ivanhoe*?"

"She did for a time, and then we lost her in a snowstorm. We spent all the next day trying to find her, but we couldn't pick her up. I admit that I didn't think it was any use, because I felt sure in my own mind that she'd gone down soon after we had left her."

"Did you take any books from the ships?"

"No. The chief engineer took the engine-room log and dropped it over the side as he was getting into the boat."

Mr. Fleming lifted a pile of books and papers from the floor on to his desk. "These came from the captain's cabin. I want you to run through them and tell me what they relate to,"

Pennington said: "They are all to do with the cargo, the manifests and bills of lading, and correspondence with the shippers." He picked up a small notebook on which, written in ink, was the word "Cargo". "The skipper kept this himself. It was only to do with the loading and unloading of cargo. He used to make out his reports to his agents from it."

"Let's have a look," Fleming said. He flicked over the pages which were filled with copy-book writing. So many standards of timber with a notation of the distinguishing marks; so many tons of bunker coal. "That certainly doesn't help us." He threw the notebook down on his desk. "Well, I think that's all for the present. I expect you're wanting your lunch." Mr. Fleming held out his hand.

When the chief officer had gone, Mr. Fleming stood for a moment staring at the carpet, thinking. So Pennington was suspicious, too. "I must see him again and tell him to keep his mouth shut. It won't do to have him spreading rumours," he said to himself. He knew nothing against Carl, and had a very lively fear of the law of slander.

But still, there it was. Someone had made erasures on the chart and in the log. Carl had told different stories about the amount of water in the fore-hold and there was the question of the position where the body had been picked up.

It was not an easy matter to decide which was the best line to follow, and Mr. Fleming had smoked his pipe right through before he arrived at an answer.

He would write to Innes and suggest that they should settle Carl Swanson's claim out of court. The question was, how much should he offer. He first thought of ten thousand pounds, decided it was too much and then scribbled five thousand on his blotter. If the claim was genuine Innes would refuse it, but if there was any sticky business, something that Innes would not like to come out, he might agree to pay. And if he did, that would be the end of the case.

Five, four, three, two thousand. Fleming's mouth widened in a smile. He'd like to see Carl's face on receiving such an offer. He thought: "It might frighten him, make him think I know something."

He opened a drawer, took out a sheet of foolscap paper and began drafting the letter. "This'll make Innes think," he muttered, as he wrote the last line and rang for his clerk.

Mr. Innes was no fool. In fact, he had a much better brain than Fleming's. His handicap was that he could always see the other side's case and give to it the consideration and importance it deserved. That was one reason why his practice in the county courts was but a fraction of that enjoyed by Fleming.

He had no illusions regarding his client, Carl Swanson.

In a pigeon-hole of his orderly mind he had docketed Carl as being a liar after he had listened to his evidence given at the inquest.

For this reason Mr. Innes waited until the crowd had oozed and spread from the council-chamber before he approached Carl with the suggestion that they should lunch together. Carl's idea of lunch was of the beer-and-cut-off-the-joint variety. Mr. Innes seldom ate anything more exciting than scrambled eggs, toast and a cup of coffee.

He quite firmly, and at his own pace, led Carl to a tea-shop at the corner of the High Street. It was a small room furnished with small tables and chairs, inadequate in size and stability for the accommodation of such a man as Carl Swanson.

A waitress, not chosen for youthful charm, asked Mr. Innes how his rheumatism was and said that she'd ordered his eggs.

Carl said he'd have the same as Mr. Innes and thought of Larry waiting for him down at the "Keel and Barge".

Mr. Innes moved a plate to one side and clasped his hands together on the cloth in front of him.

Carl thought: "I'd like to take him for a trip as a decky. Just once. With Larry to chase him around."

Mr. Innes, happily unconscious of this brutal plan, said, in a voice as dry and brittle as a match-stick: "Mr. Swanson, I—er—am not entirely satisfied with this case."

"What d'you mean, not satisfied?"

Mr. Innes released one hand to make a quietening gesture. "There's no need to get excited. No doubt you will give me an explanation which will resolve my doubts and—er—fears." He unfolded a paper napkin and spread it on his bony knees. "There are just two matters which are troubling me. The first is this question of the level of water in the fore-hold of the *Ivanhoe*."

Carl thrust out his chin. "What I said was right. It was up to the coamings."

"Quite, quite. But the newspapers this morning report you as having said that the level was four feet below the coamings, and, frankly, I am puzzled."

"They didn't get that from me."

"I suppose you gave one of the reporters an interview?"

"I dunno who I spoke to. There was a crowd in the 'Keel' last night. The papers'll say anything to make a good story."

"Yes, I quite appreciate that and, of course, I accept your statement." Mr. Innes made a prim little bow. "But you realize, of course, that one has to be very careful in a matter of this sort." He coughed, as dryly as he had spoken. "And then about the log?"

"I never saw it." The denial came quickly on the heels of Mr. Innes' question.

"You're quite sure about that?"

"Of course I am." Carl leaned forward in his chair and put his clenched fists on the table. "What are you getting at?"

Mr. Innes said: "Nothing," and was relieved to see the scrambled eggs and the toast and butter approaching. Carl Swanson was a difficult client, and Mr. Innes did not like difficult clients. As he put two lumps of sugar in his cup of coffee he said: "I must point out to you, Mr. Swanson, that in a salvage claim one must be very sure of one's facts. If it comes to a fight, any suggestion that you acted improperly would, without doubt, have the effect of the award being cut down."

"Why should they fight?"

"I don't say they will, but we must be prepared for any eventuality."

"It's clear enough what I did, and I don't see that there should be any trouble."

"And I sincerely hope there won't be."

Carl finished his scrambled eggs and stood up. "Well, if that's all you want with me I'll be getting along."

"But you haven't had your coffee."

"I can't wait. I've got to see a bloke."

Mr. Innes was left to finish his lunch alone and to pay the bill. He made a mental note to charge the amount to "Expenses" in the account which he would render to Carl Swanson when the final settlement was made.

With a cold, fish-like gaze he watched Carl go, and sighed. "A difficult man to deal with," he decided, and called to the waitress to bring him some more hot milk.

Larry was coming out of the "Keel and Barge" when Carl walked across the market-place. "You're too late," he said. "It's just gone closing-time."

Carl swore. "I was caught by that damn' solicitor."

"What did he want?"

"Come on and take a walk and I'll tell you."

Carl didn't speak again until they were clear of the fish-dock and out on the path which ran along the top of the sea-wall. Clouds, low to the southward, were banking up black and ominous, and a spatter of rain drove in their faces. "It's going to blow up again." Carl buttoned up the collar of his pea-jacket and thrust his hands deep in his trouser pockets. "Innes is a damn' fool."

"What's the trouble now?"

"There's no trouble, but he's like all these damn' lawyers, never happy unless he's asking questions. He wanted to know if I knew anything about the log."

"What did you say?"

"That I'd never even seen it."

"He can't bowl you out on that."

"Yes, but you never know what he'll turn up next. He asked me about the water in the fore-hold and I said that it was up to the coamings."

"Did he see the bit in the paper?"

"That's what started him off."

"I shouldn't worry if I were you." Larry stopped to light a cigarette. As he threw away the match he said: "He didn't say anything about the other log, did he?"

"Other log! What d'you mean?"

"I told you at the time, didn't I?"

"No, you didn't."

"Well, I meant to. It was that notebook the captain was writing in. He had it in his cabin."

"MacTaggart?"

"Yes."

"Go on. Let's have it."

"I don't know much about it except that he had a kind of an exercise-book, the sort kids use at school. I saw him writing in it, and when he was having his dinner I went into his cabin and had a look at it."

Carl began to sweat. "What had he put down?"

"Just that we had finished pumping out number one hold and had started up the main engines."

"Was there anything else before that?"

"I didn't notice. That was all I read. I meant to speak to you about it, but I forgot."

"Why the hell didn't you tell me about it before we got in? If it's found now there's going to be trouble for the lot of us."

"I told you I forgot."

"What does it look like?"

"It was a greenish colour. Not very big."

"I've got to get it." Carl stopped and stood looking out across the marsh. "I've got to get it," he repeated. He swung round on Larry. "Where d'you think it is now?"

"I dunno. Maybe where I saw it in the cabin on the *Ivanhoe*."

"If it is it'll be easy meat. But if it's not it looks like we'll be in the cart."

"We?"

"Yes, the lot of us. Dan Todd and Tubby as well."

"I'm sorry, Carl. It was my fault."

"It's done now, but I'll fix it. You needn't worry. I've been in a worse mess than this before and got out clear." Carl grinned. Confidence in himself was returning. He pointed to a man poling a boat down a creek. "That's Tom Ingleby, isn't it?"

Larry said: "Yes, he's working that eel-sett of his again."

"What a life! It would send me clean balmy. Come on, let's get back."

9

AT ONE O'CLOCK next morning a rising wind was sweeping across the deserted expanse of the market-place. Old Hoppy, muffled up in a greatcoat and with a knitted scarf wound tightly round his throat, was glad to get into the shelter of his stall.

He was too busy filling up the burners under the tea-urn and the oven in the corner to see Carl as he came down the alley which led from Hawkin's Court. Carl had dressed and got out of the house without disturbing Mrs. Mather.

There were two men at the wharf unloading boxes from a lorry under a light which swung in the wind.

Carl watched them for a minute. Then he looked over to Hoppy's stall. The old man had his back to him. He took his chance and ran to the shadow of a shuttered store, up a passage and on to the wharf.

There was an hour yet before the fish-sales would begin and he'd be back in his bed before then.

There was no one on the wharf; no one to see him as he walked quickly in the direction of the corner of the dock where the *Ivanhoe* was moored. He passed the line of close-packed trawlers, the auction-hall, silent, dark and deserted, and on round the bend of the wharf.

The light of a flickering gas lamp illuminated the white letters on the bow of the *Ivanhoe*. He slackened his pace and kept in the shadow of the fish-stores.

There was an oil lamp hanging from a stanchion on the in-board end of the gangway leading to the deck of the *Ivanhoe*, but there was no sign of a watchman. Carl stood for a minute out of the range of the light of the lamp while his gaze roved along the deck, fore and aft. Perhaps there wasn't a watchman. He squeezed out his cigarette between the thumb and forefinger of his right hand and ran quickly from the shadows, over the gangway and on to the deck of the *Ivanhoe*. Then he halted and listened. There was no sound but the lap of water against the ship's side and the creak of wood as the ship ground against the face of the wharf.

The captain's cabin was on the boat-deck and the ladder was only a dozen feet from where Carl was standing. He walked on his toes feeling his way along the side of the casing. Then his fingers closed round the rail of the ladder and he swung himself on to the first tread.

A square of starlit sky showed above his head; he reached the deck above in a couple of cat-like strides.

There was no light to show the way, but his eyes, accustomed now to the darkness, made out the bulk of the cabins and the saloon. He crept forward, his hands feeling over the smooth steel of the wall.

For a moment he stood quite still and listened. Then he edged forward to the door of the captain's cabin and his hands closed on the handle; he bent his knees and pulled. It was fast. Damn and blast! The cold iron of the handle chilled his hand. He shifted his stance and tried again, but with no result except for a faint creaking of wood. And he thought he'd fixed that lock!

He struck a match and as the flame burned up within his cupped hands he saw a hasp, a staple and a padlock. That would take some shifting! But if he could get hold of a bar or mar-line-spike he'd soon have it off.

Rain was dripping off a corner of the deck-house roof.

A bar! Where could he get one? There would be a poker in the galley. That would serve. He crept to the ladder, down to the main-deck and aft to where a splash of light fell on the deck from the galley. He pressed his face close to the cold steel of the bulkhead and looked in. An old man was sitting on a chair. His feet were on an empty grate. His head was tilted back and he was snoring. Carl stepped high over the sill and, leaning forward, gripped a short poker lying on the stove-top. That would do the trick.

The sound of rending wood roused the watchman. He blinked several times and then listened. Again came the noise. It was overhead, on the deck above. He shuffled out of the galley and shouted: "Who's there?" very loudly.

Carl swore and withdrew the point of the poker from the staple. One more heave and he would have had it out. He froze.

Footsteps grated on the treads of the ladder and again the watchman called: "Who's that?"

Carl took three steps backward. It was just like his blasted luck.

The watchman stopped on the top of the ladder and directed the beam of his lantern in the direction of the deck-house but could see no one. Uncertain and afraid, he stood quite still, listening.

Someone on the wharf called out: "What's the matter?"

The watchman walked to the rail and said: "Is that you, Bob?" He saw the glint of a silver badge on a policeman's helmet and heard the sound of heavy boots on the wharf timbers.

"Is there anything wrong?"

"I heard a noise, but I can't see nothing." The watchman went down the ladder and over the gangway.

"What sort of a noise?" asked the policeman. He had his thumbs in his belt and he was leaning forward.

"I dunno. Sounded like wood splintering to me."

"I'd better have a look round." The policeman took his lamp from his belt and switched on the light.

"It was up around the officers' cabins; on the next deck."

Carl was gone by the time Police-Constable Makin reached the top of the ladder. He dropped down on to the fore-deck, waited for a moment until he heard the policeman walk aft, and then he jumped on to the wharf and made a quick dash for the shadow of the pilot-house.

The policeman walked round the deck-house trying the handle of each door until he came to the captain's cabin. He saw the half-drawn staple and said: "This is what you heard. Someone's been trying to make a break."

The watchman put forward a hand and picked off a sliver of newly splintered wood. "He's been trying to get into this cabin."

"That's about the size of it." The policeman shone his light on the deck below and then played it on the face of the bulkhead and on the closed port-hole. "I wonder what he was after."

"There's nothing in that cabin," the watchman said. "I took all the stuff that was in it up to Mr. Fleming's office last night."

"What sort of stuff?" The policeman felt in the pocket in the tail of his tunic for his notebook.

"Just clothes and things and some books."

"Can you give me the particulars?"

The watchman couldn't. All he knew was that he had loaded three or four bundles on to a barrow and delivered them at Mr. Fleming's office in the High Street.

"I know Mr. Fleming." The constable licked his pencil and wrote a line in his notebook. Then he said: "We'd better have a look round and see if there's anything else."

Half an hour later the watchman was left alone on board the *Ivanhoe* while Police-Constable Makin proceeded at the regulation speed of three miles per hour to the police-station and woke a sergeant, who was asleep in his chair. To him he made his report and the sergeant wrote it out slowly with a scratchy pen in the report book. When he had finished and had blotted the words he rubbed his chin and said: "The *Ivanhoe*. I think I'd better tell Pollitt."

Inspector Pollitt was sitting on his bed unlacing his boots when the 'phone bell rang. Grumbling to himself he went downstairs, lifted the receiver and said: "Pollitt speaking."

When the sergeant had made his report Pollitt stood for a minute thinking. Was it worth turning out for? Bed fought a battle with the call of duty. Duty won and Inspector Pollitt arrived at the police-station when the sergeant was putting a kettle on a gas ring. It was time for a cup of cocoa.

The watchman told his story once more and led Pollitt to the captain's cabin. It told the inspector no more than it had the sergeant. He shone the constable's light through the port-hole, saw the cabin was bare and said: "Probably a casual break. He won't be back."

"If he does I'll be ready for him," said the watchman, with the courage given him by the presence of two police-officers.

"Let's have a look inside."

The watchman produced a key and unlocked the padlock.

Pollitt asked: "What's the matter with the lock on the door?"

"I dunno. It seems to be jammed." The watchman gave Pollitt a key.

"You're right." Pollitt bent down and shone his lamp on to the face of the lock. "Hullo! What have we got here?" He took a knife from his pocket and picked out a splinter of wood. "That's what's caused all the trouble."

The watchman said: "Lumme! I wonder who did that."

Pollitt said nothing and walked into the cabin. It had been stripped bare. There was not even a rug on the floor. "Whoever it was tried to get in here was a day too late. I'm going home to bed."

Carl Swanson made a wide detour and approached Hawkin's Court and Mrs. Mather's cottage from the north. Mrs. Mather came down the passage as she heard his step outside.

She said: "What's the matter, Carl?" Her hands grasped the lapels of his jacket.

"Nothing." He smiled and put an arm round her shoulders. "I just went for a walk round. I couldn't sleep."

Mrs. Mather said suddenly: "You're scared of something. What is it?"

"Nonsense. You're imagining things." He forced a smile but it faded quickly.

"We'll have a cup of tea, anyway. Come along." She put an arm through his and led him into the kitchen.

The fire was low, but it burned up as she raked out the dead ashes and threw on a handful of kindling. As she moved a kettle over the flames she said: "Jessie was here tonight. She's bothered about that man of hers."

"Larry?"

"Yes. She thinks he's got something on his mind."

"You women are all the same. What's Larry got to worry about? He'll get his share out of the *Ivanhoe*; enough to buy a house and furniture with, and leave a bit over to put by."

"Well, I don't know. I'm not easy in my own mind. There was that cup I read for you on the day before you sailed, and it said that there was going to be trouble." Mrs. Mather drew a chair up to the fire and sat down.

"I don't believe in that sort of thing."

"It's come right for me before now; scores of times, it has." Mrs. Mather looked up at a tin clock on the mantelpiece. "Mercy! It's nearly two o'clock. As soon as ever you've had your tea you must away to your bed."

In his room under the slates Carl told himself that Larry had been wrong about the notebook. He stood before the tiny window as he took off his jacket. Across the roof-tops of the houses of Gilboro' he could see the silver streak of the Gilboro' river. The moon was high.

As long as none of them spoke out of turn they couldn't be bowled out. Larry was all right, but all the same he wished he wasn't tied up with Jessie Miles. Women were an unknown and uncertain factor in Carl's mind. Dan Todd was as safe as a bank. The only real trouble was Tubby. He was too fond of beer and the bright lights of the pubs. And a lot too fond of talking.

But it couldn't happen. The truth could never come out because he alone knew the truth of the death of Captain MacTaggart. The memory of that night came back to him with the vividness of a picture on a cinema screen.

He sought to shut it out by sudden action. He turned to his bed and turned down the clothes. Then he opened the window. He was humming a tune, the one Tubby had been picking out on his zither on the night when—oh hell!

He picked up the evening paper and began to read the sport's column on the back page. The clock on St. Jude's church was striking four o'clock before he slept.

10

On the same night that Carl tried to break into the captain's cabin on board the *Ivanhoe*, Tubby spent three hours in the warmth, light and noise of the public bar of the "Keel and Barge".

His tankard was never empty for long, though he spent nothing himself on the beer which loosened his tongue, and made thumbs of his fingers as he plucked at the strings of his zither.

His rendering of "Two lovely Black Eyes" was not such as would have got him a job on the halls, but a few false notes meant nothing to the crowd which encircled him and shouted the chorus.

They felt like singing and they sang, and when breath began to get short they made Tubby tell them all over again the story of the salving of the *Ivanhoe*, and gave him more beer.

When closing-time came, Tubby was in no shape for walking and, after following a zigzag course for a hundred yards or so, he came to anchor under the lee of a fish-store. There he slept until the lights were switched on and carts came rumbling over the cobblestones.

Feeling a little better, but not much, Tubby got on to his feet and, with his zither under his arm, made for the welcoming light of Hoppy's stall. What he craved more than anything at that moment was a nice cup of hot coffee.

There was a number of lorry drivers, porters, salesmen and trawlermen talking and eating at the counter, and Tubby had to wait until the sales had started and the crowd had thinned out before he could find a place.

Mr. Hopkins looked disapprovingly at Tubby's bleary face and said: "Hullo! What have you been up to?"

"I want a cup of coffee," Tubby said with unusual distinctness. He wasn't feeling too sure of his tongue, nor of his legs and he took a firm grip of the counter.

"What you wants is twelve hours in your bed," said Hoppy severely as he took a cup off a hook and held, it under the tap of the urn.

"Now, Mr. Hopkins, don't you start getting on to me; and after all I've been through, too. I've finished with the sea."

"That's what they all say," said Hoppy and put a brimming cup on the counter. "Maybe if you drink that you'll feel a bit better."

Tubby devoutly hoped that he would and sipped noisily at the scalding coffee. It burned his mouth. "Carl's a good old scout, a good old scout, and there's not another man—not one other man could ha' done what he did." Tubby stretched out a hand and laid it on the sleeve of Hoppy's coat. "And if it hadn't been for that damn' old codger we'd have been in Gilboro' twelve hours afore we did."

A man standing beside him said: "What's that?"

"What I says. And what I says is right. If it hadn't been for him we'd have got the blooming old engines started up right away—right away, and we wouldn't have had to lie there rolling our guts out the whole of the blasted night."

"Who stopped you working the engines?"

"Who stopped us? Who? . . ." And then Tubby realized what he was saying. He put down his cup. Hot coffee splashed on his hand. He tried to think, to steady his swimming brain. Who stopped us? For a full minute he stared at a plate of pies.

Hoppy said: "You drink that coffee and get off home."

"That's right. That's where I'm going this very minute. This very minute."

"Who stopped you starting up your engines?"

Tubby turned and stared stupidly at his questioner. Then light came and he laughed. "It was Dan Todd. He said that we'd got to get the fore-hold pumped out first. And maybe he was right. Anyway, that's what we did. Me and Dan stoked them fires right through the night with the water up to our knees, and the ship rolling so that I thought every minute she was a goner. But we stuck it; me and Dan. Larry came down when it got light and gave us a hand, but she was riding a lot easier then. We had done all the donkey-work; me and Dan Todd."

"You'd better have a sandwich to go with that." Hoppy pushed a plate across the counter.

Tubby thought not. The sight of food made him feel sick. He felt in his pocket and put two coppers on the counter. "I'm going to take your advice, Mr. Hopkins, and hit the hay. Good night."

"He's got a skinful all right." The man who had been standing near Tubby laughed and walked away.

Old Hoppy looked puzzled as he watched Tubby make his way across the market-place. It wasn't like Carl Swanson to have it put across him by Dan Todd. Dan was obstinate and liked his own way, but Carl, as Hoppy knew well enough, liked his own way too and usually got it.

"I'd like to know the rights of this business," he said to himself as he started to rinse dirty mugs in a basin of water under the counter.

The watchman on board the *Ivanhoe* sold the story of the attempt to break into the captain's cabin for half a crown to a reporter from the Gilboro' *Argus*. And, as anything to do with the *Ivanhoe* was news, a highly coloured version of the watchman's story was splashed across the front page of the *Argus* in seventy-two point capitals. It told of the heroism of the watchman in beating off the invader. Inspector Pollitt had a paragraph to himself, but as it was a very short paragraph and right at the foot of a column, the inspector was not very pleased.

Mr. Innes had arrived at the marmalade stage of his breakfast when the maid brought in the paper.

"Intruder on board the *Ivanhoe*," he read, and stopped eating. What was it all about? Accustomed to read quickly and assimilate facts without effort, he skimmed through the report.

When he had finished it he thought: "I'd give quite a lot of money to know what that man was after."

That, of course, was quite untrue. Mr. Innes was a very close man and never spent a penny if he could possibly avoid doing so. But all the same he was interested and a little uneasy in his mind. He didn't like this case and he liked it even less when he arrived at his office and read Mr. Fleming's letter.

We think [wrote Mr. Fleming] *that the sum of £2,000 (two thousand pounds) would be a proper payment to make in respect of the services rendered by your clients, and we accordingly put forward this offer and await the favour of an early reply.*

Mr. Innes read through the letter again. "Very odd," he muttered to himself. He went to a bookcase and took down a calf-bound volume. It was entitled, *Salvage Awards*, 1910–1936. He searched for a similar case to that of the *Ivanhoe* and found five. In each case the award was a high one, never less than one third of the value of the salved vessel, and in two cases it was as much as one half.

Mr. Fleming claimed that the *Ivanhoe*, her cargo and freight were worth fifty thousand pounds and Mr. Innes, knowing Fleming, added twenty per cent to that figure. Of course he would have to obtain a separate valuation, but even if Fleming's figure was accepted, the offer of £2,000 was absurd.

The vague suspicion that all was not well returned, and as he put the book back in the shelf Mr. Innes' forehead was wrinkled in anxious thought. "There's a snake in this grass," he muttered. "And Fleming knows it—or suspects something."

He sat down at his desk, pulled open a side drawer and took a cigarette out of a box. It was a sign that he was very much troubled, for he seldom smoked. When his clerk came in with a basket of letters, he told him to come back later. First of all he had to decide how to answer Fleming's letter.

Five minutes later he sent a clerk to find Carl Swanson and bring him to the office, and while he waited the arrival of his difficult client, Mr. Innes paced up and down his room with short, nervous steps. He stubbed out his cigarette and lit another, and stood for a moment looking down on to the street below.

Then he went to his desk and spread out the morning paper. He began to read the account of the attempted burglary on the *Ivanhoe* for the third time, and was half-way through it when the door of the outer office banged and Carl's voice asked: "What does he want with me now?"

Mr. Innes folded the paper and put it on one side. He was sitting in his chair with Mr. Fleming's letter on the blotter before him when Carl was announced.

Carl came lounging into the room and threw his cap on to a chair. "'Morning, Mr. Innes. Now what's your trouble?"

"Please sit down, Mr. Swanson." Mr. Innes folded his hands on the desk and looked more than ever like a maiden aunt about to reprove an unruly child.

"Surely we've had enough blather about this business. What about getting the owners to cough up the dibs?"

"Er—that is exactly what I wanted to talk to you about, Mr. Swanson. But first of all I want you to read this letter." He pushed it across the desk.

Carl read it slowly and with difficulty. The greater part of it conveyed nothing to his brain, but he did grasp the fact that he was being offered £2,000 for salving the *Ivanhoe*. His face reddened with anger, and as he tossed the letter back on the desk he said: "It's a ruddy insult, that's what it is, and you can tell whoever sent it I said so, and that I'll go to law about it and then we'll see—"

Mr. Innes' dry, brittle tones cut through Carl's bluster. "I agree that it is a very small sum having due regard to the circumstances of the case as I know them at present, but—"

"Now what are you getting at?"

"I have a feeling that perhaps there was something you omitted in the statement you made to me on Monday."

"Well, there was lots happened, and maybe I did leave something out."

"Here's a copy of what you said. Perhaps you will be good enough to run through it."

Mr. Innes' eyes were fixed on Carl's face as he read, but his scrutiny told him nothing; there was no sign of confusion nor of fear. When he had finished reading, Carl said: "It's all there. And it's the truth." His tone was challenging.

Mr. Innes' eyebrows moved up a fraction of an inch. He had made no accusation. "What struck me about this letter when I first read it, was that Mr. Fleming was in possession of some information of which I know nothing."

"He can't know anything. Who'd tell him?"

Mr. Innes looked at Carl with a cold, inquiring gaze for seconds and then replied: "That is exactly what I should like to know. There's Hicks and Stevens and Todd."

"They wouldn't say—" Carl began and stopped suddenly. "I mean there's nothing for 'em to tell. Nothing that I haven't told you or said at the inquest."

"Quite," said Mr. Innes dryly. "But let us suppose that you had made a mistake about the level of water in the fore-hold and that it was not up to the hatch-coamings—"

"I don't see that that makes any difference either way."

"It might," said Mr. Innes. "The picture you have drawn is of a ship in imminent danger of foundering. Your courage in boarding her at that time would, of course, be taken into account in assessing the amount of the salvage award; as also would be the skill and perseverance you displayed in pumping out the water, securing the deck cargo and generally making the ship fit to proceed on her voyage."

Carl said: "We did have a job. It took us all the first night to get things straight and the hold dry."

Mr. Innes ignored the interruption and continued in level tones: "On the other hand, if you were mistaken as to the quantity of water in the hold and, in fact, the level was several feet below the coamings, then the owners of the *Ivanhoe* might well say: 'Our ship was in no immediate danger of sinking. In view of the subsequent weather-conditions she would have remained afloat indefinitely and could have been salved by some other vessel.'"

"If that were so, which it isn't, I don't see that it should make any difference."

"But if they were able to prove that you were guilty of fraud, it would. Doubt would be thrown on your whole story, and in consequence you might only receive a comparatively small award, say two thousand pounds."

"What d'you mean, fraud?" Carl leaned forward in his chair and put his clenched fists on the desk.

Mr. Innes raised a hand. "Merely a matter of speech. Shall we call it a mis-statement as to a material fact affecting the salvage services."

"I don't know what the hell you're getting at. You're my lawyer, aren't you? And I've told you the truth. All you've got to do now is to make the owners pay up. I reckon I'm due twenty thousand."

"You'll be a very lucky man if you get that sum," said Mr. Innes. He leaned back in his chair and, putting the tips of his fingers together, looked at the ceiling.

"Anyway, I'm not going to take two thousand. By the time the fishing-gear's paid for, there wouldn't be more than a few hundreds left after the others had got their whack."

Mr. Innes said: "Yes, I quite understand how you feel about it, and of course it is for you to decide what course you wish to follow."

"Then write and tell this man Fleming to go to hell! And if you won't, I will."

"In that case, Mr. Swanson, I will, of course, withdraw from the case."

"You mean you won't go on with it?"

Mr. Innes detached his gaze from the ceiling and said: "Exactly."

The bluster went out of Carl's manner. He muttered: "Well, I don't know." He looked rather stupid.

"You must understand, Mr. Swanson, that as long as I am acting for you, I must be permitted to conduct your affairs in the manner to which I am accustomed. The final decision as to any settlement or agreement which may be mooted lies in your hands, but you must leave the actual conduct of negotiations to me."

Words, words, words. Carl felt fogged. He said: "All right. You can write the letter your own way, but I'm not accepting the offer. You've got to make that plain."

"Yes, I quite understand." Mr. Innes coughed and then said: "By the way, would you have any objection to swearing an affidavit to the effect that the water in the fore-hold of the *Ivanhoe* was up to the hatch-coamings at the time you boarded her?"

"An affidavit? What's that?"

"A statement on oath. It would clear my mind of any doubts on that matter and regularize the position."

"Yes, I don't mind." At that moment Carl was ready to agree to almost any request. The protracted conversation with Mr. Innes was getting him down.

"Very well then. If you will return in about an hour's time I will have the draft ready." Mr. Innes got up and bowed. He was not going to risk another handshake with Carl. One had been more than enough for him.

When Carl reached the street he looked at the Town Hall clock. It said eleven o'clock. An uncomfortable time of day for a thirsty man in urgent need of strong drink. He walked to the corner where the High Street tails off into the market-place.

On his port bow lay the "Keel and Barge", still shuttered, but with a crowd of prospective customers lounging outside, smoking and talking and reading papers.

There was no one at Hoppy's stall. Carl walked over to it and said good morning.

"How's she go?" Hoppy was sitting idle on a stool, smoking a meerschaum pipe. It was one given to him by his late and only master and he loved it and cared for it as he did for everything in his stall. When not in use the pipe lived in a chamois-leather bag.

"Not so bad," Carl replied.

"Have you got your money yet?"

"No, and I don't know when I'll get it."

"It always means a bit of a wait; that sort of business. My brother didn't get his for nigh on a month, and the solicitors had their bite out of it first."

"It looks like I'll have to make a trip first. It's no use hanging around, waiting. Do you know of any ship, Hoppy?"

"There's the *Garth Castle*. There was a bloke round half an hour ago saying he was thinking of signing on with her." Hoppy picked at the ash of his pipe with a match and emptied it into a saucer. Then he rubbed the bowl against the side of his nose until it shone. "I doubt you won't get Tubby Stevens to go with you again. He told me he was finished with the fishing."

"When did you see him?"

"Last night. No, it wasn't, it was early this morning. He'd got a skinful on board." Hoppy smiled. "He was saying that Dan Todd stopped you bringing in the *Ivanhoe* as quick as you wanted."

"What?"

"That's what he said."

"How did he put it?"

Hoppy rubbed his clean-shaven chin and looked down at the counter. There was a splash of tea on it which he dried with a cloth. "I don't know exactly how it came up, but what he said was, as near as I can recollect: 'If it hadn't been for the old codger we'd have been in twelve hours sooner.'"

Carl said: "Oh, did he?"

"Wasn't that right?"

"Yes, I suppose in a way it was."

"I thought it was funny when he said it—I mean, Dan Todd putting it across you."

But Carl wouldn't be drawn. He said: "I'll be getting along." He was going to have a word with Tubby Stevens. Larry had been right. Tubby was going to give the whole show away if they weren't careful.

It was quite probable that had Tubby been available for punishment at that moment he would have suffered a different kind of headache to that which was keeping him moored to his bed. The curtains of the window of the room in which he lay were drawn, and he had no desire to play his zither which lay on the floor.

Dan Todd came into the saloon bar of the "Keel and Barge" as Carl was ordering a double White Horse. He accepted Carl's offer to have the same and drank it without the addition of water as though it was water. Then he touched Carl on the arm and said: "I want a word with you." He walked to a deserted corner of the room, sat down at a table and took out a block of tobacco the colour of tar.

Carl said: "What is it?"

"Have you seen the papers? About that business on the *Ivanhoe*?"

Carl nodded.

"I wonder who it was."

Carl said: "Yes, I wonder."

Dan looked at him. "Have you any idea what he was after?"

"No. Why should I have?"

"I dunno. I thought perhaps you might know something." Dan carved a fill of tobacco, and as he rubbed it up between his palms he said: "When are we going to get our money?"

"I wish to hell I knew."

Dan's jaw dropped and he stopped working the tobacco in his hands. "Do you mean there's something gone wrong?"

Carl answered quickly, a little too quickly, "No, of course not. It's just these damn' lawyers, they like to make a big business of a job like this so as they can get plenty for themselves out of it."

"Then we'll just have to wait." Dan paused and then went on: "Pollitt was out on that job last night. Hoppy told me."

"Well?"

"He's not such a damn' fool as he looks. And we don't want him to get too interested in the *Ivanhoe*. He might start finding out things."

Carl laughed. "Pollitt's a pal of mine."

"Policemen are pals of nobody if they think there's anything wrong. Sometimes they're slow at starting, but once they get going they're damned hard to head off."

"Oh, shut up croaking, Dan. We're on velvet. No one's going to find out anything—"

"As long as none of us talk. Now there's Tubby, for instance. He was on the jag last night, so they tell me, spinning the yarn and drinking himself stupid."

"I know. I'm going out to look for him, to tell him he's got to put a sock in it." Carl finished his drink and stood up. "I'll see you later."

Carl spent two fruitless hours searching for Tubby. On his way home to Hawkin's Court he met Inspector Pollitt, who stopped him and said: "Hullo, Carl. I was hoping I'd run into you. Do you mind walking back a bit with me."

Carl said of course he didn't, but in spite of what he had said to Dan Todd about Pollitt being a pal of his, he felt uneasy.

"It's about this job on the *Ivanhoe* last night. Have you got any ideas about it?"

"No. What happened?"

"Someone tried to break the lock on the door of the captain's cabin. I want to find out what he was after and I thought you might be able to assist me there."

"I was never in that cabin all the time I was on board the ship."

"Why not?"

"There wasn't any call for me to go into it."

"Was it locked?"

"I can't remember, but I fancy it was."

"I've been having a talk with Larry Hicks and he tells me it wasn't locked."

"What else did he say?"

But the inspector was more accustomed to asking questions than to answering them. He said: "By the way, where were you last night? It's only a matter of form, but I have to—"

"I was home in bed. I got in some time after ten."

Pollitt said: "Well, I think that's all. Sorry to trouble you."

Carl turned back towards Hawkin's Court. He walked quickly and went straight into the kitchen where Mrs. Mather was washing the dinner dishes. She turned a startled face to him.

"The police have been here."

"Yes, I know. I met Pollitt."

"He asked about—about last night." Mrs. Mather put down the plate she was holding and dried her hands. Then she walked over to Carl. "He asked where you were."

Carl's face was wooden as he asked: "And what did you say?"

"That you were in bed from eleven on."

"I never thought he'd come here. The nosy devil!"

"If you'd tell me I might be able to help a little." She put her hands on his shoulders. "I owe you a lot, Carl. If it wasn't what you give me I'd be in the Institution now."

"I've got a home here, haven't I?" He smiled down at her up-turned face.

"What is it? What's your trouble, Carl?"

"Nothing. Nothing at all," he lied smilingly.

"Maybe you'll tell me later on." She went back to the sink and picked up a plate.

"Where does Tubby Stevens hang out?"

"I don't know. You'd better ask Mr. Hopkins. He may know."

"Yes, that's an idea. I'll go along there now."

11

OLD HOPPY'S STALL was shuttered when Carl reached the mar-ket-place, and when he went to his house he found him getting ready for bed.

"No," Hoppy said. "I don't know where Tubby's staying these days. He used to be over the paint-shop, but he's moved. There was some trouble about his disturbing people with his zither."

Carl was restless. He thought of going back to Mrs. Mather's, but he couldn't abide the idea of sitting idle. He would go for a walk over the marshes. Action might clear his brain of the gnaw-ing fear that beset it.

It was good to be out of the cramping streets, with the wind and the rain in his face and the springy short marshland turf underfoot. He walked along the path on the sea-wall, past the Pride of Bedford—Tom Ingleby was nowhere about—past the Martello tower, now a shelter for sheep and cattle, on until the well-trod path petered out into a faint trail.

There was weight in the wind, and he leant forward to meet it. The river was widening now, a mile ahead was the entrance, and, beyond, seas were breaking white on the bar. Then he suddenly remembered that he hadn't sworn that affidavit for Mr. Innes. Oh, to hell with the *Ivanhoe*! He wished he'd never had anything to do with the damn' ship. He should have stuck to his own job, the fishing, rather than have landed himself in this trouble, squabbles with lawyers, conferences, everlasting questions and ever that haunting fear that the truth might come out.

He forced his thoughts away from Gilboro' to his last trip but one. That had been a winner! His share had amounted to two hundred pounds. The money was gone, but what did that matter when he had the satisfaction of recalling the bumper hauls, nets nigh bursting, fish cascading into the pounds in a wriggling, squirming, flapping grey-white avalanche; the deckies working like the devil to get them cleaned and stowed before the next haul.

It was killing work, but a grand life.

His feet were sinking now into soft sand, and he breathed short as, with short plunging strides and clutching at tufts of coarse marram grass, he climbed a ridge of dunes and saw ahead the open sea. A trawler with her mizzen set, a black square at her stern and smoke driving from her funnel, was heading for the river mouth. The funnel was streaked with salt and her sides had ragged patches of red rust.

"I'll bet she's had a hell of a trip," Carl muttered, and envied her skipper, her mate, even the deckies. They had a job and nothing to worry about. They'd be paid their share; would spend it in a week or two and then be off again.

He stood until his feet went dead and his fingers became numb. Then he turned and, with the wind and the rain on his back, ran down the sand-ridge, slipping and plunging, on to the path. For a hundred yards he ran, and then, as circulation returned and his face began to tingle and glow, he slowed to a swinging walk.

Tom Ingleby was down on his slip, prising up a sleeper for firewood. When he felt the vibration of Carl's footsteps on the sea-wall he put down his mattock and moved over to a shed, pushed open the sagging door and went inside. From a window at the back he could observe the path without being seen.

As Carl came in sight his lips moved. "He's a fine lad." He took a half-step to the door and stopped. No, it was too late for anything like that. Too late. He turned back to the window and stayed there watching till Carl was out of sight. Then he went to the slip and picked up the mattock. If he didn't get this sleeper out of it and broken up there wouldn't be any fire to cook his supper on. It was heavy work for an old man, and before the first splinter flew from the blade of his axe Carl was in sight of the fish-wharf.

Half a dozen boats had docked since he'd been away. There was a clerk from the gaffer's office leaning on a pile of boxes, writing. He looked up when he heard Carl approach and said: "When do you want to get fixed up again? The old man's been asking about you."

"I'll wait a bit yet. As soon as I've settled this salvage business I'll be crawling around asking for a ship." Carl took a packet of cigarettes from his pocket, lit one and asked: "Have you see Tubby Stevens?"

"Not today, I haven't. I expect he'll be in the 'Keel' later on."

Carl said: "Yes, I expect I'll find him there all right." He was silent for two or three minutes and then asked: "What sort of catches have they been getting?"

"Middling fair. Nothing like as big as the last three you brought in."

Carl grinned. He loved flattery. "I was lucky."

"Some say it's that, but the gaffer doesn't think that way and no more do I."

"I must make another trip before long," Carl replied, and walked off down the wharf.

At half past six he entered the saloon bar of the "Keel and Barge". One or two men nodded to him, and the barman asked him what he was going to have. It was not the reception he had expected, but the interest in the salving of the *Ivanhoe* was dying, and darts and football coupons were back in favour again.

Carl took up his usual position at the end of the bar, with his back against the wood and glass screen which separated the fourpennies from the fourpence ha'pennies. He had a good view of the room. Tubby wasn't there. He waited for an hour with his eyes on the swing doors which were hardly ever still.

"Maybe he's at the 'Flag'," he muttered to himself. "I'll have a try there."

But Tubby wasn't at the "Lamb and Flag" nor at the "Wheel of Fortune", the "World's End" or the "George and Vulture". It was nearly closing-time before Carl found him in a beerhouse, the "Magpie", half a mile out on the Birmingham Road.

Tubby had no desire to meet Carl, and when Carl came up behind him and slapped him on the shoulder he nearly upset a can of beer. He grinned nervously and said: "What cheer, Carl! Fancy you coming in here."

Carl said: "Yes, fancy," and ordered a pint. While he drank it he looked at Tubby and turned over in his mind what he was going to say to him when he got him outside. The little runt! Going round gabbing! He'd tell him where he got off. Drink kept his anger warm.

When the landlord came to collect the glasses and say, "Time, gentlemen, please," Tubby looked round for a pal to go home with, found none and lingered as long as he possibly could. It was no use. There were few customers and they had all gone when he came out into the narrow street. Carl put an arm in his and said: "Come on with me."

It was the first time in his life that Tubby had been afraid of Carl Swanson. He clutched his zither close to his left side.

The streets were almost deserted and the gas lamps were flaring in the wind. The rain had stopped, but the pavements glistened wetly in the dancing pools of yellow light.

"Where are you going?" Tubby's voice was plaintively complaining like that of a spoilt, tired child.

"Somewhere where we can talk."

Carl swung right-handed down a street which ended in an open space of sodden turf. Beyond was the river. He stopped and relit his cigarette which had gone out. "I want to know what you've been saying."

"Nothing. I mean, no more than you have. I told the chaps down at the 'Keel' about the trip. That was all."

"What did you want to say anything about MacTaggart for?"

"I didn't. I never mentioned his name."

"You told Hoppy that it was the old codger that stopped us getting in as quick as we might have done."

"Yes, I did say that," Tubby admitted.

"Well?" Carl put out a hand and gripped the collar of Tubby's jacket and forced him back against a wall.

"That was all. I tell you I didn't mention his name. MacTaggart's, I mean."

"You said it was Dan Todd you meant. Didn't you say that?"

"I may have."

"You did. God! I wonder I let you live."

Tubby struggled madly. The zither fell from his arm.

"Keep still, damn you!"

There was no sound but the breathing of the two men.

Then Tubby became suddenly limp, like a half-filled sack, in Carl's grip. "I've a damn' good mind to serve you the same as I did him."

Courage, born of desperation, came to Tubby. He wrenched himself free and backed away. "Keep off or I'll call out."

Carl stood quite still. Then he laughed; a short, hard laugh. "And who the hell's going to hear you down here?" He jerked a thumb in the direction of the river. "Can you swim?"

Tubby worked his way along the wall, but Carl blocked the way of escape. His mood changed. "All right, Tubby. I won't touch you, but you've got to get out of here and damn' quick too."

"I've got nowhere to go and besides there's my share in the salvage. I've got to wait for that."

"There won't be a share for any of us if you stay in Gilboro' and talk. You've got to leave the town tonight."

"I'll want my clothes and things."

"You've got to get out now. Take the Birmingham road. Hoof it."

"I haven't any dough."

"Here's a couple of quid. Now, get going."

Half running, half walking, Tubby disappeared into the darkness. As the sound of his footsteps faded Carl muttered to himself: "Well, that's one damn' good thing done." He took a pace forward and his foot struck against the zither which had fallen from Tubby's grasp. He kicked it; it slithered over the stones and struck the wall with a faint twanging of its strings.

12

NEXT MORNING a boy on his reluctant way to school found the zither, picked it up and tried its strings. They made such very satisfactory noises as he drew his thumbnail across them that he played with it for quite a while, so long, in fact, that the school bell was ringing when he reached the playground and he had no time to hide his prize. This was most unfortunate for the boy, for the janitor on his way to stoke the boiler found it and, with the officiousness of a janitor who dislikes boys, he took it to the headmaster.

Thus did Tubby's zither find its way to the room in the Gilboro' police-station where lost property is stored. A sergeant made an entry in a ledger, describing the zither as a "small harp"; that duty having been discharged he went to report to Inspector Pollitt that a woman wanted to see him.

The woman was Mrs. Warburton who kept a sweetshop in Town Alley and took in lodgers. Tubby had been a lodger in her house and when he had failed to return on the previous night she had, or so she said, sat up till past two waiting to let him in.

Pollitt said: "I shouldn't worry, Mrs. Warburton. He's probably visiting friends." It was the inspector's experience that "Missing Persons" usually turned up in a day or two; if they didn't, then they themselves probably wanted to get away.

"Does he owe you much?" was Pollitt's next question.

"He paid me a week in advance. Sixteen shillings. And besides that, he's left all his clothes behind—everything. That's what made me think it funny him going off without even so much as a word or a line."

Pollitt raised a hand to stem the flow. "Then, as I understand it, he took nothing with him?"

"No, that's wrong. I was telling a lie when I said he left everything. His zither isn't in his room."

"What's a zither?"

"A kind of a banjo. But it doesn't look like a banjo, if you gets my meaning."

Pollitt did not get her meaning.

"My little Albert, he's only six but smart for his age, he said that Mr. Stevens had his zither under his arm when he left the house last night."

"What time was that?"

"Round about seven o'clock it would be. The last lot of the evening papers had come in just afore then and that's how I remembers when it was."

The sergeant said: "Will you excuse me, sir," and left the room. He was soon back. He was holding Tubby's zither in his hand. As he put it on the table in front of Pollitt he said: "This was brought in this morning by the janitor from the school. He said one of the boys picked it up."

Mrs. Warburton made a gasping noise. "That's his! I'd know it anywhere."

Pollitt said: "There's no need to be upset, Mrs. Warburton."

"Something's happened to him. That's what it is. Like as not he's been knocked down and killed, and to think that only last night he and me was joking together, and he said that he'd be a rich man one of these days."

Inspector Pollitt refused to take such a gloomy view of Tubby's disappearance and sent Mrs. Warburton home in the care of Police-Constable Makin with the assurance that her lodger would soon be back.

Though he was quite sincere in this belief, Pollitt told the sergeant to make inquiries at the hospital and to question the boy who had found the zither.

If it had been anyone other than Tubby Stevens the matter would have ended with the addition of one more name to the "Missing Persons" list, but Pollitt, knowing that Tubby had been a member of the crew which had brought in the *Ivanhoe*, decided that he would make further inquiries. There was also that business of the attempted breaking on board the *Ivanhoe*, and the thought crossed his mind that there might be some connection between the two incidents.

Perhaps Tubby was the burglar and was frightened that he would be given away by someone who had seen him in the vicinity of the *Ivanhoe*.

Pollitt was a man possessed of no imagination whatsoever. Like Mr. Innes and Mr. Fleming he dealt in facts. Consequently he wasted no time in speculation.

He sent for a detective who had recently been transferred to Gilboro' and was not known to those who frequented the fish-wharf and market-place. "Kent, I want you to make inquiries into the movements of this man Stevens who has disappeared. Here's his description." He passed a typewritten sheet across the desk. "He left Mrs. Warburton's house at about seven o'clock last night and hasn't returned. There's a man who keeps a coffee-stall in the market-place, his name is Hopkins, he might be able to tell you something. And then there's Dan Todd, Carl Swanson and Larry Hicks; they're friends of Stevens', but go slow with them."

Mrs. Warburton had never kept a secret in her life and, as she said to herself, what was the good of trying to keep this one when her little Albert and Mrs. Burling, who lived next door, knew.

Her journey up the street in which she lived was therefore slow and punctuated by many whispered confidences. "Well, I'm only telling you this because I know it won't go no further, but you mark my words . . ."

She returned to her shop, opened the door and called out: "Albert! You stop here. I'm going round to see Mrs. Hopkins." And round to Mrs. Hopkins she went, much to Mr. Hopkins's annoyance. He was just taking his meerschaum pipe out of its little bag and was feeling in his pocket for his pouch.

Hoppy liked to smoke in silence without a lot of folk yattering round him. He got his fill of chat down at the stall. And, besides, he was comfortably drowsy after his night's work.

Mrs. Warburton said she hoped that she wasn't intruding and sat down before the fire. Mrs. Hopkins came out of the scullery and said: "Fancy seeing you at this time of the morning, Mrs. Warburton." She dried her reddened hands on her apron and pulled down her sleeves. A visitor was a visitor even if it was Mrs. Warburton. She sat down on the edge of a kitchen chair. "I think we're going to get some good weather after all."

Mrs. Warburton replied that she'd heard there was five boats going out that morning and tried to think of something casual to say that would introduce the subject of Tubby Stevens. It would never do to come straight out with the news.

"Have you heard how much Carl Swanson's going to get?" she asked Hoppy.

"No. Not a word."

"I suppose it'll be a tidy sum."

"It will that. Close on twenty thousand pounds I'd say." Hoppy held a lighted match over the bowl of his pipe and sucked in the smoke audibly.

"You don't say!" Mrs. Warburton was impressed.

"Well, you wait and see."

"And I suppose the others'll get their share. Dan Todd and Larry Hicks and . . ." her voice trembled a little, "and Tubby Stevens."

"Ay, they'll all get their whack."

The moment had come. "Tubby Stevens won't," said Mrs. Warburton, and fixed her eyes on a china pig on the mantelpiece.

"Yes, he will," said Hoppy. "All of 'em will."

"No he won't, because he's gone away."

"That doesn't matter. He'll find it waiting for him when he gets back again."

"Has he gone to the fishing?" Mrs. Hopkins asked.

"No, he hasn't, and he won't come back never."

Hoppy took his pipe out of his mouth and looked very hard at Mrs. Warburton. His drowsiness was gone. "Now what makes you say that?"

"Because he left my place last night and he didn't take anything with him. He's disappeared. That's what he's done, he's disappeared and we won't see him ever again."

"How d'you know that?" Hoppy asked sharply.

Mrs. Warburton shifted her gaze from the china pig to a hot coal which had fallen from the grate. "I knows all right. Something's happened to him. Something terrible."

Mrs. Hopkins gave a little squeak. "You didn't oughter say such a thing, Mrs. Warburton. Not unless you're certain sure, that is."

"He didn't take nothing with him 'cept that little harp thing he plays with and I saw it not a half-hour ago at the police-station where I was a-talking with Mr. Pollitt."

"You mean his zither?" said Mr. Hopkins.

"Yes, that's what he calls it or what he used to call it." Mrs. Warburton produced a handkerchief and rubbed her eyes.

"Where was it found?"

"I dunno, but it was proper broke up. But I could tell it all right along of a lot of little white dots it had. Mother-of-pearl they was. Tubby thought a lot of that little harp of his, and he'd never have let it got broke the way it was if he could have helped it, nor he wouldn't have left it behind him neither."

Mr. Hopkins was so interested that he forgot all about his pipe, which had gone out. He put it on the table and proceeded to ask Mrs. Warburton a string of questions she couldn't answer.

"No, I can't tell you where it was found nor who found it. I didn't ask Mr. Pollitt because I could see he was busy and, besides, it wasn't any of my business." That was one in the eye for Mr. Hopkins, and serve him right, too, for not believing her in the first place.

The orange having been squeezed dry, she left the house to continue her duties of broadcaster-in-chief.

When she had gone Mr. Hopkins went to bed, but he couldn't sleep. Somewhere at the back of his mind there was something he'd heard, something about Tubby Stevens which had made him wonder at the time and which might have some connection with his disappearance. He tried hard to remember the place and the time he'd heard it, but he went to sleep at last without succeeding.

When he went down to his stall after dinner everyone was talking about Tubby Stevens. With his disappearance the *Ivanhoe* was back on the map again and an ever-changing, smoking, gossiping crowd stood on the wharf and stared at the door of the galley where Tubby had once worked.

The general opinion was that they wouldn't see Tubby again. Most likely he'd fallen into the dock on his way home, and there was much interesting and expert calculation as to where the body was now.

Mrs. Warburton's expectations that the weather would improve were not fulfilled and, when low scudding clouds spilled their rain on the wharf, there was an adjournment to the saloon bar of the "Keel".

Detective-Constable Kent drifted with the crowd and found himself wedged up against the wall only a couple of feet from Carl Swanson.

Carl said: "Tubby's been acting a bit queer the last day or two."

The mystery deepened when it was realized that Tubby had not been seen in any of the fish-dock pubs the night before, and the correctness of the theory that he had fallen into the dock was doubted by many.

As an old trawlerman said: "If he hadn't been drinking, how could he have got into the dock? He hadn't got no call to go near it."

Then a man who had been at Hoppy's stall said that the zither had been found all broke up, and what did they think of that now?

"Who told you?"

"Hoppy, and he got it straight from Mrs. Warburton. She saw it at the police-station all smashed up."

"Whereabouts was it found?" Carl asked, and Kent thought that there was a hint of affected carelessness in his voice.

No one knew the answer to that one.

Carl said: "Maybe he's gone visiting friends."

But this suggestion did not meet with approval. It was much too tame an ending. Tubby was dead for certain sure.

Carl had ordered a drink and was stretching out his hand for the glass when Larry came into the bar. He stood for a moment looking around and when he saw Carl he pushed through the crowd to his side.

Kent saw Larry's lips move but could not hear what he said. Carl nodded, finished his drink in two gulps and followed Larry out into the market-place.

When they were fifty yards clear of the pub Larry said: "What have you done to Tubby?"

"Nothing. I've not laid eyes on him since the day of the inquest."

"Like hell you haven't." Larry's mouth shut in a hard straight line.

"Well, if you know so much what are you asking me for?"

"If he went off on his own, why did he leave everything behind?" Larry took a paper from under his arm. It was the lunch edition of the *Evening Argus*. "You see what it says here. His zither was picked up by a kid out Hanworth way."

"Well, what about it?"

They had turned the corner of the dock and had entered a street backing on Gilboro' goods station. Larry stopped and took Carl by the arm. "I'm going to get out of this business. I don't like it."

Carl's under-jaw shot forward and he clenched his right fist.

Larry saw the movement. "And you needn't come any of that stuff on me. I'm not Tubby Stevens."

For seconds Carl stood tense; a pulse on his temple was throbbing; his breath came fast. He saw nothing but Larry's eyes, Larry's mouth. And then he became conscious of footsteps approaching. The danger passed, the high tide of his anger ebbed.

He looked at the slouching, shuffling figure of Detective-Constable Kent, saw him pass and watched him till he was out of sight. Then he said: "Come on, Larry, what's the use of us two beating it up?"

"I'm getting out. I'm going to see Mr. Innes and tell him."

"You'll lose your share."

"Tubby's lost his."

"Oh, for God's sake leave him out of this. I swear I never laid a hand on him. I'll tell you what happened. He was talking too much round the pubs and I told him to clear out of the town and stay away till everything was fixed up."

"What happened?"

"I just had a talk with him, that's all, and he saw sense." Carl grinned. "It was lucky for him he did." Carl put a hand on Larry's shoulder. "Let's go and have a drink."

Larry said, "All the same, I'm not going to make a claim. It won't make no difference to you. You can go right ahead."

"Jessie won't like that."

"And you can leave her out of it as well."

"All right," Carl said easily. "But if you do this it's going to start people talking. They'll want to know why you've done it, and I don't want any more questioning. I've had my fill of that."

"I'll tell Mr. Innes not to say anything about it. He'll keep it under his hat."

"Why not put it off for a day or two? There's no almighty hurry."

Larry said nothing. Damn Carl! When he was pleasant it wasn't easy to say no to him. He allowed himself to be led into the "Keel" and accepted the double whisky Carl ordered. It was the first he'd had that day and it made him feel a lot better. As he watched Carl leaning on the bar talking to the potman about the fishing, he thought to himself, "I don't believe he could have done anything to Tubby."

He said: "What about the other half?"

"Sure. It's good stuff this."

The other half put paid to the last remaining misgiving in Larry's mind, and when at half past one he set off to meet Jessie he had decided not to call on Mr. Innes—at least, not just yet.

Kent followed Carl and Larry back to the "Keel" and, when Larry went off, he set out on a round of the public-houses within a quarter-mile radius of the market-place. At every one of them he drew a blank. No one had seen a man with a zither on the previous night. It was after closing-time before he reached the "Magpie", and then he had to travel a couple of miles to the potman's home.

Albert Mann was at once thrilled and nervous to find himself questioned by a police-officer, and at first he could remember not one single incident which had occurred in the bar of the

"Magpie" on the previous night. Then Kent described the zither and painted a very fair picture of Tubby. Light came. "Yes, I remember now. That bloke or his twin brother came into our place and he did have something under his arm. I remember thinking at the time that he was a busker."

"Did you have any talk with him?"

"I suppose I did, but I couldn't rightly say what passed."

"What did he have to drink?"

"Beer. That's all we've a licence for at the 'Magpie'."

"Do you remember what time he came in?"

"No, I couldn't say."

"Was it about six o'clock?"

"May have been. He was in the bar quite a time, sitting by hisself at a table over in the window, and then a bloke come in and he went out with him."

"What was the man like?"

"I didn't notice him hardly."

"Did you hear him speak?"

"If I did I don't remember what he said. But he did raise his hand like this, and the bloke with the zither got up and went out."

Kent wrote down a brief account of what the potman had told him, made him sign it and took a tram back to the town.

Inspector Pollitt was signing papers when Kent came in to make his report.

"I've found out where Stevens went after he left Mrs. Warburton's."

Pollitt said: "Good," and took the statement which Kent handed to him. When he had read it through he said: "We'd better follow this up. There may be nothing in it, of course, but . . ." He fiddled with a pencil. "Get a-hold of Dan Todd and Larry Hicks and bring 'em along here."

"What about Carl Swanson? He's the boss of the party."

"No. Not Swanson. He can wait."

Kent went to Larry's house where he lived with his mother and found he was out. Mrs. Hicks was tearfully anxious. "I don't know where you'll find him I'm sure. He went out with Miss Miles. They're going to get married soon."

"Perhaps you'll be good enough to give him a message when he comes in. Ask him to come down to the police-station."

"I will. Of course I will. What shall I say you want him for?"

"Oh, don't bother about that. It's just a formal business."

Mrs. Hicks shut the door behind Kent and said to her cat, which was standing with arched back and a ramrod tail in the passage, "This is some of Carl Swanson's trouble I wouldn't wonder. It's high time Larry got married and settled down to a steady job."

The cat said nothing, straightened out and picked a delicate way into the kitchen. There was something in the pig-pail which had attractions for her.

Dan Todd, fatheaded from a sleep before the fire, was standing at his street door when Kent came along and asked if Mr. Todd was at home.

Dan asked him what he wanted, and when he heard that Inspector Pollitt would like to have a word with him he thought for quite a long time before he said: "I'm Daniel Todd."

He thought a lot more as he had a rinse in the sink, put on a collar and tie and his jacket. If this was going to be the start of trouble, he'd have to watch out for himself. Carl would do the same and so would Larry Hicks. Every man for himself was Dan Todd's motto.

Slightly self-conscious, and trying hard not to show it, he walked into the Gilboro' police-station.

Kent told him to take a chair in the charge-room and went in to report to Pollitt. "I've got Dan Todd."

"All right, let him wait." It was Pollitt's practice to keep witnesses waiting. It took some of the starch out of them and sometimes made 'em want to talk. He had obtained quite a number of confessions that way, and, if there was one thing that pleased Pollitt more than another, it was a confession. It saved him a lot of trouble and time.

Unfortunately, in the case of Dan Todd, enforced silence had no such effect. He hadn't done no wrong, and no one was going to make him say he had, he said to himself, and turned his mind to the farm he was going to have one of these days. It was a pleasant and a familiar dream and he was annoyed when the sergeant broke in upon it with the words: "The inspector'll see you now."

Dan's face was without expression as he stumped into Pollitt's room.

Pollitt said, "Sit down, Todd," and pointed to a chair.

Dan sat down and stared at the desk in front of him.

"You know Stevens, don't you?" Pollitt asked.

"Yes, I know him all right."

"Where is he now?"

Dan shook his head slowly from side to side. "He's left the town, so they tell me, but I don't know where he went."

"Where were you last night?"

"Last night? What time?"

"From six o'clock on."

"At home, where I always am at that time."

"Did Stevens say anything to you about going away?"

"I haven't seen him since the inquest and then I didn't hardly say anything to him."

Pollitt, with his arms outstretched across his desk and his hands clasped together, leaned forward. "Why did he go away?"

A hint of a smile widened Dan's mouth. "He wasn't all that gone on the sea. That's maybe the reason. He spoke to me a lot of times about clearing out."

"When?"

"When we were aboard the *John Goodwin* and on the *Ivanhoe* as well."

"He didn't like his job, then?"

"He didn't like the sea, but I'll say this, he did have guts. He was the only one of us that ever answered Carl back."

"So he didn't get on with Carl?"

"I didn't say that." Dan's eyes closed to slits. He saw what Pollitt was after.

"But you said that he answered Carl back?"

"He did, but they never had words."

"Did you see Carl last night?"

"No."

"Or Larry Hicks?"

"I was home all the night."

"You don't live far from the 'Magpie' do you?"

"No."

"Do you ever go there?"

"Sometimes."

"When was the last time you went there?"

"A couple of days ago."

"Did you ever see Stevens there?"

"No. The 'Magpie' is right out of his line. He lodges down by the market and uses the 'Keel' mostly."

Pollitt stared at Dan for quite half a minute. Then he said: "That's all I want from you. You can go."

When Dan had left the room, Pollitt rang for Kent. "Keep an eye on him. I wouldn't be surprised if he went to see Carl Swanson."

But Dan had not the slightest intention of looking up Carl. Carl could look after himself, and the less he, Dan, mixed himself up in this business, the less chance there was of getting himself into trouble. Tubby had cleared out. He'd read all about it in the papers, but where or how Tubby had gone was no business of his. He went straight home to feed his hens.

<h1 style="text-align:center">13</h1>

LARRY HICKS was standing with Jessie Miles outside a new little house in a very new road. Jessie had a key in her hand and was saying: "I don't think it'll be too big for us, Larry. There's three bedrooms, but we could take in a lodger to start with. That would help things."

Larry looked at the heaps of clay and broken bricks which was the front garden. "It'll take a time to get that into shape, let alone the back."

But Jessie wasn't listening. She was picking her way between a string of puddles which led to the front door. As she fitted the key in the lock she said: "I do like green paint, don't you?"

"Yes. It's all right."

Together they pressed into the tiny strip of a hall and Jessie opened a door under the stairs. "Oh, what a lovely big cupboard!" Larry put his head in, said, "Smells a bit damp to me," and ran the tips of his fingers over the wall.

"It'll be all right once we get the fires going." She ran into the kitchen. "Oh! It's just perfect! When do you think we'll be able to move in?"

"We'll have to wait a bit yet."

"Yes, I know. Until you get your salvage money, but that won't be long now, will it?"

"I don't know." Larry was staring at the floor and he was frowning.

"Larry, what's the matter with you? You said that first night, when you came back, that everything would be all right."

"Yes, I know I did, and I thought so then, truly I did, but I'm not so sure now."

"Why not?" Jessie's lips were trembling and tears hung in her eyes.

"I can't tell you now, you'll have to wait."

"You mean you're keeping something back? And you promised that we'd never have secrets from each other."

Larry felt acutely miserable. First it was Carl and now Jessie. "It's got to do with other people besides me, and I gave my word I wouldn't speak."

"It's Carl Swanson. I know it is. I never wanted you to have anything to do with him. I asked you not to go with him and you wouldn't listen." She began to cry.

Larry put an arm round her shoulders but she wrenched herself free. "And I thought everything was going to be all right and that we'd have a lot of money and you'd get a job ashore, and now it's all spoilt—by Carl. I could kill that man."

"Carl's all right," Larry mumbled unhappily. "If you take him the right way."

"What's he done? That's what I want to know."

"Nothing."

Jessie blew her nose on a scrap of a handkerchief, folded it into a pad and dabbed at her eyes. "We'd better go home. It's no good staying here any longer." She walked quickly out of the kitchen and by the time Larry had locked the front door she was twenty yards down the street.

He loved Jessie Miles, and the sight of her crying was just a little bit more than he could stand. After all, what would it matter if he did tell her? He'd make her promise not to tell anyone, and maybe she could help him. Anyway it would ease his own mind if he were to share the secret.

As they reached the corner a tram came swinging down the street. Jessie was about to step off the pavement when Larry took her by the arm. "Let's walk and I'll tell you all about it."

When he had finished Jessie was silent for a minute and then she said: "How do you think it happened? I mean, how did Mac-Taggart fall over the side?"

"He must have been leaning on the guard-rail of the port side of the bridge and it carried away. I saw the lanyard myself. It was frayed right through."

"If it was found out, would there be trouble?"

"It would mean the salvage money would be cut down a lot. You see, as MacTaggart was on the *Ivanhoe* when we boarded her, she wasn't a derelict. That makes a lot of difference."

Jessie said: "Yes, I see." She pressed close to Larry's side. "I'm awfully glad you told me. Nothing matters now."

"What d'you mean?"

"I don't mind waiting, even if it's months, now I know there's nothing between us." She gave a little laugh. "I hope the boy won't be sold before we get the money to buy it."

"I'll speak to them in the shop about it. Maybe they'd put it by for us."

They were passing a newsagent's shop when a placard caught Jessie's eye: "Mysterious Disappearance of Gilboro' Fisherman." She said: "I read about that this morning. I wonder what happened to him."

"It was Tubby Stevens."

"Did you know him?"

"He was our cook on the *John Goodwin* and he was with us on the *Ivanhoe* as well. Wait a minute and I'll buy a paper. Maybe there's some news about him."

Larry came out of the shop reading the paper. Jessie came close to him and saw a photograph of Tubby Stevens broadly smiling. Below was a photograph of the zither and the caption, "Any person who saw this man within the last twenty-four hours is asked to communicate with Inspector Pollitt at Gilboro' Police-Station."

"And to think he may be lying dead somewhere." Jessie shivered. "He looks such a cheery little man."

Larry read in the stop-press: "Stevens is believed to have been in the company of a man who met him at the 'Magpie' public house in Spurling Street." That must have been Carl, he thought to himself.

"What do you think happened to him, Larry?"

"I don't know," he replied slowly. He folded the paper and put it under his arm. "Anyway, it isn't any of our business."

"You said he was on the *Ivanhoe*?"

"Yes."

"And he knew about this man, MacTaggart?"

"Yes."

"Do you think he had anything to do with him falling over the side?"

"Who? Tubby? No, not a chance of that, and, besides, it was clear enough the way MacTaggart went. I tell you I saw the broken rail myself." He grinned. "Tubby couldn't have done a hurt to a dog, let alone a man the build of MacTaggart." Then, as quickly as it had come, the smile faded and a half-formed, half-forgotten fear returned to his mind. He was back on the bridge of the *Ivanhoe*, in the chart-room. Carl was there too, sprawling across the table, a half-smoked cigarette in the corner of his mouth. He remembered the way Carl had looked; hard, insolent, and his words: "We'd be a lot better off with that damn' captain out of it. He's going to spoil our ruddy pitch."

And then that morning when Carl had announced that MacTaggart had gone overboard. There had been a challenge in his voice, and Larry remembered, now, that his first thought had been that Carl had killed MacTaggart. But when he had seen the broken guard-rail, his suspicions had died.

"I know why Tubby's gone," he said to Jessie.

"Then why don't you tell the police?"

"Because if I did it might come out about MacTaggart."

"I don't understand."

"Tubby's fond of beer and he's fond of talking, too. Carl found that he'd been letting out about MacTaggart being on board the *Ivanhoe* and told him to clear out."

"So if Tubby stays away everything'll be all right?"

"Yes, that's the idea."

"Well, don't let's talk about it any more. I expect it'll come out all right in the finish, and we'll get our house—and the boy." She slipped her hand in his.

"Same with me. I was meaning to tell you when I came to your house, but somehow I couldn't make a start. Now what about going to Doughty's for tea and shrimps?"

"I'd love to, but I promised Mrs. Mather we'd go to her, and I know she's been baking this morning, so we can't disappoint her."

Larry said: "That's fine," with no enthusiasm, and added: "We'll have a pennyworth of tram. I expect you've had your fill of walking for one day."

Mrs. Mather had been baking, and on the table in her kitchen there was a fruit-cake, a simnel cake, a pile of scones, warm from the oven, and a good big slab of the best dairy butter. There was also a basin of shrimps caught that morning by Tom Ingleby and brought by Mr. Hopkins.

"Well, if that ain't fortunate, Mr. Hopkins. Me with a party this very afternoon. Come along in and join us, won't you?"

Mr. Hopkins did not need much pressing, and settled down in the chair which Mrs. Mather pushed up to the fire.

"I don't want to be odd man out."

"And you won't be because there's only Jessie Miles and Larry Hicks coming, and it's cosier with four." She put the teapot on the hob to warm, opened the tea-caddy and laid a spoon beside it. Then she went to the window from which she could see down Hawkin's Court. "I told Jessie not to be late, but she's been out looking at the house they're going to buy, and you know what young folk are."

Mr. Hopkins said that he did and sat looking at the hot coals. He was glad he wasn't out looking at houses in this weather.

A blatter of rain rattled on the windowpane and Mrs. Mather looked up from her knitting to say: "I hope they had the sense to take their coats with them."

As she spoke the latch on the front door clicked and a draught of cold air swept round Mr. Hopkins's legs.

Mrs. Mather called out: "Is that you, Jessie?" Then she bent forward, raked a flat bed on the coals and put the kettle on to boil.

Jessie's cheeks were red and her eyes were shining as she came into the room. "It's lovely and warm in here." She kissed Mrs. Mather and then saw Mr. Hopkins awkwardly getting on to his feet. "Afternoon, Mr. Hopkins. Don't get up."

"Draw up to the fire, Jessie, and warm yourself." Mrs. Mather took Jessie's hands in hers. "You're frozen, girl!" She turned to Larry. "You shouldn't have kept her out so long."

Mr. Hopkins, now that he had been roused from his contemplation of the fire, was eager for his tea and he was very fond of shrimps. He drew his chair up to the table and said: "Is Carl coming?"

"Maybe he will," Mrs. Mather replied. "But I don't know what's happened to him these last two days. He's not the same as he used to be."

Mr. Hopkins looked at the basin of shrimps and hoped that Carl would not be one of the party.

The air of Gilboro' is a destructive force when translated into four hearty appetites, and the mound of scones had shrunk, the shrimps had disappeared and the cakes had suffered considerable damage by the time Mr. Hopkins lit his pipe and Larry a cigarette.

Mrs. Mather and Jessie carried the remains to the back kitchen. The red-and-white check tea-cloth was replaced by one of a rich shade of maroon; it was one of Mrs. Mather's most treasured possessions. Carl had given it to her last Christmas.

The old lady sat in her favourite chair, one with high sides and a very straight back, and picked up her knitting. As her needles flashed and clicked, she said: "Now, Mr. Hopkins, tell us the news. What's all this talk about Tubby Stevens?"

Mr. Hopkins contrived to look very important. He took his pipe from his mouth and turned his head towards his hostess. "I wouldn't care to be Tubby at this moment."

Mrs. Mather's needles were still. She said: "Why? What do you think's come over him?"

"They found his zither didn't they? All kicked about and left lying down in Smith's Field. Well, that don't look too good to me. Like as not he's in the river."

"But no one would have wished Tubby any harm, surely?"

"I don't know as to that," said Mr. Hopkins. "There's been a lot of queer goings on that no one knows the rights of." He puffed at his pipe conscious of, and satisfied with, the effect he had produced.

"What do you mean, goings on?" Jessie asked. She was looking down at the cloth, at a whorl in the pattern.

"That's not for me to say," said Mr. Hopkins, implying that he knew a great deal more than he could tell at this moment.

"What about a turn of the cards, Mrs. Mather?" Jessie suggested. "Perhaps they'll tell us something."

For a full minute Mrs. Mather's needles clicked, and she gave no sign that she had heard. Then her hands fell on her lap and she said: "I don't like to—I'm afeared."

Larry added his weight to the request. "It won't do any harm. Come on, Mrs. Mather, give it a go."

Mr. Hopkins was silent. He didn't believe in fortune-telling.

"All right, then, I will." Mrs. Mather wound her wool on the ball and stuck in the needles. Then she got up, opened a drawer in the dresser and took out a pack of cards. "But I don't say they'll work." She gave the cards to Larry. "You shuffle 'em."

In spite of his affected indifference Mr. Hopkins sat up in his chair and turned to the table.

"You have to say a name, don't you?" said Jessie. "Else we won't know what the cards say."

"That's right," Mrs. Mather replied. "Who's it going to be? What about you, Mr. Hopkins?"

But Hoppy wasn't having any of that. Of course he wasn't superstitious, but all the same he didn't want no one to tell him the day he was going to die.

Neither Jessie nor Larry was keen to try their luck. Larry said: "What about Tubby Stevens?"

"I don't like to," Mrs. Mather said. But her fingers were already engaged in dealing out the cards, face downwards in seven rows, seven cards in a row. "That's the magic number. Seven." She turned the three remaining cards face upwards and looked at them for a long time. The first was the knave of spades, the second the three of hearts and the last one, the five of hearts.

"Five and three is eight." She picked up the first card of the second row and turned it over. It was the ace of hearts. "He's coming back," she muttered.

"When?" asked Mr. Hopkins.

But Mrs. Mather did not answer. She was doing another sum in her head. "Eight and one is nine." Her right hand crept towards the second card in the second row. "I'm feared," she said.

"Nonsense," said Mr. Hopkins. "Go on." He was anxious to get home to his wife but wanted to know the answer first.

"If it's a spade it means he's dead," said Mrs. Mather. She was sitting as still as a statue.

"Then how can he come back?" asked Larry.

"In a coffin," said Mr. Hopkins. "Or on the tide. And that's where he is at this very instant, in the river."

Jessie said suddenly. "Please stop. I don't like it."

But Mrs. Mather's fingers were moving, feeling round the corner of the card. Jessie shut her eyes but the matter-of-fact Mr. Hopkins leaned farther over the table. Larry was looking at the toe of his boot.

"It's a heart," said Mr. Hopkins, and there was disappointment in his voice.

Jessie gave a little gasp of relief. Then she laughed. "It gave me quite a turn for a minute."

Larry took a cigarette from a packet and lit it. As he threw the match into the grate he said: "Can you find out anything else?" His face was wooden.

"Maybe I can," said Mrs. Mather. "Now let me see where I was." She thought for a moment and then turned over the last card in the last row. It was the queen of spades. "There's going to be trouble," she muttered.

"Going to be what?" said Mr. Hopkins, getting up and reaching for his coat.

"Trouble. I can't tell what it'll be, but it's going to be the worst kind of trouble. It was the same when I worked the cards for Sim Barton and his brother was drowned at the fishing three weeks afterwards. It came true then all right."

As Mrs. Mather gathered up the cards Jessie put a hand on her sleeve. "Does it mean that something's going to happen to Tubby Stevens?"

"No, not him. Someone near to one of us, maybe. You never can tell exactly." Mrs. Mather's face was grave and she did not smile when she said good-bye to Mr. Hopkins.

Mr. Hopkins's sight was bad, he was in a hurry and the passage to the front door was dark, so that when he blundered straight into something he received a very great shock. He dropped his hat and called out, "Mercy me! Who's that?"

The cry brought Larry out from the kitchen. Jessie and Mrs. Mather were close behind him.

The obstruction which had so startled Mr. Hopkins was Carl Swanson who laughed at Mr. Hopkins, picked up his hat and patted him on the shoulder. "You're in an almighty hurry, Mr. Hopkins."

Mrs. Mather said: "Carl, whatever are you doing there? We never heard you come in, did we, Jess?"

"You were too busy talking, I reckon," Carl said, and nodded to Larry. "You're starting your training early. Tea-parties. You'll get your bellyful of them, time you're spliced."

As the front door banged behind Mr. Hopkins, Jessie said she must be going, too. She had her father's supper to cook. Larry said he'd see her home, and as she was getting her hat from the back bedroom he whispered to Carl. "Is there anything new?"

"There's nothing in the papers."

"Someone saw you with Tubby last night."

"I saw that bit." Carl lounged back against the dresser, took his cigarette from his mouth and blew out a cloud of smoke. "But they don't know who it was."

"I wouldn't be too sure about that if I was you."

"Well, what does it matter? I never did nothing to him."

Larry was about to reply when Jessie came back wearing her coat and hat. She kissed Mrs. Mather good night and took Larry's arm. "Come on, we must hurry."

For five minutes after they had gone, Mrs. Mather fussed about the room putting things straight. Then she poked the fire and was about to put on fresh coal when Carl took the bucket from her hand. "Here, let me do that."

When he had finished he walked to the dresser and saw the pack of cards lying there. "Have you been telling their fortunes?"

Mrs. Mather picked up her knitting and drew out the needles from the ball of wool. She said: "Yes, I was," but didn't look up.

"How did it work? Is Larry going to come into money?"

"It wasn't Larry's fortune I was telling."

"Who's was it then?" Carl stood behind her chair and, leaning with his elbow on the back, put his hands on her shoulders.

"Tubby Stevens, if you want to know," Mrs. Mather replied. Her voice was low.

"Tubby Stevens." Carl stood up. "What made you pick on him?"

"It was Larry who suggested it."

Carl walked over to the window and parted the curtains. He said: "It's still blowing."

"It came out that Tubby was alive and would come back."

"Anything else?"

"Yes." Mrs. Mather's hands fell idle on her lap. "There's going to be trouble and I have a feeling it won't be far from here." She shivered and drew her shawl close about her shoulders. "It's silly, I know, to think such things but that's what the cards said, and it's what I feel myself."

Carl sat on the arm of Mrs. Mather's chair. "I wouldn't go too much on what the cards say. They don't always come right. Same as that night when I sailed in the *John Goodwin*, they were wrong then."

"That wasn't the cards. It was tea-leaves and you did have bad luck. You lost a couple of trawls."

"But we fell in with the *Ivanhoe* and that was a real bit of luck. It's going to mean thousands of pounds to me, and when I get the money I'm going to buy you anything you want."

Mrs. Mather smiled. "Will it run to that bit of lino I spoke about?"

"Lino! I'll be buying you a motor-car with a man to drive it. And lots of shawls, and I'll pay someone to come in and help you in the house."

"I've managed on my own the last fifty years, and I couldn't have a girl about the place. She'd be more trouble than she was worth." Mrs. Mather looked at the clock. "Mercy mighty me! It's time I was getting the supper on instead of sitting here talking." She got up. "Carl, promise me that if ever you get into any sort of trouble you'll tell me. Maybe I'll be able to help you."

Carl said: "I wish you'd leave these cards alone. They always get you down." He sat before the fire and put his feet on the fender. If Tubby did come back there might be trouble, but what was the good of worrying? He'd tell Innes to push his claim through, get the money and then he could snap his fingers at the lot of them; buy a trawler of his own and be his own master.

14

WHILE CARL WAS forcing his thoughts into pleasant channels, Tubby Stevens was tramping along a country road. It was a very hard road, and the soggy grass verge was flanked by a deep ditch filled right up to the top with brown and very cold water. The only bright spot in the situation was that the wind was on his back, and at times he had almost to run to prevent himself falling on his face.

On either side, beyond straggly hedges, stretched flat, grey fields. Tubby kept his eyes straight ahead of him, for he did not like the wide open spaces. He was a lover of good company, a fire and a full pint pot; as he strode on he said to himself, "Surely there must be a pub soon," which was a reasonable hope, he having covered five miles without finding anything more exciting and inviting than a wayside coffee-stall.

Then the ditch stopped, and its place was taken by a footpath. "Getting somewhere now," he muttered to himself and quickened his pace. Ahead there was a row of lights of a filling-station. As he came abreast of it he called out to a man standing at the door of a shed. "How far to the town, mate?"

"A mile and a half."

A trickle of water ran down inside his collar, but Tubby was past caring about such trifles. There was a town ahead; he began to forget about this hellish tramp in the rain. His thoughts went ahead of him and found a pub with a fire in the bar, a cheery crowd, a good supper and a bed.

As so often happens, expectation outran reality. There was but one word to describe the town of Brickwell. It was "mouldy". No trams ran on the lines on its cobbled streets. The fronts of two out of its three picture-houses were dark, and there was little life in its streets.

Then Tubby sighted a lighted window with the glad sign "Burrows' Beers" on it, and pushed open a swing door. There were two men at the bar; they made grunting noises when Tubby said good evening. But on the other side of the counter was the more cheerful sight of bottles and bottles and bottles, ranged on shelves against a mirror.

Tubby took off his dripping coat and put it on the back of a chair. There was no fire, and where there should have been a sylph of a barmaid a fat woman stood. She looked sulky and was wearing a dirty overall.

"I'll have a rum hot, if you please," said Tubby.

"Hot?" said the woman.

"Hot," repeated Tubby firmly. That's what he felt like, a rum hot, and nothing else would do. It wasn't the sort of night for beer.

"You'll have to wait," said the woman, and went reluctantly into a room at the back of the bar. Through an open door Tubby could see the dancing flames of an open fire. Later, he'd maybe be able to work his way in there, but he'd have to go slow with the fat woman.

One of the men at the bar looked up from the paper he was reading. "Have you come far?" he asked.

"Gilboro'," said Tubby.

"Today?"

"I got a lift a bit of the way."

"Gilboro'?" said the man and tilted his cap on to the back of his head so that he could see Tubby more easily. "There's been a murder there."

Tubby stared at him. "A murder! Who was it?"

"A bloke called Stevens."

"How was it done?"

"Doesn't say."

It was the first time in his life that Tubby had been told that he had been murdered. He goggled. "Murdered! Let's have a look." He snatched the paper and saw a photograph of himself dressed in his best suit, grinning broadly. He remembered now. It had been taken that time he had spent a week at Scarborough.

"Do you know him?" asked the owner of the paper, suspiciously.

"Never seen him in my life before," lied Tubby.

The fat woman was a welcome interruption. In one red wrinkled hand she carried a kettle. "I'll have a double," said Tubby. The sound of rum gurgling from the bottle was a very cheerful sound at that moment. "And easy on with the water."

"That'll be one and tuppence."

It was the best one and tuppence' worth he had ever had, Tubby decided, as he rolled the spirit round his mouth, savoured it and swallowed it.

"I needed that," he said as he put down the glass.

"He says he comes from Gilboro'," said the man with the cap.

"What about it?" asked the fat woman. She had never been more than twenty miles from Brickwell in her life, and the name Gilboro' meant nothing to her.

"Where the murder was."

"You don't say!"

"You can read about it there." The paper was pushed across the bar counter.

The woman, breathing through her mouth, spelt out the first few lines of the announcement. "It doesn't say nothing about a murder. It's only that this bloke Stevens has disappeared and I expect he had a good enough cause. The police were after him for something he'd done, I wouldn't wonder."

This swift change from being murdered to becoming a fugitive from justice made Tubby blink.

"Well, what do you say?" asked the man in the cap.

But Tubby had no explanation ready and mumbled that he didn't rightly know what to make of it.

"You mark my words," said the Tweed Cap. "That bloke Stevens'll never drink another pint."

As though to give the lie to this pronouncement Tubby ordered a pint. The rum had warmed him up and his taste for beer had returned. As he drank his beer he said: "Do you think you can give me a bed for the night?"

"Bed?" said the fat woman and scratched her head with a hairpin. Apparently the word was a stranger to her for she repeated it in the same surprised tone.

"That's right. Just for the one night. I'm going on to Birmingham in the morning."

A shrill cry of "Elsie!" brought a tousled head into view round the door at the back of the bar. "Is Bill coming in tonight?" asked the woman.

"No, he won't be back till Saturday."

"Then you can have his bed," the woman said to Tubby, "and it'll be half a dollar."

Bill's room was not over-furnished. There was a bed, a chair and a table, and, tacked up over the fireplace, a misty, spotted, six-inch square of looking-glass.

Tubby shut the door, putting the back of the chair against it and walked over to the mirror. He compared what he saw in it with the photograph of himself in the paper. They weren't much alike, especially if he kept his hat on and didn't smile. As he got into bed he said to himself, "I wish to hell I hadn't told 'em I came from Gilboro'."

Tom Ingleby, when he had delivered the shrimps to Mr. Hopkins, received in return a copy of the *Evening Argus*. It wasn't often he read a paper these days and he took it only out of politeness to Mr. Hopkins. "It would come in handy to light the stove with," he thought to himself as he walked down to the fish-dock where his dinghy was moored under the bows of the *Ivanhoe*.

As he pulled away from the wharf he looked up at the black sides of the *Ivanhoe*. "That was a damn' good job," he said aloud. "No one else could ha' pulled it off the way he did."

Then he bent his back to the oars and there was a gurgling rush of water past the sides of his boat. As the blades came clear of the surface glowing drops of phosphorous dripped from them like molten silver.

Out in the river the wind, blowing up against the strong ebb-tide, had raised a short, steep sea through which the dinghy plunged and drove her way, raising showers of fine spray which beat on Tom Ingleby's broad back.

Half an hour's hard pulling brought him to the ramshackle jetty at the Pride of Bedford, and, cat-like, he found his way up the path to the house without a lamp. He threw the paper on the table and lit the wick of a hanging lamp. As the light strengthened he glanced at the paper and saw Tubby's smiling face.

He knew him well by sight; knew that he had been on board the *Ivanhoe* with Carl and read every word of the account of his disappearance. Then he stood for a long time, with the paper in his hand, staring at nothing. He was trying to work it out but found no answer. He was frightened; frightened for Carl.

Jessie forgot all about Larry's story of what had happened on board the *Ivanhoe* until she had finished washing up the supper dishes in her father's house; then, as she reviewed it, misgivings arose in her mind. Her conscience, a very lively member of Jessie's make-up, began in a very small voice to say that surely it wasn't right to claim a reward for saving the *Ivanhoe* and back up that claim with a lie; for to say that the ship had been a derelict was a lie; her captain had been on board.

Jessie replied that she didn't really understand these things and, if Larry thought it was all right, then it wasn't for her to interfere. Conscience said, "Nonsense. You know very well it's wrong."

And then the thought of the little house, the furniture she had set her heart on—and the boy dealt conscience a very shrewd blow. Jessie thought: "You've got to think of yourself these days or you'll never get anywhere." Conscience, sagging on the ropes, said weakly: "Yes, I suppose you're right."

But Jessie knew she was wrong, refused to admit it and told herself she had waited long enough for the house, the furniture, the boy and—Larry.

Mr. Fleming, when he read of Tubby's disappearance, said to his inkpot: "There is something wrong about this *Ivanhoe* affair." And the inkpot remaining mute as inkpots are in the habit of doing, he went on, "I'd like to know what Innes is thinking now. He'll be damn' sorry one of these days he didn't accept that offer I made him."

But Mr. Innes was thinking of nothing of the kind, for he did not possess Mr. Fleming's imagination. A missing man was but a missing man to him and he was quite incapable of picturing Tubby lying foully murdered in a ditch. If one of his clients liked to leave Gilboro', well that was his business, not that of Mr. Innes. True, he didn't like it, but then Mr. Innes did not like any case which did not run true to form.

Mr. Fleming picked up the receiver of his telephone and called the Gilboro' police-station.

Ten seconds later the voice of Inspector Pollitt asked: "Well, have *you* seen Tubby Stevens?"

"No," said Mr. Fleming, "but I was just ringing you up to—"

"Five hundred people have seen him," said Pollitt. "I was wondering if you were going to be the five hundred and first."

Mr. Fleming said that no thought was farther from his mind that he should seek this distinction. He was interested in Tubby Stevens, so he said, merely in relation to the claim Carl Swanson was bringing against his clients, the owners of the *Ivanhoe*.

"You don't want to take any notice of what the papers say," Pollitt replied. "It's my private opinion that he's gone off on some business of his own and'll be back tomorrow."

"What about the zither?" asked Mr. Fleming.

"I expect he got fed up with it because he couldn't play the damn' thing. And who wants to play a zither anyway?"

This was a question which obviously called for no answer and Mr. Fleming ignored it. "Do you think Carl Swanson's mixed up in this in any way?"

"I don't see why he should be." Pollitt was tired of answering questions. He was also tired of the subject of Tubby Stevens.

Mr. Fleming, realizing that there were no fish to be caught in these waters, said he was sorry he'd troubled Mr. Pollitt, said good night, and rang off.

Pollitt was about to read through a pile of reports when Kent came in. "I've been keeping observation on Carl Swanson," he said.

"Yes," said Pollitt with an awakened interest in his voice. Kent had spoken with the repressed excitement of one who had found a pearl in a Whitstable oyster.

"He nearly had a scrap with Larry Hicks."

"What about?"

"I don't know. Carl was drinking at the 'Keel' and Larry came in and they went off together. I followed them and I could see they were arguing about something. They stopped in a gate leading into the goods yard and when I came up abreast of them Carl was squaring up to Larry."

"And after that?"

"They started back to the town."

"Where did they go?" asked Pollitt.

"To the 'Keel' and had a drink. After that Larry went off on his own. I waited for Carl and trailed him to Mrs. Mather's house in Hawkin's Court."

Pollitt gave Kent half of a pile of telegrams. "They're all about Tubby Stevens. We've got to go through them tonight."

Kent, who had had his dinner at four o'clock and hadn't managed to catch up with tea, said he wasn't in a hurry to knock off, which, strangely enough, was not a black lie. Kent was young and keen on his job.

When the last report had been read, checked with Tubby's description and filed and the clock in Pollitt's room said that it was a quarter past ten, Pollitt decided that he would let today take care of itself and wait the coming of tomorrow in the comfort and warmth of his bed.

That was a vain hope and all because of a fat woman in Brickwell who had a more lively mind than her bulk and manner indicated. From the moment when she had seen the photograph of Tubby in the papers she decided that she was heading for headlines and fame.

There was no other reason which would have made her accede to Tubby's request for a bed. She had never done such a thing before, and she had risked Bill's wrath when she had told Tubby that he could have his room. The owner of the head which had appeared in answer to her cry of "Elsie" was summoned by a hoarse whisper as soon as the door of Bill's room had closed behind Tubby.

At the same time as Tubby was comparing his reflected face with that of the photograph in the paper, Elsie was half running, half walking in the direction of the Brickwell police-station bearing the news that the man who was missing from Gilboro' was about to sleep in the "Bull".

Elsie was overcome by the importance of her mission, and when she saw a policeman trying the padlock on a shop door her heart did very funny things, and her legs became as rotten cabbage stalks.

The policeman thought, "Drunk," hitched up his belt and said: "Now then."

Elsie let out a gasping "Oh!" and clutched at a lamp standard for support.

The policeman was confirmed in his first diagnosis and advanced on Elsie very much like a grizzly bear on its prey.

Elsie said: "I'm going to the police-station. I've got a message."

The policeman stared at her and decided that she was not drunk, at least not very drunk. Her speech was reasonably clear and drunks were not in the habit of paying voluntary visits to a police-station. He said: "What's it all about?"

"We've got him round at our place. The missus sent me to tell you to come quick."

"Let's have your name," said the policeman.

By the time he had finished with his questions Elsie felt limper than ever.

The policeman said: "You come with me and we'll see what the sergeant has to say about this."

If the fat woman expected the sudden arrival of a car loaded with police and with a siren wailing, she was disappointed. She had smoked four cigarettes before there came a double knock on the street door unheralded by the sound of screaming brakes.

She got up, went into the bar, stood for a moment listening for a sound of movement from Bill's room, and then shuffled to the door and drew the bolts. The first person she saw was Elsie, beside a blue pillar with a helmet on the top of it which was a policeman, and a man in plain clothes who was a detective.

The policeman said: "Does she live here?"

"Yes, come along in, but step quiet. He's not long been gone to his room."

The policeman took off his helmet and at once looked strangely different. "What makes you think he's Stevens?" he asked.

"Because of the photo in the papers and him saying he'd come from Gilboro'."

The detective said he'd go up if the fat woman would show him the room.

"You'll find it easy enough. It's the second door on the left down the passage at the top of the stairs." She would dearly have liked to have been in at the death, but as her legs were not in entire agreement with her on that point she remained seated.

Tubby was dozing off when he heard the sound of voices downstairs and he wondered lazily if it was Bill come back to claim his bed. He heard two sets of footsteps on the stairs and half a minute later they stopped outside his door. Then the door opened and the policeman walked into the room and shone the light of a flashlamp on his face.

Tubby shut his eyes to the glare and asked what the something something they wanted waking him at that time of night.

The detective said: "You're Stevens, aren't you? Tubby Stevens?"

Tubby said: "No."

"What's your name then?"

Tubby's brain wouldn't work. He'd been a fool not to have thought of a name and a story to tell if he were questioned. It was too late now.

The detective lit the gas and picked up the paper which was lying on the floor. He looked first at the photograph and then at Tubby. Then he said: "You'd better come along to the station with us. You'll maybe remember your name on the way."

As Tubby was lacing his boots the policeman said: "You've got nothing to be scared of."

"I know that."

"Then why did you want to clear out? You've given us a lot of trouble."

Tubby got up and put on his hat. His old grin came back. "If I like to leave Gilboro' for the good of my health that's nothing to anyone, or shouldn't be."

At the police-station he admitted that he was Tubby Stevens and that he had left Gilboro' of his own free will. He didn't know when he'd be going back and hinted that if he did it wouldn't be soon.

Inspector Pollitt was drinking a cup of tea at Gilboro' police-station when a call came through from Brickwell to say that Tubby was alive, and asked what was to be done with him.

Pollitt looked at Kent and said: "He's been found. You can burn that lot"—he pointed to a pile of telegraph-forms and type-written reports.

Brickwell wanted to know what they should do with their captive. Would Gilboro' send an escort for him in the morning?

Gilboro', in the person of Inspector Pollitt, said there was no charge and that Stevens was to be told to return.

"He says he won't go back," replied Brickwell.

"Ask him why he ran away?"

"We have, but all he'll say is he left for the good of his health."

"Keep on at him. Try and make him talk."

Brickwell said they'd done all they could.

"All right. Let him go but keep an eye on him." Pollitt put down the receiver. "Well, that's finished that," he said to Kent. Then he laughed. "Fleming had an idea that Carl Swanson had done Stevens in."

Pollitt wiped his mind clean of the Tubby Stevens disappearance, finished his tea, which was almost cold, and went home to bed.

15

The inhabitants of Gilboro' were disappointed next morning when they learnt that what had promised to blossom into a first-class mystery, if not a cold-blooded murder, had fizzled out in such a matter-of-fact fashion.

Mrs. Mather read the news as the kettle boiled for the cup of tea which she took up to Carl every morning. "The cards told true again," she murmured to herself. "I must tell Carl." She mounted the ladder and lifted the trap of Carl's room.

He sat up in bed and said: "'Morning, Granny."

"Here, take a look at this." She gave him the paper and then went to the window to draw the curtains. It was another wild morning. Low clouds, ragged and undershot with purple, were driving to the northward. "I doubt we'll get some more rain when this wind goes down."

But Carl wasn't listening. They'd found Tubby and what the hell was going to happen now? He picked up the paper he had let fall on his knees and read the account again. Tubby hadn't talked—yet. But you never knew with these damn' papers. They usually got a story wrong or left out the important bits. It wasn't likely the police would have said anything even if Tubby had told them about MacTaggart.

"Oh hell!"

"What's the matter?" Mrs. Mather turned towards the bed.

Carl's eyes met hers and then he looked quickly away. "It's nothing. Nothing to worry about anyway."

She said: "I'm going to get breakfast ready."

Carl waited until he heard her reach the kitchen. Then he threw back the bedclothes. It was time he was out of all this. He'd go down to the gaffer and tell him he was ready as soon as there was a boat free. He'd get Larry Hicks. No, Larry was getting soft; Jessie Miles was spoiling him. But he'd have Dan Todd; Dan hadn't got mixed up with women.

Down in the kitchen Mrs. Mather was unwrapping a half-pound of bacon. With a sharp knife she cut the rind off each rasher; Carl didn't like rind. Then she spread the red-and-white chequered cloth on the table and set out plates and cups and saucers. "And I'll fry him a slice of bread. He does fancy a bit of fried bread."

She told herself that there were good times ahead for Carl, and yet—and yet in the back of her mind there lurked the fear born of the cards. They'd never told her wrong, and only last night they'd said there was going to be trouble, the worst kind of trouble, and she'd felt it, too, like a cold wind which chilled her old bones.

Mrs. Mather looked at the fire. It hadn't burned up bright enough for the frying. She hesitated for a moment and then opened the passage door and walked through to the front room. It was cold, and she clutched tightly at her shawl with her left hand as she turned the handle of the door.

By the dim morning light the centre table stood out black and silhouetted against the window. She picked up a plush-framed photograph of the late Mr. Mather, an uncompromising figure, standing belligerently four square in a square frock coat. She recalled his words: "Don't you have nothing to do with the brat."

But she had been obstinate as she had never been before and he'd given in: "All right. Have it your own way." And she'd had her own way. Had he been right and she wrong?

She put the photograph back in its place on the table, bent to pull a corner of a rug straight, and then went back to the kitchen.

Mr. Hopkins felt himself to have been cheated when he read the news about Tubby Stevens. His reputation as a minor prophet would suffer, and as he sat down to a late breakfast at half past ten his brain was busy in an endeavour to find a loophole of retreat from the position he had adopted. He had told his customers at his stall that without one shadow of doubt they would never again see Tubby Stevens alive. And now the papers said that he had been found at Brickwell.

"I don't believe it," he said as Mrs. Hopkins put before him a plate of bacon and eggs. "He's dead."

"Who's dead?" said Mrs. Hopkins.

"Tubby Stevens."

"Oh, never. You'll see he'll be along one of these days."

"You've been reading the papers."

"Yes, I have."

"You don't want to believe all they print."

But Mrs. Hopkins refused to be damped. "It'll come out all right, you see if it don't."

"I'll believe it when I sees him with me own eyes," replied Mr. Hopkins and proceeded to do damage to the bacon and eggs.

Jessie Miles didn't see the morning paper until she had fed her father and washed up the dishes. She wouldn't have bothered to have looked at it even then if Mrs. Warburton had not come in. "They've got him." Mrs. Warburton's face and eyes were shining. Which was brighter it was hard to say.

"Who?" said Jessie. Her heart did funny things that made her catch her breath.

"Tubby Stevens, of course."

Jessie flopped down on a chair. She said: "Oh!"

"Yes, and he hasn't been murdered as Mr. Hopkins said he'd been. The silly old yaffler."

"What happened?"

"Nothing. You can read for yourself." Mrs. Warburton held the paper under Jessie's nose. But of course she didn't let Jessie read it for herself. "He's right as rain and only went away because he wanted to."

Jessie thought: "Then Larry was right. Carl had had nothing to do with it."

"Just wait a minute and I'll tell you all it says." And, Mrs. Warburton being Mrs. Warburton, Jessie did wait a minute and did listen.

After a very long time Mrs. Warburton went off in search of a fresh audience, but Jessie still sat in her chair with her elbows on the kitchen table and her chin cupped in her hands. Conscience was having another go at her and was saying that she'd got to tell—she'd got to. She'd never be happy with the money if it wasn't come by honest.

Jessie cried and said it wasn't fair, but she had to give in. How was she to do it? She couldn't go to the solicitor and tell him; she'd never have the courage to do that, and when all was said and done it was nothing to do with the police; besides she couldn't face Inspector Pollitt, nor even the sergeant, though he'd spoken to her once or twice and he seemed quite a decent sort of man.

The only thing to do was to write a letter and tell him everything she knew; every word Larry had told her. She took down a penny bottle of ink from the dresser, found a pen and a sheet of pink, scented notepaper.

Writing a letter is very often much more difficult than thinking about it and that is what Jessie found. Three crumpled sheets bore witness to an inability to marshal her thoughts and reduce them to writing, but at the fourth attempt she achieved a result which satisfied her. Then the question of to whom to send it arose. Larry had mentioned the name of Innes as the solicitor who was acting for them, but she didn't know his address.

At first she thought of asking Mrs. Warburton, but decided that that wouldn't do. Mrs. Warburton would be sure to ask a lot of questions and go round telling people. So she just put "Mr. Innes, solicitor. Gilboro'" on the envelope and went out to post it.

She had to walk a mile before she found a pillar-box in a street where she wasn't known. As she heard the letter fall she thought, "I ought never to have done it." But she had done it and was miserable and forgot at least two things she had meant to buy for her father's dinner.

At three o'clock Mrs. Mather, who was sleeping soundly in a chair before her fire, woke with a start. There was a knock at her front door and she called out, "Come in," and hurriedly tucked away little stray wisps of hair that will get out of place when you sleep in a chair.

As soon as she saw Jessie's face she said: "Why, whatever is the matter, girl? Is it your father?"

"No, he's all right."

"Come along and sit down and I'll make you a nice cup of tea."

"Is Carl in?"

"No. I don't know where he's got to. Did you want to see him?"

"Well, not exactly."

Mrs. Mather became very still and she forced fear from her voice when she asked: "What is the matter, Jessie?"

"Larry told me. It's about the *Ivanhoe*." Jessie hesitated.

"Yes. Go on." Mrs. Mather moved over to Jessie's chair and put a hand on her shoulder. "You can tell me—everything."

"It's not anything bad really, but—but . . . Oh! There was a man on board that ship when Carl and Larry went to her first; the captain, and he fell over the side; it was all an accident, but they never said anything about it because they knew if they did they wouldn't get so much money for bringing her in."

"He fell over the side. Did Larry say that?"

"Yes. It just happened as they said at the inquest. One of the rails broke or something."

Mrs. Mather's brain worked slowly. She was trying to realize what this would mean to Carl.

"It's only a matter of the money. None of them did any wrong."

"The cards said that there was going to be trouble," Mrs. Mather said. She was afraid—for Carl. "We'll have to figure what's the best thing to do," she said, and looked down at a scrap of paper on the floor.

"I've done it. I know I shouldn't have. But it's too late now."

Suddenly Mrs. Mather came alive. She turned on Jessie almost fiercely. "What have you done? Tell me! Tell me!"

"I wrote a letter and put in what I've said."

"You shouldn't have! You should have spoken to Carl first and asked him if it was true. Most likely it's not." Mrs. Mather grasped at this brittle straw of hope.

"Larry wouldn't lie to me. He said Captain MacTaggart was on board, so it must be true."

Mrs. Mather relaxed and clasped her hands together. She bent over Jessie. "Where did you send the letter?"

"To Mr. Innes, the solicitor."

"That's not so bad," Mrs. Mather muttered.

"Oh, I do wish I hadn't done it. I should have asked Larry first. When he first told me I believed him when he told me it wouldn't do anyone any harm if nothing was said, but later on I got thinking."

"Well, never mind, it's done now." Mrs. Mather's voice was without emotion.

"But if they find that it was me."

"They'll know soon enough."

"No, they won't. I didn't put my name to it."

"Well, that's something." Mrs. Mather moved the kettle on to the glowing coals. "It's just on the boil."

"I can't stay." Jessie pulled herself to her feet and made for the door.

"Wait a minute. You've got to promise me one thing before you go."

"What is it?"

"Don't say a word of this to another living soul. If you do maybe you'll never marry Larry Hicks."

"But it was nothing to do with him," Jessie protested.

"Perhaps it wasn't, but promise me all the same."

Jessie said, "Yes," and with her handkerchief to her eyes ran down the passage to the street door.

As soon as she had gone Mrs. Mather took a shawl off a peg and draped it over her head. There was one thought in her mind: she must find Carl and warn him.

She hurried, hobbling over the rough cobblestones, down Hawkin's Court into the market-place. It was a slack time of day on the fish-wharves and there were few men in sight. If it had been an hour or two later she'd have known where to find Carl; he'd have been in the "Keel and Barge", but at that moment she had not the slightest idea where to start her search.

She was standing irresolute at the corner of the street, trying to make up her mind where to go, when she saw a man come out of one of the passages between the salesmen's stores. It was Tom Ingleby. She would have known him a mile off with his black beard and swinging stride. He was carrying a basket in one hand.

Mrs. Mather drew her shawl down over her face and walked westwards twenty yards to the corner of Carnaby Street. "He's going to see Mr. Hopkins; that's where he's going," she muttered.

"Good afternoon, Mr. Ingleby."

Tom Ingleby peered down into the face before him and there came a startled look on his face. He was as awkward as a boy caught out by a schoolmaster.

"Why, Jenny! Fancy you being down this way. I thought you never left your house these days."

Jenny! It was a long time since anyone had called her by that name, but this was no time for chat and reminiscence. "The doctor said it would kill me to walk a hundred yards, but I've done more than that and I'm still alive." She smiled and then clutched at her chest. "I spoke too soon, seemingly."

Tom Ingleby put an arm around her. "You'd best get right back to your house and lay down."

"I'm all right. It's gone now."

"Where was you a-going anyway?"

"To find Carl."

"Carl!"

"Yes, I've just heard something. I've got to tell him."

"They've found Tubby Stevens," Tom Ingleby said. "Carl's got nothing to worry about."

"It's not that. There's something else."

"I'll get him for you. You go back home as I said and rest yourself. I'll send him right along as soon as I find him."

"All right. Thanks, Tom. I do feel a little tired. I'm not quite so spry as I thought I was."

Tom Ingleby waited until he saw Mrs. Mather reach her cottage. Then he walked quickly to Mr. Hopkins's house and when Mrs. Hopkins opened the door he gave her the bass bag. "Here's some fish for you. I won't be able to stop to tea today."

"Whyever not?" said Mrs. Hopkins. "My husband'll be real disappointed."

But Tom Ingleby was not to be thus deflected from his purpose. He'd got to find Carl Swanson and he meant to find him if he was in Gilboro' town.

Carl Swanson was not a man who liked being idle. But here were no jobs to be had on the wharf so he had set out to walk down to where the river ran into the sea and watch the boats coming in. There he stayed until darkness drove him back to the town. Tom Ingleby saw him coming along the sea-wall and went to meet him. He said: "Excuse me, Mr. Swanson, but I've got a message for you from Mrs. Mather. She wants you to go to her house right away." The two men, well matched in height and physique, faced each other.

"What does she want?"

"I don't know. She was down in the market-place looking for you."

"She shouldn't have been out. Her heart's bad."

"I know. I said I'd come and find you."

"Thanks, mate." Carl strode on towards the town. Whatever had made Granny leave the house? She must have heard some-thing! His anxiety increased as he neared Hawkin's Court and as he lifted the latch of the front door he was frightened.

"Is that you, Carl?"

"Are you all right?"

"Of course I am. Why shouldn't I be?"

"I met Tom Ingleby and he said you'd been out looking for me. You shouldn't have done that."

"I had to. Even if it killed me, which it didn't. Sit down. I've something to tell you."

Mrs. Mather picked up her knitting which she had laid aside when she had heard the door open. "Jessie Miles was down to see me this afternoon and she says Larry told her that there was a man on board the *Ivanhoe* when you got to her."

"Well?"

"Is it true?"

"Yes."

The needles flashed in the firelight and as she drew a length of wool from the ball in her lap Mrs. Mather said: "And she's written a letter to Mr. Innes telling him all about it."

Carl sat quite still. His lips moved but he did not speak. And he thought he'd been safe when he'd got Tubby out of the way! He'd forgotten Jessie.

He brought a packet from his pocket and took out a cigarette. As he blew out smoke between clenched teeth he said: "I might ha' known it would have been a woman."

"It was Larry who told her. She'd never have known else."

Carl had a curious feeling that he was standing outside his body, listening to this conversation.

The import of the news so quietly spoken by Mrs. Mather did not at once register in his mind. Jessie had written a letter to Mr. Innes; she had told him that MacTaggart had been on board the *Ivanhoe*.

Realization of what it would mean came slowly. He got up and began to pace up and down the room. He forced himself to think.

"Is there nothing that can be done?" Mrs. Mather looked up from her work but he did not meet her gaze.

"No. I don't think so."

"It'll only mean you'll lose money, won't it?"

Carl said: "Yes."

"Then isn't it better this way? It would have come out sooner or later."

"I'm going away," Carl said suddenly. "And I don't know when I'll be back."

Mrs. Mather saw the look in his eyes. She pulled herself to her feet. The ball of wool rolled unheeded across the floor. "Where'll you go?"

"I don't know. Up North, maybe."

"That's no good, Carl. They'll follow you and bring you back."

He looked down into her eyes and was about to speak. He was going to say, "What does that matter?" but he read in Mrs. Mather's face the understanding that the loss of the salvage money was not all he had to fear.

He sat down in a chair and stared fixedly at a crack in the wall. Funny, but he'd never noticed it before. You could almost put a finger in it.

"I know where you can go. To Tom Ingleby's. No one'll ever think of looking for you there."

"You mean down at the Pride of Bedford?"

"Yes. He'll take you in if you tell him I sent you."

"I didn't know he was a friend of yours."

"He was." Mrs. Mather sighed. "A very long time ago."

"I'll go first thing in the morning."

"Mr. Innes'll get the letter tonight. Jessie posted it at dinner-time."

"Then I'll pack my things now."

"It'd be better so."

When Carl came down from his room with a bundle of clothes under his arm Mrs. Mather was sitting in her chair drawn up close to the fire. She was so very still that he caught his breath as a fear passed swiftly through his mind.

"Granny!"

She turned her head wearily. "I must have been asleep."

He bent down and kissed her on the cheek. "If—if anyone comes asking for me, say I've gone to Newcastle to visit friends."

"All right." She put out a hand, blue-veined, white as milk, and laid it on his. "Now you will stop with Tom, won't you? I'll try and send word how things go here."

"I'll be all right. Try not to worry." He put a hand in a pocket and brought out a half-crown and three pennies. "Have you any money you can lend me?"

"Yes." Mrs. Mather rose slowly and walked with short, unsteady steps into her bedroom.

Carl could hear a box being pulled across the floor, a lock snap back and then the rustle of paper.

She came back to the room with five one-pound notes clasped tightly in her hand. It was her "burying money". The sum she had saved over many long years as an insurance against lying in a pauper's grave.

"Will that be enough?"

"Plenty." Carl put the money in his pocket and picked up his bundle.

"And here's a line to give to Tom Ingleby."

He took the note, said good-bye, and was gone.

Tubby woke up in Bill's room at the Bull Hotel at Brick-well and stretched out a hand for his trousers which were lying on a chair. He felt first in one pocket and then in the other. They were both empty.

He began to sweat and sat up in bed. Perhaps the money was in his coat. But that hope was a false one for there was no trace of the two one-pound notes Carl had given him. He tried to think back to the time when he'd last seen them, but could only remember stuffing them in his trouser pocket when he had left Carl.

Now he was in a blooming mess and no mistake! And he didn't like the fat woman. She was just the sort to turn nasty.

A photograph on the mantelpiece of a man with the face of a prize-fighter and signed "Your ever-loving Bill", caused Tubby to make a noise like a dying-duck balloon. Life was being very difficult and became even more so when the fat woman's voice came shrilly up the stairs telling him breakfast was ready.

He had no appetite for food nor desire for conversation, but there was nothing else for it but to go downstairs and eat and discuss his experiences of the previous night.

The fat woman said she was sorry there had been trouble, but there now, you never knew these days, did you? with all sorts of people on the road.

Tubby agreed that this was undoubtedly a fact and that she had had good reason for sending for the police and he didn't hold it against her.

"And now I suppose you'll be leaving us?" she said.

"Well, if you don't mind I'd like to stop another night, I'm still a bit tired after yesterday."

"All right. But I've just got word this morning that Bill'll be back at dinner-time."

Tubby spent an hour after breakfast smoking and reading the local paper. But at the back of his mind was the nagging thought that he had no money to pay for his night's lodging.

At half past ten he went out and bought a sheet of notepaper and an envelope. These purchases he carried to the post-office and wrote a letter, addressed it to Carl Swanson and, as an afterthought, printed the word "Urgent" at the top of the envelope.

As he dropped the letter into the post-box he was grinning and feeling much more like his old self.

When Tom Ingleby had given Carl Mrs. Mather's message he went straight to Mr. Hopkins's house.

"You're late, Tom. What's ailed ye?" Mr. Hopkins called from the kitchen as he heard the familiar heavy step in the passage. He was in his shirt-sleeves fastening his dicky, for it was nearly the time for opening the stall.

Tom Ingleby said that he'd had a job that had kept him, and it was time he was getting back, but Mrs. Hopkins, who came out of the back kitchen drying her hands, would have none of this.

"You sit right down, Tom Ingleby. The kettle's not far off the boil and it won't take me a minute to wet a pot of tea."

Tom Ingleby was too nervous of Mrs. Hopkins to refuse. He sat on the edge of a kitchen chair.

Mr. Hopkins clipped a tie into place between the wings of his collar and picked his coat up off a chair. "What was your job, Tom?"

"Mrs. Mather."

Mr. and Mrs. Hopkins exchanged startled glances.

"Mrs. Mather! Have you been to her house?" It was Mr. Hopkins who asked the question.

"No, I met her down by the market. She was looking for Carl to give him a message. I found him for her."

"She didn't ought to have been out," said Mrs. Hopkins severely. "With that heart of hers."

"She wasn't looking too good. I told her to go right back home."

"What was it she wanted Carl for?"

"I dunno." Tom Ingleby shook his heavy head slowly. "She didn't say. I saw him later on and told him to go to her house and that's all there was to it."

This was news. Mr. Hopkins forgot about his customers. He stood with his back to the fire and faced his guest.

"Are you sure there wasn't anything else?"

"Certain sure. I was only with her two—three minutes."

"Well, I don't know." Mr. Hopkins fingered his side whiskers. He was thinking very hard. At last he said: "It must have been something serious for Mrs. Mather to have come out like that."

"She's been keeping her house this last three months back," Mrs. Hopkins commented.

"I wonder if there was anything wrong?" Mr. Hopkins decided that he would call on Mrs. Mather on his way down to the stall.

Mrs. Hopkins poured out a cup of black, steaming tea and gave it to Tom Ingleby. "Just wait a minute and I'll bring you the milk."

When she had left the room Mr. Hopkins said that he would have to be getting along. "There'll be a crowd waiting for me, I expect. There's a dozen boats due in."

Tom Ingleby nodded. "I won't be stopping long. I'm setting my eel-nets tonight. If they run all right maybe I'll be up tomorrow with a bag for you."

Mr. Hopkins called out, "So long, Maria," to his wife and hurried down the passage.

Three minutes later he was knocking on the door of Mrs. Mather's cottage in Hawkin's Court. He heard a chair scrape over the kitchen floor, the sound of shuffling steps and then the voice of Mrs. Mather asking who was there.

"It's me, Mrs. Mather."

The lock turned, the latch clicked and the door opened. "Come along in, Mr. Hopkins. I'm glad to see you." She shut the door and followed him down the passage into the kitchen. "I keep the door locked now Carl's gone away."

Mr. Hopkins tried to conceal his surprise at this news and he asked casually: "Where's he gone?"

"Newcastle. Bring your chair up to the fire."

"I can't stop long, Mrs. Mather. It's time I was on the job."

"Oh, there can't be all that hurry."

"Business is business," said Mr. Hopkins. As he compared his watch with the cuckoo clock on the wall he asked: "And what's taken Carl to Newcastle?"

"Visiting friends," replied Mrs. Mather. "And I don't know when he'll be back," she added, forestalling the next question.

"Oh, I see," said Mr. Hopkins, who saw nothing. There was something in Mrs. Mather's manner and voice which discouraged further questioning.

She stretched out a hand to the table and picked up a letter. "This has just come for Carl by tonight's post and I don't rightly know what to do with it."

"You can send it on to him, can't you?" Mr. Hopkins suggested.

"I don't know his address."

"Then you'll have to keep it till he comes back."

"But it's marked 'Urgent'." Mrs. Mather gave Mr. Hopkins the letter.

He read the address and then twisted the envelope so that he could decipher the postmark. "Brickwell," he said. "Where's that?"

"I'm sure I don't know. And I don't know who it's from neither. Do you think I ought to open it."

Mr. Hopkins pouted his lips. "That wouldn't hardly be right, seeing it's meant for Carl." And then his curiosity got the better of his principles. "Of course it is urgent and that makes a difference."

"That's what I was thinking," said Mrs. Mather.

Mr. Hopkins's hopes rose. "But as Carl didn't leave his address I can't see as he can blame you if you were to open it."

Mrs. Mather took the letter from Mr. Hopkins. "I don't like to but it's hard to know what to do for the best."

"I'd chance it if I was you," said Mr. Hopkins.

"All right. Then I will." Mrs. Mather took a knitting-needle out of her ball of wool and slit the envelope. She drew out a single sheet of notepaper and handed it to Mr. Hopkins, saying, "You read it. My eyes aren't so good these days."

Mr. Hopkins was not backward. He held up the sheet to the light of the lamp on the table. "It's from the Bull Hotel, Brickwell, and it starts:

"Dear Carl,

"I am here at a place called Brickwel and i have lost the munney you gave me which makes it very hard for me seeing i have nothing to pay wot i owes so will you please send by return sum more munney it would not be nice for you if i was to tell wot i knows."

Mr. Hopkins stopped reading and Mrs. Mather leaned forward in her chair. "Who's it from?"

"That's what I'm trying to make out," answered Mr. Hopkins. "It's difficult to read, the writing's that niggley." He got up and spread the letter on the table under the lamp. "I can make out a 'T'. That's clear enough."

Mrs. Mather said: "I can't think who it could be."

"Stevens! Tubby Stevens! That's who it is." Mr. Hopkins was as excited as a boy who has found a long-lost sixpence in the lining of his coat.

"What do you think we ought to do, Mr. Hopkins?" Mrs. Mather asked anxiously. "I don't like to think of that poor man stranded in—what is the name of the place?"

"Brickwell," replied Mr. Hopkins. "But I shouldn't worry about him if I was you."

"I gave Carl all the money I had in the house before he went away and unless I borrow it . . ." She looked at Mr. Hopkins, but he did not respond to the unspoken request.

"Don't you think no more about Tubby Stevens. He ain't worth it," said Mr. Hopkins. "And now I really must be off or I don't know what folks'll be saying about me."

Mr. Hopkins did not take his own advice. As he walked down Hawkin's Court his mind was full of the letter and Tubby Stevens, for he scented a mystery. Before he came to the end of the street he remembered what Tubby had said to him that night at the stall. "If it hadn't been for the old codger we'd ha' been in twelve hours sooner. He wouldn't let us start up the main engines till the hold was dry." At the time, the remark had puzzled him, but he'd been too busy to think about it.

"There was something happened aboard that there old *Ivanhoe* that never came out at the inquest," Mr. Hopkins said to himself. Tubby's last words in the letter were clearly a threat to Carl that if he didn't send money he, Tubby, would give Carl away.

As he took down the shutters on his stall Mr. Hopkins tried hard to think of the answer and went on worrying as he lit the burners under the urns. After that he was too busy serving out tea and coffee and meat pies to bother any more about Tubby Stevens, and it was not until the flow of custom eased that he was able to give the problem his full attention. The easiest way out was to tell the police and leave it to them to deal with the matter, he finally decided.

The desk-sergeant at the police-station was reading the latest sports news when Mr. Hopkins came in. He took down Mr. Hopkins's name and address, though he knew them well enough already. "Now, what is it you want to tell me?"

Spoken slowly and in time to the sergeant's slow-moving pen, the story which Mr. Hopkins had to tell did not sound half so exciting as it had when he had rehearsed it in his own mind. When he had finished he wondered if he hadn't been a fool to waste his time like this.

"All right. Take a seat there while I get on to the inspector," the sergeant said, and lifted the receiver of his 'phone.

He was some time getting on to Pollitt, and Mr. Hopkins had ample opportunity for examining the inside of a police-station. He had never been in one before and experienced a thrill when he saw four pairs of handcuffs hanging on a green, baize-covered board over the fireplace.

"I've got a man here, Hopkins is the name, who says he knows something about Tubby Stevens." The sergeant gave a summary of Mr. Hopkins's statement, was silent for a minute while the receiver clacked, then said: "Very well, I'll keep him." He put down the receiver and turned to Mr. Hopkins. "The inspector's coming down. He wants to have a word with you."

Mr. Hopkins began to be sorry that he had ever come to the police-station.

A quarter of an hour later there was an angry humming outside, a door slammed and footsteps on the pavement told of Inspector Pollitt's arrival in his eight-horse-power buzz-box.

He looked at Mr. Hopkins much as a scientist might regard a new type of beetle. "Your name's Hopkins, is it?"

Mr. Hopkins said it was.

Pollitt read the statement through. "Why didn't you say anything about this before?"

"I didn't think there was anything in it."

"Has Mrs. Mather sent any money?"

"No."

"Have you heard anything more? Has there been any talk round your stall?"

"No."

Pollitt took a pouch from his pocket and began to fill a pipe. "I want you to forget all you've told me, but keep your ears open, and if you hear anything about Tubby Stevens or any of the others who were on board the *Ivanhoe*, let me know."

Mr. Hopkins said the inspector could rely on him, and went home.

"He's a proper old gasbag, that man," was the sergeant's comment when Mr. Hopkins had gone.

Pollitt took a telegraph-form from a drawer. He addressed it to Stevens, Bull Hotel, Brickwell, and wrote in the body of the form, "Impossible send money as asked", and signed it "Carl".

Then he put through a call to the police at Brickwell and spoke with them for fully ten minutes. When he was satisfied that his instructions were understood he put down the receiver and sent a constable to fetch Detective-Constable Kent.

When Kent arrived Pollitt gave him Mr. Hopkins's statement to read. "You'll see that he says there that Carl Swanson has gone to Newcastle."

When he had read the last line Kent said: "I wonder why he did that?"

"It's got me guessing," Pollitt replied. "And until we can get something out of this man Stevens, I don't see what we can do. Anyway you'd better check up on Swanson's movements. Try and find out what train he went by. I'll get through to Newcastle and tell them to trail him when he arrives."

When he left Mrs. Mather's house Carl walked to the station by way of the High Street and Station Road, which were crowded at that time of night.

He joked with the man in the ticket-office when he bought a ticket for Newcastle, and while he waited for the train to come in he stood under a lamp. But when the train drew in the desire for publicity faded and he got into an empty third-class carriage.

The train was a slow one and, according to the time-table, was not due to reach Newcastle until a quarter to ten, but Carl did not settle down on a seat. He stood at the off-side window looking out until the train started.

A quarter of an hour later it drew up at a wayside halt. Carl turned the handle of the door and opened it an inch or two. A porter with his back to him was walking down the train calling out the name of the halt.

Carl opened the door, stepped out on to the platform and ran quickly a few yards to the shelter of a bush growing on the edge of a grass embankment. From far down the train came the faint shrill of the guard's whistle, and slowly the string of lighted carriages slid past.

The way was clear now; over the line and over a fence; across a field and he would be on the road which led back to Gilboro'. There were five miles to go, and a fine rain spilling from the low clouds was driving in his face and soaking into his coat, but he didn't care.

He walked quickly with his long swinging stride, his shoulders bent and the brim of his hat pulled down over his eyes. For a couple of miles he followed the road which ran parallel to the railway and then turned left-handed down a track which led across the marshes.

It was rutted and the thick mud pulled at his feet; there was a string of gates to be opened and shut. He stopped for a breather in the lee of a marshman's hut and lit a cigarette. The wind, whipping round the corner of the hut, blew the tip to a fierce red glow. The smoke tasted hot. "Might as well go on," he muttered.

"No use stopping here." He threw away the cigarette and left it glowing as he plunged on through the mud. "Not a blooming light to steer by, I wish to hell I hadn't come this way."

Somewhere ahead was the sea, somewhere on the right was the river. Overhead the clouds blotted out the stars.

And then over the sandhills showed dimly the loom of the bar lighthouse. Three flashes.

"I'm all right," Carl said to himself. "I've got my bearings now."

The track ended in a brimming dyke. Carl turned right and jumped a ditch. He could see the Martello tower silhouetted against the sky; if he kept it on his port bow he'd strike the path on the sea-wall which led to the Pride of Bedford.

As he approached the house on the piles and called out there came no answering cry. The door on the landward side was ajar; he kicked it open. Inside it was as black as the pit. He struck a match and leaned back on the door to shut it; the match flared up and he saw a table, two hard chairs and a chest.

Above the table a lamp hung in a bracket.

The match burned down to his fingers; he dropped it, glowing red, and swore.

The chimney of the lamp felt ice-cold to his fingers as he raised it and rubbed a finger over the charred wick.

As he waited in the dim light for the glass to warm, Carl looked round the room. It was as bare as a hermit's cell. True there was the table, the two chairs, a bunk built in to a wall, and on the walls photographs torn from papers, but that was all the furnishing there was.

Then, as he turned up the wick and as the light from it grew stronger, he saw a cup on the table, half filled with tea and covered with a film of curdled milk; a plate on which two rinds of bacon and a skirting of white of egg had congealed in greenish grease.

Depression, complete and all-enveloping, fell on Carl, and, for a moment, he thought of going back into the night, back on to the marsh. He began to feel afraid of Tom Ingleby. He fumbled for the note Mrs. Mather had given him, brought it out, crumpled and dirty, and threw it on the table.

Now he was here he might as well stop. It was too late to go anywhere else, and, besides, he was wet through. He pulled off his coat and hung it on the back of a chair. As he did so he saw a stove in a corner of the room. A stove! Fire! Warmth!

The ashes were cold; he raked them out into a pan. In a box at the back of the stove was splintered driftwood and a pile of newspapers.

Soon he had flames leaping high in the stove and he held his hands outspread to the blaze. He did not hear footsteps on the path outside, nor the creaking of the door as it opened.

Tom Ingleby had been down in the creek setting his eel-nets, for the tide was making and it was the period of full moon.

He lengthened his stride when he came in sight of the Pride and saw a sliver of light shining out of a window on a tussock of marram grass.

When he saw Carl kneeling before the stove he felt a tightening in his breast and for a moment he stood without speaking. Then he said: "Good evening."

Carl swung round on his heels and looked up into the black-bearded face of the owner of the Pride of Bedford. Then he got on to his feet and said: "I'm sorry to come in like this but—"

The booming voice of Tom Ingleby said: "That's all right, Mr. Swanson."

"You know me."

"I've read about you in the papers."

Carl was as absurdly pleased as a child and for the moment forgot that he was a fugitive. He picked up Mrs. Mather's note and handed it to Tom Ingleby. "That'll explain."

Slowly Tom unfolded the paper and slowly spelled out the words, speaking them half aloud. When he had finished he gave it back to Carl. "That's all right. You can stop here as long as you like, and if you want to lie up there's the tower."

Carl felt unexpectedly humble in the presence of Tom Ingleby. He said: "Thanks very much. I hope it won't be for long."

"As you've got the stove going we might as well have supper." Tom Ingleby opened a cupboard door. "There's bacon and there's a mess of tripe which only wants heating up. What'll you have?"

"Tripe," said Carl. He was too tired to care what he ate. All he wanted to do was to turn in.

Out in the river a ship's whistle was moaning. Tom Ingleby walked to a window. "Sounds to me like the *Penrith Castle*." Two minutes later he said: "Yes, it's her all right."

And Carl felt a strong envy for the captain of the *Penrith Castle*, and a smile crossed his face as he remembered that day, not so very long ago, when he'd passed the Pride of Bedford outward bound on board the *John Goodwin*. He had been contemptuous then of the owner of this derelict boat-yard with its rotting slips and crazy wharf—a failure!

And now he was glad enough to seek sanctuary in the very house he had derided. He had laughed at the name, Pride of Bedford.

Tom Ingleby said: "Mrs. Mather's not too well."

"She's all right."

"She didn't look too good to me when I saw her this afternoon."

And then Carl realized what he had not appreciated at the time, that Mrs. Mather had looked ill, really ill when he had left her. He had been so intent on his own trouble that he'd had no time to notice that of anyone else. "She's getting on, that's all there is to it," he said defensively.

"Maybe," replied Tom Ingleby; he picked up the cup and plate and carried them out of the room.

16

MR. INNES WAS GETTING ready to go home when the evening post came in. He had put his pince-nez in their case, had wiped his pen and put it in its place on the rack and had tidied the papers on his desk.

"They can wait till the morning," he said to his clerk, who laid three letters on his blotter.

And then he saw the spidery blotted writing of Jessie Miles: "Mister Innes, Solicitor. Gilboro'."

"What's this, Smith?" he said, and picked up the envelope gingerly by one corner.

"I'm sure I can't say, sir."

"And no stamp. Very curious."

Mr. Innes dropped the envelope and brooded over it. It was past six o'clock and high time he was on his way home. Two friends were coming in after supper for a rubber of bridge, and his wife would be cross if he were late. Still he peered at the letter. He opened his spectacle-case and put his glasses on the end of his nose. He had never had a letter quite like this before. And without a stamp! He worked his right thumb under the flap, tore it apart and drew out a sheet of paper, pink and smelling of scent.

"I think you ought to know," Mr. Innes read, *"that there was a man on board the* Ivanhoe. *It was the captain and his name is MacTaggart."*

"MacTaggart," repeated Mr. Innes. "Yes, that's right. He was the captain. Dear me, what does this mean?" He read on. *"He was on the ship for a day after Carl Swanson got to her. He fell over the side of the* Ivanhoe *by acident."* Mr. Innes pursed his lips at the misspelling. *"The boat was on her way to Gilboro' and it wasn't nobody's fault except his because he leaned on a rail and it broke."*

There was no signature.

Mr. Innes didn't like it. He turned over the sheet, found nothing written on the back, and dropped it on the blotter. Then he studied the address on the envelope, but that conveyed nothing to him.

It was awkward, very awkward. Mr. Innes took off his pince-nez and put them back in their case. Ought he to show Fleming the letter? And, if he did, what effect would it have on the claim he was making on behalf of Carl Swanson?

By no stretch of imagination could it be considered as evidence, but it would put Fleming on inquiry, and one never knew what the result of that might be.

But if it came to that he, Mr. Innes, was of the opinion that Fleming already suspected that the story told by Carl Swanson was not the true one. There was that letter offering to settle the claim out of court for two thousand pounds.

Mr. Innes did not like Mr. Fleming, nor did he approve of his method of conducting a case. He locked Jessie Miles's letter in a drawer and put on his bowler hat and raincoat. He'd sleep on it and make a decision in the morning. Meanwhile he'd have to hurry if he wasn't going to be late for supper.

He was hurrying along the High Street when a man who had crossed the road stepped in front of him. It was Carl Swanson. He didn't recognize Mr. Innes and Mr. Innes made no effort to speak to him. He saw Carl turn into the station yard.

"Wonder where he's off to?" muttered Mr. Innes, and then thought of something else.

The wire dispatched by Inspector Pollitt was delivered at the Bull Hotel when Tubby was sitting down to breakfast.

Elsie brought it in. "A telegram for you, Mr. Stevens, and the boy's waiting for an answer."

Tubby's hand was trembling as he clumsily tore open the flap. The flimsy paper rustled as he read the message.

Impossible send money as asked. Carl.

He read it again. The utter finality of the refusal robbed him of all power of thought. He didn't even hear the fat woman asking if it was bad news.

"Are you feeling all right, Mr. Stevens?" He heard her this time and forced himself to reply. "No. It's nothing." He crumpled the telegram and thrust it into his pocket.

And Bill was coming at lunch-time! He'd got to get out of Brickwell. His health would suffer if he stayed.

Unfortunately for the success of this project the fat woman had become suspicious and greedy for the money Tubby owed her. She was very forceful about it. Five shillings and ninepence was the price she demanded for Tubby's freedom, and if she didn't get it he could just stop in the house till Bill came home.

Bravely Tubby replied that she was making a lot of fuss about nothing and said he was expecting money by the next post.

"That's as it may be," said the fat woman sourly, as she locked the front door and put the key in her pocket.

Then help came in the most unlikely form—a police-officer in plain clothes. He came to the back door and said that he'd like a word with Mr. Stevens.

Elsie said vaguely that she didn't know and fetched the fat woman who stated belligerently that: "Mr. Stevens don't go out of this house till he's paid me my money."

The police-officer explained that he had come for the very purpose of liquidating the debt, but, of course, he put it rather differently. The effect, however, was the same, and Tubby was soon out in the street drinking in the free but soot-laden air of Brickwell.

"I must say that's real handsome of you, mate," said Tubby. A man bearing a close resemblance to Bill was coming down the street. "And just in time, too," he added, and lit a cigarette. He was beginning to feel better already. "Now all I wants is to get out of this damn' town. It's giving me the willies."

"If you come along to the station, I'll buy you a ticket to Gilboro'."

"You'll buy me a ticket to Gilboro'?"

"That's right. If you promise to go there."

Then Tubby remembered Carl and said: "I want to go to Birmingham."

"Would it make any difference if I was to tell you that Carl Swanson has gone to Newcastle?"

"How do you know that?"

"It's true enough. We got word last night."

Tubby took his hat off and ran his fingers through his hair. "If I thought that was right . . ." he muttered.

"The police in Gilboro' want to ask you a few questions, but you've got nothing to be afraid of. If you had I wouldn't be letting you go on your own."

"And if I don't go to Gilboro', what happens then?"

"That'd be up to you, but as you're broke I should think you wouldn't have too easy a time. If you go back the police'll give you something to carry on with till you find a job."

This was a side of the police-force of which Tubby had never before had experience. He said: "Well, I don't know what to make of all this. You comes along just when I'm in a bit of bother. You pays my bill and now you offers me money to get back home with." He thought for a moment and then asked suddenly: "You ain't got nothing on me, have yer?"

"I tell you if we had you'd be under arrest now."

"Yes, I suppose that's right. And you give me your word, cross your heart and hope to die, that Carl Swanson ain't in Gilboro'?"

"Yes, of course I do."

"All right. I'll go."

17

MR. INNES ARRIVED at his office at ten o'clock sharp to find Inspector Pollitt sitting in his room smoking a pipe.

Mr. Innes sniffed and then said: "Good morning."

Pollitt pulled himself out of his chair. "I must apologize for this early morning call, Mr. Innes, but there's rather an important matter I wish to consult you about."

Mr. Innes said: "Oh yes, quite," and sat down at his desk.

"It's about a client of yours, Carl Swanson. Do you know where he is now?"

"At his home, I expect," replied Mr. Innes.

"No, he isn't," said Pollitt bluntly. "He caught the six-forty train last night for Newcastle, but he didn't get there."

"Swanson! Now let me see." Mr. Innes rested his chin on his hand. "I saw him last night as I was on my way home. He went into the station and the time was about half past six."

"Was he alone?"

"Oh yes. And he was carrying a bundle."

"Do you remember how he was dressed?"

"I'm afraid I don't. You see I was in rather a hurry because we were going to have a rubber of bridge after supper and—"

"Did you speak to him?" Pollitt interrupted.

"No, I didn't."

"Had he told you at any time that he was thinking of leaving Gilboro'?"

"No. I hadn't seen him since the day of the inquest. By the way, may I ask what is the purpose of this inquiry?"

"Oh, I just want a word with him, that's all. A question has been raised and, though I have not much reason to believe that there's anything in it, I want to get an answer to it."

"Has this question got anything to do with the salving of the *Ivanhoe*, by any chance?"

"As a matter of fact it has. Why?"

Mr. Innes took a key-ring from his pocket, selected a key and unlocked a drawer. "In that case perhaps you would like to see this." He pushed the anonymous letter across the desk.

Pollitt read it. "When did you get this?"

"By last night's post. Here's the envelope it came in."

"I'll keep it if you don't mind."

"You're very welcome, Inspector. And I don't mind telling you that I should be very glad to get out of this case. There are certain aspects of it which I do not—er—like."

"What do you mean?"

"Well, it's not easy to put into words, for I have no facts to go on, but I have a feeling that Mr. Swanson has not told me the whole truth."

"You mean you believe that MacTaggart was on board the *Ivanhoe* when Swanson came up to her?"

"Suspect," corrected Mr. Innes. "It's no more than a suspicion, and it would never have occurred to me but for this letter. Of course it is absurd to place any reliance on it, but sometimes one is ruled by one's instinct rather than by cold reason."

It was Pollitt's turn to agree. He was satisfied that he had got all he could out of this very dry solicitor and was anxious to get back to the station and continue the inquiry. He thanked Mr. Innes for the help he had given him and hurried from the office.

Kent was waiting for him with the news that Tubby Stevens was on his way back to Gilboro'.

"That's good," Pollitt replied. "Now I think we'll get some-where." He took the anonymous letter from his wallet. "Innes got this last night."

When he had read it, Kent said: "Well, that confirms Hopkins's story." He examined the postmark. "Posted at dinner-time yesterday."

"Yes, and now we've got to go right ahead. Get out a description of Carl Swanson. 'Wanted for questioning in connection with the salvage of the S.S. *Ivanhoe*.' You know how it ought to go."

When Kent had left the room Pollitt sent out men to watch Dan Todd and Larry Hicks. "If they try to make a getaway arrest 'em," Pollitt ordered.

Then he went to Mr. Fleming's office.

Mr. Fleming was dictating letters when the inspector was announced. He said to his clerk: "I'll finish them later. Ask Mr. Pollitt to come in."

His piggy eyes were bright when he welcomed Pollitt and asked him to take the comfortable chair. "Have you got news about Stevens?"

"He's coming back today. We expect him about noon, and I think I know why he went away."

"That's interesting," said Mr. Fleming, and pushed a box of cigarettes across his desk. Then he leant back in his swivel chair till the spring groaned in protest.

Pollitt spoke quickly. He told of Tubby's remark about the "old codger" having prevented Carl starting up the main engines of the *Ivanhoe* before the hold had been pumped out, and of the anonymous letter received by Mr. Innes. "It looks as though MacTaggart had been on board when Carl arrived in his trawler."

"I've thought that ever since the inquest."

"Why?" asked Pollitt.

"Well, the first thing that made me suspicious was the fact that Carl Swanson told two different stories about the height of the water in the fore-hold. If the level had been, in fact, four feet below the coamings when he boarded the ship, that could only have been effected by pumping. Pennington said that the hold was awash when he left the *Ivanhoe*.

"The inference was that MacTaggart, who had been left behind, had done the pumping. And then there was that evidence of the position of the body when it was picked up. If it was correct and Pennington's recollection of the place of abandonment was accurate, then either the body had drifted approximately forty miles, or MacTaggart had fallen over the side after the *Ivanhoe* had been manned by Carl Swanson and his crew and had steamed that distance.

"And I've got evidence here which supports Pennington's statement." Mr. Fleming took from an envelope two full plate photographs. "This one is an ultra-violet photograph of the deck log of the *Ivanhoe*, the other an ordinary photograph."

"Ultra-violet light? What's that?"

"It's difficult to explain but the effect is that this type of light, which is invisible to the human eye, shows up the ridges and indentations made by pencil-writing on paper—even after the grains of graphite deposited by the pencil have been entirely removed."

Pollitt said: "Yes, I understand"—doubtfully.

"As a matter of fact there are traces of graphite still remaining, embedded in the fibres of the paper."

"I can't see any."

"No, you need a microscope for that. But the important thing is to compare these two reproductions." Mr. Fleming got up and leaned over his desk. "Look here."

"You mean these white lines?"

"Yes. You can read figures."

"What do they mean?"

"They give the position of the *Ivanhoe* at the time of her abandonment."

Pollitt looked at Mr. Fleming for ten seconds. Then he said: "Does it agree with what Pennington told us?"

"Yes."

Pollitt examined the photographs again. "Of course if these are going to be any use to us we shall have to get expert evidence on them."

"I can arrange that," replied Mr. Fleming.

"I'm very much obliged to you for taking all this trouble."

"Well, I am not entirely disinterested in this matter. The present owner of the *Ivanhoe* is my client."

Pollitt looked at his watch. "It's time I was getting along. That man Stevens is due in half an hour."

That man Stevens sat in the corner of a third-class carriage of a train which bore him swiftly to Gilboro'. He was glad enough to get away from Brickwell, but he would much rather have been travelling in the opposite direction.

The thought of Carl and the memory of his own dispatch from the town raised a groan. The two other occupants of the carriage dealt him two startled glances. One of them glanced at the communication cord above his head.

"He's acted funny all the way," thought the woman in the opposite corner. "Sitting there mumbling to hisself and tapping with his fingers on his knees." She clutched the handle of her umbrella so tightly that there were spots of white on each one of her knuckles. It was a fast train, too, and there was no stop before they got to Gilboro'.

If she regretted that fact, Tubby regretted it more. He looked out of the window and saw the Gilboro' river and the roof-tops and smoke of the town. He also saw the close-packed masts of the fishing-fleet and shut his eyes.

Three minutes later the train ground to a stop in Gilboro' station, and Tubby got out and made a bee-line for the exit. He had an idea of losing himself somewhere where neither the police nor Carl Swanson could find him.

But Kent knew his job. He also knew Tubby from his photograph, and as Tubby approached the gate he put a hand on his shoulder. "You're Stevens, aren't you?"

Tubby said he was. He never had liked policemen and he did not enjoy his free ride to the police-station one little bit. He did, however, manage to work up a grin for the benefit of the sergeant, but it faded when he was pushed into the presence of Inspector Pollitt.

Pollitt had put on his "Now don't try any tricks with me" expression, and barked, "Sit down." Then he went on writing, and Tubby sat rigid in his chair. Five times he wetted his lips with his tongue and tried to think pleasant thoughts, but Pollitt was too much for his imagination. He coughed and swallowed and looked at the ceiling and the floor, and at a notice pinned on the wall which was too far away to read.

Pollitt finished a page, put down his pen and thumped blotting-paper over what he had written. Then he put his elbows on the desk and glared at Tubby. "You're in a bit of a mess, Stevens."

Tubby opened his mouth, but no sound came out of it.

"It'll be a lot better for you if you tell me all about it. I want to know what happened on board the *Ivanhoe*."

"Nothing," Tubby mumbled. "We brought her in. That's all."

"You knew MacTaggart, didn't you?"

"I've never set eyes on the man."

"Oh yes, you have. He was the captain of the *Ivanhoe*, and he was on that ship when you and the others went aboard her. I know that."

The man was bluffing, Tubby told himself. All he'd got to do was to deny the truth of the suggestion and everything would be all right. "There wasn't a living soul on board that ship when we got to her. I'll swear that."

"Now just wait a minute. Isn't this what happened? You went on board and found Captain MacTaggart there. All that first night was spent in pumping out the hold. Carl Swanson wanted to get under way, but MacTaggart wouldn't agree to that till the hold was dry. Next morning the ship was got under way, and at some time during the following night MacTaggart fell over the side. No one saw him go, but one of the bridge rails was found to be broken."

"I never saw MacTaggart on board the *Ivanhoe*."

"Well, perhaps you didn't actually see him, but you knew he was there. Perhaps he stayed in his cabin."

"No, he didn't. I mean he wasn't anywhere in the ship."

"How can you say that? Did you search the ship?"

"No, of course I didn't." Tubby's confidence was returning slowly and he began to find speech less difficult.

"Someone saw him there," said Pollitt. He produced the letter written by Jessie Miles and folded it so that only a few lines could be seen. "Read that."

Tubby leaned forward in his chair. He spelled out the words slowly, *"I think you ought to know that there was a man on board the* Ivanhoe. . . . *He was on the ship for a day after Carl got to her. . . ."* Tubby looked up. His lips were trembling. "Who wrote that?" he muttered.

"That doesn't matter. It's the truth, isn't it?"

"Was it Larry?"

"Come on, Stevens. Let's have it straight. MacTaggart was on board when you got there. Now, wasn't he?" Pollitt dropped his bullying tone. "You've got nothing to be afraid of."

"Then what are you asking all these questions for?"

"I just want to get the true story, that's all. There's been a lot of talk, and we've got to stop it." Pollitt opened a packet of cigarettes and held it out. Tubby took a cigarette and lit it. He read the remainder of the letter.

Pollitt said: "If this is true and MacTaggart did fall over the side by accident, there's nothing for you to worry about."

"Do you mean that?" There was a world of relief in Tubby's voice.

"Of course I do."

Tubby thought for a minute, tapped ash into a saucer on the desk and, without looking up, said: "It is true. What that letter says—every word of it. It was on the Thursday night we came up with the *Ivanhoe*. The skipper was on board and him and Carl did have a bit of a argument about putting steam on the engines. I didn't see him hardly at all, because I was helping down in the stoke-hold, and a blooming awful job that was."

"Did you see MacTaggart any time during the next day?"

"Yes, I think I did, but I never spoke to him. The last time was when he came into the saloon and I gave him supper. He took it straight along to his cabin."

"What did you do after that?"

"I had my chow, and when we'd all finished I took the dishes to the galley and cleaned them."

"And it was on that night that MacTaggart fell over the side?"

"Yes, that's right. Next morning Carl told us he'd gone, and Larry told me that there was a rail bust on the bridge and said that was how he must have gone."

"Were you turned in all night?"

"No blooming fear. I was stoking most of the first watch."

"I suppose that was pretty hard work, with the ship rolling?"

"No, it weren't so bad. She'd steadied down a lot and was just holding her starboard list."

"Where were you before you went to the stoke-hold?"

"In my cabin on the boat-deck."

"Did you hear anything when you were there?"

"No. I was asleep from the time I got me head down till Dan Todd came and turned me out."

"Right. Now we'll get all this down in writing, and I'll get you to sign it."

One hour later Tubby walked down the steps of the police-station. There was a smile on his face, for he had a ten-shilling note in his pocket and had received the assurance that Carl Swanson was not in Gilboro'. He had his zither under his arm.

Mr. Hopkins saw Tubby as he was steering a straight course for the "Keel and Barge", and so far forgot his dignity as to call out to him. But the call of beer was strong, and Tubby only waved an arm and kept his course and speed.

Mr. Hopkins knew how a tiger feels when he sees a fat sheep outside his cage. There was no one he could leave in charge, and if he didn't follow Tubby he would only get the story second-hand.

And if that wasn't bad enough, Dan Todd and Larry Hicks hove in sight, accompanied by Detective-Constable Kent. They were heading for the police-station. "Things are moving," he muttered, and gave tuppence too much change to a fish-porter.

Dan Todd hid his nervousness beneath his customary sick-horse expression. Larry looked stupid because he was afraid.

Pollitt came into the charge-room and chose Larry as his first victim. When he had got him into the chair lately vacated by Tubby he said: "Stevens has told me everything. I've got his statement here." He pointed to a paper on his desk. "And it'll save you both and me a lot of time if you do the same."

"You mean about the skipper of the *Ivanhoe*?"

"Exactly."

"I've been wanting to speak about it the last day or two, and Jessie said it was the best thing to do, but Carl said we was to keep mum and so—"

"And so you didn't bother. But Carl's run out on you. We can't find a trace of him."

"I heard that—last night."

"Did you see him before he went?"

"No."

"What was the talk you had with him the day before, down by the goods yard?"

Larry's eyes opened wide. "How did you know about that?"

"You came near to a scrap, the two of you. What was it about?"

"Tubby Stevens. I thought Carl had done him in, and I told him I was going to chuck the whole business even if it meant losing my share in the *Ivanhoe*."

"What did Carl say to that?"

"We had a drink and a talk, and I agreed not to do anything."

"And why did you want to forgo your share?"

"Because the story we'd told wasn't true. The *Ivanhoe* never was a derelict. Her skipper was on board all the time until—"

"He fell over the side the night after you boarded her; when you were on the way back here to Gilboro'."

"That's right." Larry relaxed in his chair. His relief was obvious.

Pollitt followed up his advantage. "Then I suppose you'll have no objection to telling me what happened on the day MacTaggart disappeared."

"There's nothing much to tell. I don't think I set eyes on MacTaggart after four o'clock in the afternoon. He was on the bridge, then. Next morning Carl—"

"Where did you sleep that night?"

"In a cabin next to Tubby Stevens on the boat-deck. I kept the morning watch, and Carl called me at four o'clock. I lashed the wheel at eight, as the ship was steering well and there was nothing in sight, and I came down for breakfast."

"Who was in the saloon, then?"

"Nobody. I sat there and smoked a cigarette, and after a little while I heard the skylight rattling. I'd lashed it up the day before with a bit of cod-line, but—"

"Cod-line!" said Pollitt.

"Yes." Larry was surprised at the interjection. "Why?"

"Oh, nothing. Go on."

"The catch on the light had snapped off short and every time the ship rolled it lifted."

"And the lashing you'd put on had come adrift?"

"There wasn't a sign of it on that skylight, so I went along to the store and cut another length and put it on the same place. When I was finishing the job Carl came down."

"When did Carl tell you that MacTaggart had gone?"

"As soon as he came into the saloon."

"Can you remember his exact words?"

"No. He just said that MacTaggart had fallen over the side sometime in the night. I told Tubby."

"When did you know that the bridge rail had been broken?"

"It was some time in the forenoon, after we'd had our breakfast, that Carl showed me where the rail lanyard had carried away. It was after we'd altered course."

"Why did you alter course?" Pollitt asked.

"Well, in the first place when MacTaggart was alive, him and Carl had agreed to make for the Thames and we steered for the

Edinburgh lightship. After MacTaggart had gone Carl said we'd make straight for Gilboro'."

"What was the weather like at that time?"

"The sea had gone down a lot. Of course we still had a heavy list to starboard, but the ship wasn't moving much; pitching a bit to the swell that was all."

"What time are you talking about?"

"From supper-time on the first day onwards."

"There was something rubbed out in the deck log. Did you do that?"

"No, I never touched the log. It was Carl done that."

"Why?"

"He didn't say, but I knew that wasn't going to do any good seeing as MacTaggart had a log in his own cabin."

"Did you tell Carl that?"

"No. I didn't think about it at the time. It wasn't till we were back in Gilboro' that I said anything to him about it, and that's why he tried to break into the skipper's cabin when the ship was in the dock."

"So that's who it was!" Pollitt said. "I thought it might have been Tubby Stevens when he disappeared."

"Carl made Tubby clear out in case he gave the show away."

"I see," said Pollitt. "That's very interesting."

"By the way, where is the log which MacTaggart kept?"

"I don't know. I only saw it the once in his cabin."

"Was it like the log which was kept on the bridge?"

"No. It was a little book, no bigger than a piece of notepaper."

"Wait a minute." Pollitt got up and went into the charge-room. "Get me Mr. Fleming on the 'phone," he said to the sergeant. "And put him through to my office."

Then he went back to his office and said to Larry: "Now is there anything else you've got to tell me?"

Larry said he thought he'd told everything.

"All right, then you can wait outside."

18

POLLITT SAT DOWN at his desk and fiddled with a pencil. If MacTaggart had fallen over the side by accident, as all the evidence tended to show, then why had Carl run away? The worst that could happen to him would be that his claim for salvage might fail on the grounds of fraud.

Then the 'phone bell rang and he lifted the receiver. "Good afternoon, Fleming, Pollitt here. . . . Do you know anything about a small notebook which MacTaggart used as a log . . . ? A notebook, yes. Quite small. . . . Thank you." He put down the receiver.

Mr. Fleming got up from his chair with the speed and the agility of a much younger and lighter man and walked to the window. He picked up a bundle of books and put them on his desk.

"A small notebook," he muttered to himself as he shuffled through the books. They were for the most part textbooks on navigation and seamanship; there was a tattered copy of the *Channel Pilot*, and—"Hullo, what's this?"

"This" was a yellow-covered notebook. On the outside in ink was written in a schoolboy, copybook hand, "Cargo". As he turned the pages, he remembered having looked at it on the day of the inquest. His eye skimmed the entries relating to so many tons of cargo loaded, so many tons discharged. "Nothing here," he muttered, and then as he turned a page he said: "Well I'm jiggered!"

Nov. 25th.

7.15 p.m. Party from *John Goodwin* boarded ship. 10.15 p.m. Commenced pumping number one hold. Wind N.W. Heavy swell and sea.

Nov. 26th.

7.30 p.m. Drained number one hold. Steam on main engines. Set course for Edinburgh light-vessel. W. by N. 10 a.m. Ship proceeding at slow speed. Estimated speed 2½ knots. 4 p.m. Wind moderating and veering to southward. 8 p.m. Wind a light breeze from S.S.W.

That was all.

"Damn' fool I was to have missed this. I wonder what put Pollitt on the track." Mr. Fleming turned over the remaining pages of the book but they were blank. "If we can prove this is MacTaggart's writing we're on velvet."

He shut the book and got up and put on his hat.

Dan Todd, as yet unsummoned and unquestioned, gave Mr. Fleming a fraction of an uninterested glance as he came into the charge-room.

Mechanically the sergeant asked, "What name, please?" Then he recognized Mr. Fleming and said, "Will you please go straight in. The inspector's expecting you."

Fleming nodded and drove through the doorway. He threw the notebook down in front of Pollitt. "That's what you want. It ties it all up. MacTaggart was—"

Pollitt said: "One minute," and got up and shut the door. "We don't want everyone to hear about it." He picked up the notebook.

Mr. Fleming said: "You'll find the material entry near the end," and leaned back in his chair and tapped with his fingers on his knee.

"This is clear evidence." Pollitt looked up from his examination of the notebook. "Now we're getting somewhere."

"It's what I've thought all along," Mr. Fleming said smugly. "From the first minute I heard Swanson speak I knew he was a liar."

"There was that broken rail," Pollitt said half aloud. "I suppose that's how MacTaggart went. It must have been an accident."

"A very lucky accident—for Swanson."

"Yes, but how do we know that it isn't the true explanation?"

"We don't. At least I don't," said Mr. Fleming, "but I shall resist all claims made against the ship and what's more I shall succeed. I'm looking forward to seeing Innes' face when he sees this log."

Pollitt said yes, absently, and wrote a few words on a clean sheet of paper. Then he put down his pen. "Well, I'm much obliged to you, Mr. Fleming." He got up and held out his hand.

Mr. Fleming took it reluctantly, for he would have liked to have stayed and found out all that was in Pollitt's mind. He had, however, no alternative but to accept his dismissal.

When he had gone Pollitt sent for Dan Todd, who came into the room with extreme caution as into the cage of a very hungry man-eating lion.

When he was uncomfortably seated Pollitt took the first sheet of Tubby's statements and read extracts from it. He did the same from that of Larry's and concluded by reading the log which Mr. Fleming had produced. Then he arranged the papers in a neat pile and looked at Dan, who was staring woodenly at his own feet. "What have you got to say?"

Dan detached his gaze from his toes and transferred it to the top of the desk. "You seem to have got it all," he muttered.

Pollitt said: "Yes. But I'd like to hear your version of what happened when MacTaggart went over the side."

"I don't know nothing more."

"I dare say, but I'd like to check over one or two points with you. First of all, where were you on the night when MacTaggart went over the side?"

"Up and down between my cabin and the stoke-hold. I was keeping an eye on the pumps and stoking the fires."

"Stevens said that he kept the first watch in the boiler-room. Is that right?"

"He did."

"Where were you at that time?"

"In my bunk, asleep."

"Where was that?"

"At the after-end of the boat-deck on the port side."

"Did you hear any noise during the night?"

"There was plenty noise. The ship was working and the pump was on and the main engines as well."

"Nothing else?"

"No, I sleep sound."

"When did you wake?"

"Round about midnight when Tubby came to call me. I dressed and went down below. The fires were going fine so I didn't do more than give them a shovel of coal all round. At half past three I set to and took out a couple of fire-bars that were burnt out in the port-wing boiler. That took me half an hour, nearly."

"And after that?"

"I went up to get new bars that I'd left out ready by the fiddley door, but I couldn't find them, so I had to get a lamp and go into the fiddley and get them from there."

"Are you sure you put out these fire-bars?"

"Of course I'm sure. Why shouldn't I be?"

"No reason. I was just asking."

"Fire-bars are a tidy weight as you'd know well enough if you'd ever handled one—and dirty, too. My hands were all over red rust."

"How did Carl get on with MacTaggart?"

"They did have a bit of a barney once."

"What about?"

"Carl wanted to get the engines going right away as soon as ever we had the steam, but MacTaggart would have it that we'd got to get the hold dry first, and I won't say that he wasn't right. You see Carl was keen to finish the job. That was all he was caring about."

"Yes, I understand," Pollitt said. He thought for a moment. "You can go now."

Pollitt went out into the charge-room. Kent was writing up his diary. "I want you to come with me down to the dock," Pollitt said. As he walked to the door he turned to the sergeant: "Keep Hicks and Todd here till I come back."

Pollitt and Kent were crossing the market-place when Tom Ingleby came from the dock where he had moored his boat. He watched them until they were out of sight, then he went over to the coffee-stall where Mr. Hopkins was getting ready to go home. He had taken off his black alpaca jacket and was putting on his coat.

Tom Ingleby said: "What are they after?"

"That's just what I'd like to know," replied Mr. Hopkins. "They've had Tubby Stevens up at the station and Dan Todd and Larry are there now."

Tom Ingleby bunched up his beard with his right hand. His eyes were troubled. "Is there nothing in the paper?"

"Only that Carl's gone and there's a description out."

"What do they want him for?"

"That's something else I'd like to know," Mr. Hopkins replied. "And so would a lot of folk." He stepped out of the stall, lifted a shutter and put it over the space above the counter.

Tom Ingleby took a paper from under Mr. Hopkins's arm and unfolded it. Yes, there it was, right in the middle of the front page, a full description of Carl Swanson. "Any person knowing the whereabouts of the above man is requested to communicate with Gilboro' Police Station."

Mr. Hopkins, having secured the shutter in position, locked the door of the stall and stood for a moment while he struck a match and lit his pipe. Between the puffs he said: "The captain of the *Ivanhoe* was on board of her when Carl got to her. I do know that much."

"Who did you get that from?"

"A bloke who's been talking with Tubby Stevens."

Pollitt walked on board the *Ivanhoe* and went up on the bridge. He went straight to the port wing and picked up a hanging strand of the broken lanyard. He looked at the ends of the strands for a moment and then he said to Kent, "Have a look at this."

"What do you mean?"

"Tell me how you think that break occurred?"

Kent, puzzled, held up the ends of the broken lanyard. "I can't see anything."

"What about this one? It looks like a clean cut to me."

"By Jove, yes." Kent looked at Pollitt, a question in his eyes.

"I don't know what the answer is, but I've got a damn' good idea."

"What?"

"MacTaggart didn't fall over the side by accident. He was killed on board the ship. His body was weighted with fire-bars, and, if the lashing hadn't slipped, his body would never have been recovered."

"How do you work that out?"

"I got it out of Tubby Stevens and Larry Hicks that on the night that MacTaggart disappeared there was hardly any motion on the ship. She had a heavy list to starboard."

"Yes, but where does that take us?"

"MacTaggart was supposed to have fallen over the port side. But that's not all. There was a length of cod-line round the body when it was picked up. A cod-line lashing that Hicks had put on one of the saloon skylights disappeared the same night, and two fire-bars which Dan Todd had put out on the deck were missing when he went for them at four o'clock next morning."

"Carl Swanson'll have a bit of explaining to do if we get him."

"We'll get him all right." Pollitt cut the end of the lashing and pulled it clear of an eye-bolt.

"Looks like a cast-iron case," Kent said.

"Yes, if the others aren't mixed up in it. If they were accomplices, of course, there are difficulties. We'd have to have independent evidence."

"There's that private log that MacTaggart wrote up."

"That's something," Pollitt agreed. He walked to the top of the bridge ladder and looked down on the engine-room casing and then at the strip of deck on the port side. "The bulwarks aren't any height; it wouldn't be difficult for one man to heave a body over them."

"But you'd think the others of the crew must have heard something. MacTaggart was a big man and probably put up a fight for it."

"If Swanson isn't picked up by tonight, I'll have another go at them, but I have an idea that they were speaking the truth."

The caretaker came out of the galley as Pollitt jumped down on to the deck from the engine-room casing. He had a cup of tea in his right hand. He said: "I thought you'd finished here."

"There's a few loose ends to tie up," Pollitt replied and asked for the key of the captain's cabin.

"There's nothing there. It was cleared out the day the ship came in. You'd better see Mr. Fleming."

"Let's have the key all the same."

When the door was opened Pollitt examined the floor. Then he stepped over the high sill and went inside. The bunk was bare, stripped to the wire mattress. Under it were some newspapers. Pollitt pulled them out, looked at the dates and said: "These don't help us."

There was nothing on the shelves or in the drawers or wardrobe. He examined the woodwork for signs of a struggle, bloodstains or scratches, but found none.

Then he went into the saloon and saw the skylight which Larry had lashed with cod-line. The catch had been snapped off short. "Well, that part of Larry's story seems to be true enough," he muttered, and cut off a length of the twine. "We'll compare this with the bit that was round MacTaggart's waist."

"We'd better check what Dan Todd said about the fire-bars," Kent suggested.

Pollitt agreed and told the caretaker to take them to the fiddley. There he found a stack of fire-bars, coils of wire, shovels and slices.

"There's only engine-room stores in there," the care-taker said. "If there's anything particular you're looking for, maybe I can help you."

But the hint that Pollitt should divulge the purpose of his visit was ignored. "We'll have a look in the cabins and I think that'll be all."

The clock on St. Jude's Church was striking five o'clock when the search was completed; no weapon which could have been used to kill MacTaggart had been found. "I suppose he chucked it over the side." Pollitt stood for a minute at the top of the gangway and lit his pipe. "It's not going to be quite so easy as I thought at first."

When Pollitt and Kent had gone, the caretaker left the ship and went as fast as his aged legs could carry him to the office of the *Evening Argus*. After he had told his story of the visit of the police to the *Ivanhoe* he was rewarded with half a crown, and an hour later the paper came out with a headline, "Dramatic turn in *Ivanhoe* mystery", and below in smaller type, "Police visit ship. Cabins searched for clues."

Tom Ingleby walked with Mr. Hopkins to the foot of Hawkin's Court and there he said good night. Then he walked quickly in the direction of Mrs. Mather's cottage. But as he neared it his pace slackened and at the gate in the whitewashed wall he stopped.

Twenty-eight years had passed since he had last smoked his pipe in Mrs. Mather's kitchen; he had no desire to revive the memory of that day when he had come to Jenny Mather and she had told him that his wife was dead.

In a corner of the room there had stood a cradle.

"I've got to do it. I've got to find out," he muttered to himself, pushed open the gate and reached the front door in half a dozen strides.

He knocked twice and waited, listening. Light steps came down the passage, the door opened and he looked into Jessie's white face; she had been crying.

"Is Mrs. Mather in?"

"What do you want?" Jessie asked nervously.

"Tell her Tom Ingleby's here."

She stared at him for a moment and then said: "Wait a minute," and shut the door.

A minute or two later she opened it again. "You can come in, but don't stay long. She's not well."

Tom Ingleby shuffled down the passage and into the kitchen. Mrs. Mather was sitting before the fire. Her hands were lying on her knees. She looked up but did not smile as she said: "Come along in, Tom. Jessie, bring up a chair."

Tom Ingleby looked for one fleeting second to the corner where the cradle had stood—twenty-eight years ago.

He said thank you to Jessie and sat down.

Minutes passed in silence and then Mrs. Mather spoke. "You've come about Carl?"

Tom Ingleby nodded. "I hear he's in some sort of trouble."

"He's at your place, isn't he?" Mrs. Mather asked.

"Yes, but he hasn't told me anything. It was only half an hour ago I saw in the paper that the police were after him."

"They've found out that MacTaggart was on the *Ivanhoe* when Carl got aboard of her," Mrs. Mather said.

"What happened after that?"

"I don't know."

"MacTaggart fell over the side by accident, that's what was said at the inquest."

"I wish I could believe that, but I can't."

"Why not?"

"If it had been an accident the police wouldn't be after him now." Mrs. Mather turned to Jessie. "I'd like a cup of tea, and you'll take one, too, Tom, won't you?"

"No. No, thanks. I'll have to be getting back. I shouldn't have left him." Tom Ingleby slouched to the door. "I'll maybe come in again later in the week and let you know how he is."

When he had gone Jessie asked, "Who was that?"

"A friend of mine. A very old friend." Mrs. Mather leaned back in her chair and shut her eyes.

Jessie, frightened, put down the kettle. The colour was ebbing from Mrs. Mather's cheeks so that they became as white as ivory. Jessie tiptoed to the door and ran out into the street to the house of Dr. Thompson.

19

CARL SWANSON was coming along the sea-wall with a bundle of driftwood under his arm when he saw the boat returning. He waited while Tom Ingleby moored her to a ring-bolt in the rotting wharf and came up the slipway, his shoulders bent forward and his arms swinging in time to his stride.

"You're back early," Carl called out.

Tom Ingleby looked at the bundle of wood. "You hain't done so bad. Come along in and we'll get the stove going."

Carl followed him up the ladder on the verandah of the Pride of Bedford and into the living-room. As he shut the door he said: "Did you hear anything in the town?"

"Plenty. Read that."

Tom Ingleby pulled a crumpled newspaper from his pocket and threw it on the table. He struck a match and lit the lamp.

"I was expecting this." Carl gave a short laugh.

"Dan Todd and Larry Hicks are up at the police-station."

"Oh!" Carl kept his head bent and his fingers were gripping tightly on the edge of the table. "How do you know that?"

"Hopkins told me. They've had a go at Tubby Stevens as well."

Carl turned over the paper and looked at the stop-press column. "There's nothing about it here." He stood upright.

The lamp-glass was warm now, and, as Tom Ingleby turned up the wick, Carl went to the window and drew a cotton curtain across it.

"I went to see Mrs. Mather and she told me what was the trouble."

"How is she keeping?" Carl asked.

"Not too good—but there was a girl there, looking after her."

"What did she tell you?"

"Just that MacTaggart had been on board the *Ivanhoe* when you got to her." Tom Ingleby knelt down before the stove and raked out the dead ashes. Then he turned and took the paper off the table, crumpled the sheets into balls and put them on the bars. "Give us over some of them sticks."

Carl said: "I don't know why they're making all this fuss. It hasn't got anything to do with the police anyway." But there was no conviction in his tone.

"That's what I was thinking," Tom Ingleby said, and held a lighted match to the paper. He shut the door of the stove and opened the draught-plate. Then he stood up and faced Carl. "What did you want to run away for?"

"Because I knew that it would come out about MacTaggart and I didn't want to have to answer a lot more questions. I've had my fill of that from that damn' lawyer, Innes, and at the inquest."

"It'll make 'em suspicious. You should ha' stopped in Gilboro'."

"Suspicious of what?" Carl's lower jaw shot out.

"I don't know, but I can make a guess." Tom Ingleby stood rugged and four square as the bole of a tree.

"There's nothing I'm afraid of." Carl turned away. In Tom Ingleby he had met a man who did not fear him.

"I'd go back if I was you."

"And if I don't I suppose you'll be going along to Inspector Pollitt and telling him where I am," Carl sneered. "Mrs. Mather said I could trust you."

"And so you can." Tom Ingleby opened the door of the stove and put in more wood. Then he put a kettle on the stove. "I'll get the supper started."

Out on the river a trawler was blowing. "That's the *Kent Maid*," Tom said. "Must be a bit of fog." Again came the wailing, melancholy note.

Carl stood listening for a moment and then he opened the door and looked out. "It's coming in pretty thick." Then he shut the door and sat down on a chair. Tom Ingleby was cutting bread and had his back to him.

Carl thought, "Now, what the hell am I going to do? I can't stop here for ever." He stared at Tom Ingleby's broad back. Suppose he told the police! Like as not he would and then . . . But what was there to be scared of? No one had seen MacTaggart die. And besides, it had been an accident. He'd fallen and hit his head. That's all there was to it. No one had seen him pitch the body over the side, and, if he kept his mouth shut, everything would be all right.

Confidence returned, driving out fear. "What's for supper?"

"We'll have to make do with eels again. I forgot to get the bacon." Tom Ingleby moved the kettle to one side and put a saucepan on the stove. "There's dripping in that jar by your right hand."

The two men supped on stewed eels, stewed tea, and bread and dripping.

Afterwards they sat close to the stove, smoking. Carl's pipe was drawing well. He said: "When this business has blown over I'll have to be looking for a ship."

"You'll have to square yourself before you can do that." Tom Ingleby took a deep pull at his pipe and blew out a cloud of smoke. "You'll have to tell the truth."

"Mebbe you're right. But there's not all that hurry."

"I wouldn't leave it too long if I was you."

And then there came to Carl Swanson the desire to talk, to tell Tom Ingleby everything. Why this sudden urge was born he could not have explained, nor did he try to find the cause; perhaps it was something about Tom Ingleby, his very silence as he sat there with his head thrust forward, a hand under his chin, staring at nothing.

"I'd like to tell you how it happened," Carl said suddenly. He had to talk, to break the silence of that little room.

Tom Ingleby took his pipe from his mouth to say, "If it'll ease you any, go ahead. I've got a short memory."

But it was harder to make a start than Carl had thought. He said: "Well, it was like this," and then stopped and pricked the ash from his pipe with a match. Then he tried again, stammering disjointed sentences. "I was up on the bridge on the second night. MacTaggart came up. I was at the wheel. He came up the port ladder."

And then as the memory of that night returned and became as real as though he were living it again words came more easily.

"He stood at the top of the ladder and I turned round. He had a grin on his face. 'You think you're going to run this ship your own way, Mister Trawlerman,' he said. I asked what was biting him and he said, 'The logs. I've seen what you've been up to, but that's not going to do you no good.' I got mad and I hit him with my right. I don't know quite where I hit him. He kind of swayed for a minute. I heard his nails scrabbling on the canvas screen and then he fell backwards down the ladder. He never cried out or anything.

"I went down after him. He was lying on the top of the casing. His head was right back. He was dead."

"How did you know?"

"I've seen too many stiffs in my time not to know one when I see it. He was dead all right. I was scared and I thought the only thing was to get the body over the side, and not say anything about it to the others."

Tom Ingleby's face was without expression when he said: "So you did that?"

"Ay. I lashed on a couple of fire-bars and dropped him in the drink. I made it look like he'd fallen over the side of the bridge by breaking the lanyard on the top rail; and that's all there is to it."

"What did you tell the others?"

"Nothing. Just that he'd disappeared in the night. I showed Larry Hicks the rail."

Tom Ingleby smoked in silence for some minutes and then he said: "It looks to me as if the police had got hold of something agin you. If not, why should they be wanting you so bad?"

"They don't know anything. They can't." Carl half whispered the words as though he were talking to himself, were trying to convince himself of their truth.

"Well, I don't know why there should be all this trouble if no one but you knows about it." Tom Ingleby looked at Carl. "Did you hit him hard?"

"No, just a tap. It must have been a roll of the ship made him fall. It wasn't any fault of mine he was killed."

"Then why not go back to Gilboro' and tell what happened? They can't do anything to you if it was an accident, and there's no one seemingly that can say that it wasn't."

"Why should I speak?"

"Because you'll never have no rest until you does. I know that, for the same kind of thing happened to me once. I hit a man and he fell and hit his head on the edge of a pavement and he died. I ran away and left my wife and kid.

"There was a lot of talk in the papers same as there's been here, and I thought I could get away where I wouldn't be cotched.

"For a whole month I stopped in an old lead mine up in the hills, Derbyshire way. I was starving and all the time I wanted to tell someone what I'd done. I wanted to explain that it had been an accident and that I'd never meant to hurt the bloke, which was true enough. That month was hell, and when they found me and took me to a house and gave me a meal I was crying and I told the police all about it. I felt better then. I didn't worry no more; even when they said I was to be tried I didn't care much. I'd told the truth and my mind was at rest again."

"What happened?"

"It was brought in manslaughter and I was given eighteen months. When I came out my wife was dead but the kid was all right. I got a friend of the wife's to take him in and I changed my name and started down here, building barges."

Carl got up and walked to the window. The fog was thick now and he could not see the verandah rail, three feet away.

"My lawyer told me after the trial that if I hadn't run away I might have got off altogether. That's why I'm telling you all this. You can never live happy if your mind's not easy."

"I'll think over what you've said."

Tom Ingleby got up and opened the door. "I was meaning to set the nets tonight, but I doubt it's too thick. I think I'll turn in."

Carl nodded, but did not move from his position at the window. He was still standing there when Tom Ingleby climbed into his bunk.

20

"THEY'VE BEEN at the police-station all night and if that doesn't mean something, I don't know what does." So spoke Mrs. Warburton as she stood in the Hopkins's kitchen.

"You mean Dan Todd and Larry Hicks?" said Mr. Hopkins, putting down his cup.

"And Tubby as well. They came for him last night. After midnight it was and I didn't half get a fright I can tell you. They knocked at my door—"

"Who knocked?" asked Mr. Hopkins. He didn't want to miss anything.

"The police of course. Tubby kept asking what they wanted him for and one of 'em said there was some questions they wanted to ask him and off he went. I sat up waiting for him to come back but he never did, and now just take a look at this." Mrs. Warburton took a paper from under her shawl and put it on the table.

It was a Birmingham paper. "Just you read that and tell me what you thinks of it." Mrs. Warburton pointed to headlines which ran across three columns. "Mystery of Salved Vessel". "Country-wide Search for Missing Man". And underneath in smaller type, "The police desire to interview a man who, it is believed, can give valuable information concerning the death of Captain Roderick MacTaggart."

"It's Carl Swanson they're after. There's a photo of him on the back page."

"It's the same as was in the *Argus* yesterday afternoon," said Mr. Hopkins. "There's nothing new here."

"They've found out something and they want him bad, else it wouldn't have been put in a paper like this."

"I wonder what it can be," said Mrs. Hopkins.

"Murder," said Mrs. Warburton with relish. "Carl Swanson did him in. There ain't no doubt about it and they'll get him, you see if they don't. There never was a murderer got away yet except he killed himself."

"You didn't ought to say such things," said Mrs. Hopkins.

"Everybody's saying it. And I don't know I'm sure what'll happen to Mrs. Mather. I heard from Jessie Miles that they'd had the doctor to her and he sent her straight to her bed." Mrs. Warburton picked up her paper and left the house.

For the first time for many years, in fact since the day of the fire at the fish-wharf, Mr. Hopkins didn't put on his collar and tie before he followed in Mrs. Warburton's wake down the street. He'd open up his stall early, that's what he'd do. And if he knew anything, he'd get plenty of customers.

He was quite right. By the time the urns were half warm there was a crowd of men round the coffee-stall counter. Most of them had papers, most of them talked, very few listened, even to Mr. Hopkins when he retailed Mrs. Warburton's story of Tubby's arrest.

It was an exciting subject for discussion and there was no theory left unaired by the time the coffee was hot.

"They're all in it if you ask me. Up to their blinking necks."

"I knew as how that Carl Swanson would land up in jug."

"And Dan Todd. I never did trust that man."

"I wouldn't ha' thought it of Larry Hicks."

"He just did as he was told."

"Hit him over the nut with a spike. That's what happened."

"Carl always was a devil."

"A proper nasty temper he had, too, if you got the wrong side of him."

"They won't hang the lot of 'em, will they?"

Mr. Hopkins, by virtue of his position on the raised floor of the stall, could see over the heads of his customers. Why he should have bothered to look in the direction of the dock is not clear, but he did and suddenly cried out, "Look!"

The talk died and everyone stared at Mr. Hopkins, who pointed across the market-place. "It's—it's him." His customers turned as one man to see Carl Swanson walking towards them. There was no mistaking Carl's swinging stride.

"Good morning, Mr. Hopkins," Carl called out as he approached. The crowd parted and he walked up to the counter. "You're open early."

Mr. Hopkins said yes, rather breathlessly, and knocked over a cup which fell on the floor with a crash. Those who had newspapers put them in their pockets or under their coats. No one spoke.

"A cup of coffee if you please, Mr. Hopkins," Carl said, and took a sandwich off a plate. The audience watched him wonderingly.

Here was a man that all the police in England were looking for, eating and drinking as though he hadn't a single thing to worry him.

It was a situation far beyond Mr. Hopkins's powers to handle.

Carl finished his sandwich, drank his coffee and said: "So long, chaps."

"Well, I'm everlasting damned," said a fish-porter. "And do you see where he's heading for? Have you ever seen the like of that?"

No one bothered to reply, but all kept their eyes fixed on Carl until he had disappeared through the door of the Gilboro' police-station.

Inspector Pollitt thought the policeman was pulling his leg when he came into his office and said, "We've got Swanson outside, sir."

Pollitt looked at the policeman very hard and said, "Who?"

"Carl Swanson, sir. You know, that man in the *Ivanhoe* case."

"All right. Send him in and tell Kent I want him too."

And Carl came lounging into the room. He was smiling. "Didn't think you were going to see me so soon, did you?" Pollitt pointed to a chair. "Sit down. Where've you been?"

"Visiting friends in the North. I only got back an hour ago."

Pollitt asked himself if he hadn't been a fool to send out that description, but comforted himself with the thought that the responsibility was that of the Chief Constable who had endorsed his action.

Carl Swanson certainly didn't look like a murderer. He was still smiling and was apparently very sure of himself.

"I've been having a talk with your crew and they tell me that MacTaggart was on the *Ivanhoe* when you boarded her."

"That's right." Carl leaned back in his chair and crossed his legs. "What about it?"

"That wasn't what you said at the inquest."

"I dare say not."

"Why didn't you tell the truth then?"

"Because I wanted to get all the money I could. I made out she was a derelict."

"What happened to MacTaggart?"

"He fell over the side. You saw the rail, didn't you? It must have carried away when he was leaning on it."

"I saw the rail all right. And I saw the lanyard." Pollitt's voice was hard as cold drawn steel.

Carl's body became tense. He sensed danger but he forced himself to speak casually. "Well, that's how it must have happened."

"The ship had a heavy list to starboard, hadn't she?"

"She had a bit of list, yes."

"And she wasn't rolling much."

"Not a great deal."

"Then it's curious that MacTaggart fell over the port side, isn't it?"

"I don't think so. There's no other way it could have happened."

"The lanyard of the rail was cut with a knife."

Carl opened his mouth and shut it again without making a sound. He sat up straight in his chair. His hands were gripping the arms of his chair. He said: "That's absurd."

"I don't think so. It's an easy thing to do."

"Well, I don't know anything about that. It didn't look to me as if it had been cut."

"You can take it from me that it was." Pollitt leaned across his desk. "Now come on, Swanson. Tell me the truth."

"I tell you I don't know anything." Carl raised himself an inch in his chair. "If that lanyard was cut I don't know who did it."

"You pointed it out to Larry Hicks, didn't you?"

"I may have done, I forget."

"He says you did."

"I tell you I can't remember."

"You killed MacTaggart."

Beads of sweat formed on Carl's forehead. He put up a hand to wipe them away. It wasn't working out the way he'd planned, and for a split second he thought of making a dash for it. This was a very different Pollitt to the man who had met him on the wharf the day he'd brought the *Ivanhoe* in; to the man who had taken him home the night he was drunk. Pollitt was his friend. He was dreaming all this; he must be.

Everything was blurred and unreal. Then his brain cleared and his eyes focused Pollitt who was still staring at him across the desk.

"You killed MacTaggart."

The words were as a blow in the face, and he half raised an arm as though to ward them off.

"That's the truth, isn't it?"

"No, it isn't. It's a damn' lie."

"And after you'd killed him you weighted the body with fire-bars and threw it over the side."

Carl tried to laugh. "Nonsense"—his voice sounded as though it were someone else who had spoken.

"You found two fire-bars outside the fiddley door and you got the line, cod-line it was, from a skylight in the saloon."

"Who told you that?"

"It's the truth, isn't it?"

Carl made an effort to fight back. "No, it isn't. I never did that."

"You did. I know you did. It's no good denying it, Swanson. Now, why not get it off your mind? Tell me the truth. If I can help you, I will."

"All right," Carl said. Suddenly he felt very tired.

Pollitt turned to Kent. "Take down what he says." Then he said to Carl: "I must caution you that you need not say anything, but whatever you do say will be taken down in writing and may be used in evidence. Do you understand?"

"Yes; but I didn't kill MacTaggart. It was an accident."

"All right. Now tell me what happened and take your time."

"I was up on the bridge at the wheel on the second night after we got on board, and MacTaggart came up the port ladder."

"What time would that be?"

"Some time after midnight."

"Were you alone?"

"Yes."

"All right. Go on."

"I heard his step on the ladder and I turned round. He said something about my not having it all my own way and that he was still captain of his own ship."

"What did he mean by that?"

"I don't know."

"Had you had a quarrel with him?"

"No."

"I thought you were going to tell me the truth. I know you and MacTaggart had a dispute. It was about starting up the main engines."

"It wasn't a quarrel. He said he wanted to wait until we'd got the hold dry and I agreed with him. That's all there was to it."

"All right. What happened next?"

"I told him that I was willing to work in with him and that I'd no wish to take command of the ship. I turned away from him to look at the compass, and when I had my back to him I heard a noise. When I turned back to the ladder he was gone. He'd fallen down on to the casing."

"What did you do?"

"I went down and found him stretched out. He was dead. At first I thought of calling the crew but I didn't—I don't know why. Then I thought that if I was to put the body over the side and tell the others not to say anything about him having been on board, we could say the ship was a derelict when we found her."

"And then?"

"As you said I got a couple of fire-bars. They were lying on the deck by the fiddley door, and I remembered that Larry had put a lashing on a skylight in the saloon. I cut it adrift and lashed the bars to the body and hove it over the side. I never killed MacTaggart."

"You hit him. That's why he fell down the ladder."

"I didn't."

"There was a bruise on his cheek. You remember what the doctor said at the inquest."

"I don't think I did."

"Come on, Swanson. You did hit him, didn't you?"

"Yes, I did. He was coming for me. But I didn't strike hard. It was just a light blow."

"Why was he coming for you?"

"I don't know. I think he must have been drunk. I never said anything to him."

"Well, let's get back to the point when you found him stretched out on the casing."

"He was dead then."

"No, he wasn't."

"He was, before ever I touched him."

"MacTaggart was alive when you put him over the side. His death was due to drowning. That was the medical evidence at the inquest."

Carl Swanson was convicted of the wilful murder of Roderick MacTaggart at the Gilboro' Assizes on the 12th January and was sentenced to death.

His solicitor saw him in his cell below the court before he was taken to the gaol. "Is there anything I can do for you, Swanson?"

"Yes. See that Mrs. Mather isn't told. Tell her that—"

"Mrs. Mather died this morning."

Mr. Hopkins was doing a good trade in gossip and coffee and pies. Someone said to him, "I wonder who it was paid for Carl's lawyer."

"His father, Tom Ingleby," replied Mr. Hopkins. It was the only secret Mr. Hopkins had ever kept.

THE END